The Laying Out of Gussie Hoot

SOUTHWEST LIFE AND LETTERS

*A series designed to
publish outstanding new
fiction and nonfiction
about Texas and the American
Southwest and to present
classic works of the region in
handsome new editions.*

*General Editors:
Suzanne Comer, Southern
Methodist University Press,
and Tom Pilkington,
Tarleton State University.*

The
Laying
Out
of
Gussie
Hoot

. . . .

MARGOT FRASER

Southern Methodist University Press

DALLAS

This novel is a work of fiction. Any
resemblance of its characters, setting, or
plot to actual persons, places, or events
is entirely coincidental.

First edition, 1990

Requests for permission to reproduce

material from this work should be sent to:

Permissions

Southern Methodist University Press

Box 415

Dallas, Texas 75275

LIBRARY OF CONGRESS CATALOGING-IN-PUBLICATION DATA

Fraser, Margot.

The laying out of Gussie Hoot / Margot Fraser.—1st ed.

p.   cm.—(Southwest life and letters)

ISBN 0-87074-317-1   *14.95*

I. Title.   II. Series.

PS3556.R3545L38   1990

813'.54—dc20   90-52659

Design by Molly Renda

To Suzanne Comer for her vision, her courage,

and her sense of humor

. . . .

Part I

CHAPTER I

. . . .

Gussie Hoot was counting her money. Same as she did every single morning of the world. It was a thing you could depend on, like noon. There wasn't a person in town who didn't know that around about eleven A.M., Augusta Houghton would be found at her kitchen table, a Coke at her elbow and her box of cash open on the table in front. It was equally well-known that she was not to be disturbed during that time—too many had been left for dead on her front porch, fingers fused to the doorbell in the August heat. Telephone callers met with the same fate, were left ringing until either the phone gave out or they did. Nobody bothered Gussie at that particular time of day. When she was counting her cash neither hell nor high water would have fazed her, even arriving on her doorstep simultaneously in a kind of boiling eruption. No, Gussie would have gone right on.

That special morning, still wearing her wrapper and mules, she unsnapped the old metal box, surveyed the contents with satisfaction and took a long pull on the Coke. She smiled as the familiar aroma of river mud and catfish escaped, allowing memories of the Rio Grande to swirl around her kitchen. For more years than she cared to count, that box had carried Carter's fishing tackle. Hauled around in the back of the pickup, jammed between rocks, scratched, dented, with even a bullet hole right through the middle, it was a sorry thing to look at. But now instead of fishhooks and leaders and lopsided lead sinkers it contained money—clear up to the top. Gussie lifted out the stacks of bills lovingly and laid them in neat rows. Somebody who didn't know any better, a stranger for instance, would have taken her for a little old lady playing solitaire to pass the time. Nothing could have been farther from the truth.

Still smiling, Gussie licked her thumb and began to count. It was so comforting, reassuring. She could just let her mind run on. . . . After she had been at it for a while, she observed that the morning was starting to get hot. Going to be another scorcher. That little old breeze seeping through the screen door had the breath of a branding iron. Gussie glanced over her shoulder, noted that the door was unhooked as usual and chuckled to herself. Bubba would pitch a fit if he saw it. Well, he could just pitch one since he was the one who left it open all the time. Went on at *her* to keep the place locked up like a bank vault—like a *tomb* with her sealed up inside, her *and* the money, oh yes—then went off and left everything wide open himself. She had told *him*:

"Screen doors! Don't you go on at me about screen doors! All those years down yonder on the ranch . . . only you in diapers, one Messkin and that old dog to save me from whatever it is you think is out there and trying to get in . . . ! Lord, Bubba! I declare. Sometimes I don't think you've got the sense you were born with. Before you were born I didn't even *have* a screen door. When Carter was away—which was most of the time, him and the rest of the men—why, I just set me a shotgun by the door and left it. Only thing between me and Mexico was sixty miles of open country and that old shotgun. One time a desperado did crawl over that sill come to think of it—a little old brown tarantula trying to get out of the rain. Law! I haven't got the time or inclination to fool with screen doors. Never locked a door in my life and I'm not fixin' to start in now."

He had gone white with anger. It wasn't her he was worried about—oh no, make no mistake about *that*—it was the money. He despised more than anything to watch her counting it, would go out of his way to keep from it.

"Mama," he said, "I wish to *God* you wouldn't spread that old money all over the kitchen table! It isn't *sanitary*."

What he meant was, it wasn't his.

Phew. It was going to be hot all right. Funny how May was nearly always hotter than July. Her Coke was standing in a puddle of its own sweat. Gussie went on counting. My word . . . it was beginning to add up. Lordy, if her friends knew . . . ! Gussie laughed out loud. Amity would gasp, flutter a hand to her throat. But Amity's throat was not what it used to be. Even in those high-necked frilly collars it was still all cords and folds. And besides that, flirty gestures did not become a woman of seventy-two. Gussie shook her head. Susannah Bledsoe would meanwhile be waving her fan around like a windmill in a March wind. Susannah, like Amity, would never see sixteen again. In fact, those years were so far away that they might not ever have happened. Yet these women lived out that illusion, just like they were still there, fluttering and fanning—sometimes

Gussie felt as if she were surrounded by faded photographs rather than real people. Not Effie Sue though, thank God. If Effie Sue knew about the money she would merely pull her thin lips together and say no more about it. But Charlotte—Charlotte would lean forward, jaws working like a starving praying mantis green with envy.

"Gussie, *dear?*" Charlotte would have said. And glance around like she suspected that Pancho Villa himself was lounging in the corner. "Honey? I mean . . . do you think it *wise* to keep, well, so *much* here at home? Why, only last week those wetbacks broke into the Valle Seco ranch, went right on up to the main house, smashed the picture window and made off with all the food and blankets they could lay their hands on including the ham Kitten Wills had in the oven. In broad daylight! While she was at *church*! Course they caught 'em a couple of days later . . . but you really do have to be careful these days."

Gussie let out a snort and shoved a pile of twenties to one side. She had no use for twenties, couldn't imagine how they'd gotten mixed up with the real money. . . . She slammed down a royal flush of hundreds in disgust. What in hell were they all so scared of? There were always those people who tore out first thing and bought up a supply of mothballs. Like measuring themselves for their own coffins. The world was divided right there, along those lines— those who put their faith in mothballs and the hooks on screen doors and those who didn't. Gussie herself had no use for such puny temporary measures. They were like fresh spreader dams in the face of a flash flood, would never hold out. Yet people persisted in putting their faith in such things.

*

Take Lincoln Winters now. Was Lincoln a mothball man? Gussie paused in her own tallying and gazed off, seeing not the sink and the drainboard but the slender Lincoln Winters remote in gray and silver glory. Lincoln habitually wore banker's gray. He made it look elegant and, since he was a banker, it suited him. Yes, she concluded, Lincoln was definitely a mothball man. Always and forever after her to stash her money in the bank. HA! He just wanted to make use of it himself. She knew how banks made money— very cautiously. And they were often wrong to boot. Lost it all and had to start over, get the taxpayers to bail them out. No, a bank was no place for money. Cash ought to be out and working, like a good cutting horse, not sit-ting around earning increments of interest as thin as sliced peaches. She could speculate much better on her own and Lincoln knew it. She, for her part, was aware that he envied her shrewdness, her *sagacity*, and would have begged her advice in a minute if his pride had permitted it. Damn fool. He wouldn't know what to do with her kind of money if he had it. Lincoln lacked both grit and savvy. Not that she didn't like him—Lincoln Winters was a handsome and highly respected man—but liking and respecting were not the same thing. Oh, she respected Lincoln, too, as far as it went. But she mainly loved to tease him, to make his life momentarily miserable and settle like a blowfly on his well-groomed hide. Not with malice exactly—just to *tease*.

Every so often when she had collected a considerable pile of money, like now, for instance, she would cram it all in that old tackle box, drag it down to the bank and force him to help her count it. Gussie had never in her life con-sidered dealing with an ordinary teller, land no. They were cheap, chintzy little things so loaded down with makeup and perfume that it gave a person the blind staggers. God no. Instead, Gussie would lug that smelly old box directly into Lincoln's office, dump the contents all over his rosewood desk and watch him cringe. Lincoln Winters was the most fastidious man in the world and it delighted her to smother his fine old desk with filthy money—just like snipping the wires from a bale of alfalfa. Money all over—and Lincoln's face as long as a heifer's in heat. Then she would insist that he help her count it, making mistakes on purpose just to tax his patience. His face was a study. It would start out a mixture of distaste and envy, but before long it was the color of thin putty. When the two of them finally agreed on the sum she would order him to put it away for her. She did not mean credit her account—oh no—or open up still another one with some silly little book. Not at all. What she meant was: Put it away. That very money, not some mythical amount written down in washable ink. She simply wanted her funds in storage, she was running out of space at home.

Lincoln always groaned. Then he would explain in the most *tiresome* detail why he could not do that, how it was against the law and so on and so forth. Then she would jog his memory just a little, about how that bank and him along with it would have gone under, not only in the '30s but several times since if it had not been for her and one or two others, would have folded in fact once and for all. About how she and Carter, how her *family*, had always banked at home and there was her daddy's name in brass on the plaque listing the original board of directors. She would remind him gently of these facts, sometimes with no more than the lift of an eyebrow and a word of admiration about how nice the portrait of her daddy (done by a famous artist) looked hanging on the wall directly behind Lincoln's desk.

*

Lincoln Winters would sigh then, say he would see what he could do. And every time Gussie nearly laughed out loud. She knew full well what he would do. He would make up some tacky little book with her name on the front in gold letters. And just as soon as her back was turned, the minute he had bowed her safely out the big glass doors, he would rush back to his office and see to it that her money was shipped to Washington, D.C., or Fort Knox or wherever it was they sent money when they had too much of it. And presently she would receive still another statement in the mail with a piddly little bit of interest on the amount.

Well, Gussie didn't want any part of that business but she did love to tease Lincoln so she devised a little scheme of her own. She concocted a method by which she would know *without a doubt* which money was hers. In other words, she marked the money in a special way, put a brand on it you might say. And kept a record, a *careful* record. That way she planned to go down to the bank some afternoon and demand all of her money—every cent—back. Exactly the same bills she had poured all over Lincoln's desk. HA! She speculated on how composed Mr. Winters would be then. He would bring her an armful of money—all neatly stacked and wrapped—and she would be forced to thumb through it, regret and consternation on her face. Forced to say, "Lincoln, this is not *my* money! I am sorry but you have made an embarrassing mistake. Now you take this back and bring me the money I asked you to keep."

Of course he couldn't.

She would look at him, stunned. "But Lincoln, I asked you to keep *my* money, to take care of it yourself and give it your personal attention! And you have let me down. Lincoln, you have let me *down*! Here I have depended on you, counted on you, on our *longstanding friendship* . . . and now you, the one person in this world I thought I could *trust*! . . . you, too, have let me down."

He would be crushed. Caught out. And he wouldn't have the faintest idea how she could possibly know. Gussie chuckled and continued counting. Of course getting the best of Lincoln Winters was not the main thing, what she really loved was the money itself, the feel of it and the sight of it around her. Like seeing the whole upper pasture two feet high in grass and heading out. It wasn't a need to be somebody or buy things, but a sense of knowing exactly who she was, and where, down to the last square inch.

Gussie took another slug of Coke and wet her thumb. Money had a way of sticking together in this heat. It was said that having it attracted more. Well, that was a fact. All this (and much more: this was only the tip of the iceberg, a hobby) was purely her own money. Not Carter's—which *was* in the bank—nor her daddy's either. The Colonel—her granddaddy, granted that distinction for his outstanding service in the Civil War, leader of the famous Lone Star Battalion—Colonel Mayhew Merriwether had left her well-off when he died. Left her everything, in fact, called her The Little Colonel. By now she had multiplied that money. As for Carter, he hadn't had all that much to begin with so she let Lincoln sit on that. But she had run that ranch far better than he ever had. (Some people had employed the word "ruthless" and applied it to her. Well, they could go to hell.) Carter never had any imagination. No gumption, either. She knew more about the business of ranching and the cattle market than he could have learned in a lifetime. She was the one willing to take chances, go out on a limb. She had made investments when everybody else was scared to make a move, come through drouth when they were forced to sell out. She knew when *not* to loan money and who not to loan it to, she bought when others were selling and sold when they said buy. So, she had gone her own way, taken the risks and now the money was hers. She *owned* it—and she could keep it at home in a cookie jar, bury it in the back yard or wear it in her shoe if she wanted to. But, my word! She hadn't realized so much had accumulated. That old box was full to running over. Likely she'd have to go downtown and pester Lincoln soon. Humming a little tune, she took another long pull on the Coke and counted on.

Presently she glanced up at the kitchen clock. Law, time to get going on that cake. Still, she put it off, idly observing her own hands as they moved over the bills. Old hands— the skin loose and webbed with high blue veins, the fingers knotted and heavy with diamonds—well, they *were* old hands! She chuckled at her own joke. Those hands had been around, done a thing or two in their day. And they still worked fine for her—Augusta Euanthe Houghton née Merriwether—never called Gussie in her life until she married Carter and moved off down to that ranch. Well, there was a lifetime of thinking could be done about *that*.

She had better get busy on that cake. It was her turn to bring refreshments and she had promised the bridge club a shortcake. Before she started counting her money she had set out bowls and spoons right there on the end of the table. Before she sat down she had fetched her favorite mixing spoon, a heavy maple one carved in Vermont and brought across the continent by her grandmother. Gussie loved the heft of that spoon but at the moment she would just as soon leave it be. She didn't feel like baking any cake. It was too hot. Besides, the ladies in her bridge club were in no need of cake—not the Mmes. Asa (T. D.) Hines, or Reid Spence or even Austin Bailey. No, they were pretty well fleshed out already. And cake wouldn't do Lady Lynn Reeves any good either, not so long as she continued to worry over her old mother. Ada Reeves, nigh on ninety-seven, had made her daughter's life a living hell. Mean as a cornered javelina. She had sapped all the juice out of Lady Lynn. Lady Lynn was as flat and pale as a tapeworm and had just about as much spunk. Strawberry shortcake wasn't going to help her any.

Gussie let her mind run on. Went to thinking about the ranch. Time to take a little *vuelta* down there. Casey was as fine a foreman as you'd ever hope to find. "He'd do to ride the river with," as the saying went. But he still looked to her for direction. And the last time he'd been up to town he had been worried. "Rains came too early," he said. "Grass come up short and headed out. Dry as a bone down yonder now." After that he had waited quietly, regarding her from under the shade of his hat. "I'll come on down directly," she had replied. He nodded. "Them calves are lookin' poor."

Gussie pictured how it would be—seared over and the soil aching for rain. Tanks shriveling up and the mud cracking all around the edges like squares of chocolate curling up. Bubba always said when he was little, "Look, Mama! Look at all that chocolate!" Didn't he wish! Well, he ought to be home for lunch soon. Another reason why she ought to get a move on. But it was so nice just to sit there, quiet. A hot little midday wind came up, banging the screen door, ruffling the loose bills and warming what was left of her Coke.

. . . .

CHAPTER 2

A short while later Bubba pulled into the driveway. Bubba's real name was Hugh Merriwether Houghton and he was forty-three years old, the sole offspring of Augusta and Carter Houghton. Ever since childhood he had maintained a body which resembled a soft, plump pear and now his hair, always fine and slightly reddish, was beginning to thin on top. Bubba took great pains over his appearance and was even relieved to arrive at middle age since the mature years allowed a person to wear weight with a certain dignity. Still, he had always been self-conscious about his figure. However, as his mother was fond of pointing out (not without a certain malice), he was also regular for meals. With the air of resignation that comes of choosing comfort over risk, and the certainty of knowing that his life was one of small dimensions, Bubba had years ago settled into the task of teaching history at the high school. He knew it was a thankless task—attempting to recreate the glory that was Rome for a bunch of randy adolescents whose own dreams would never transcend the splendor of becoming cheerleaders and cowboys. Teaching as a career was not what he would have chosen had he ever allowed himself to think about it. But since he didn't allow himself to think about it, since the faculty lounge was a horror of old banana peels and librarians, and since the drive was only a matter of blocks, Bubba always came home for lunch. On that particular day he was anticipating a taste of his mother's shortcake. She was baking for her bridge club—she never baked for him, said he ran to fat.

He climbed out of his new Buick (one of the benefits of choosing comfort), swore mildly as he burned his hand on the door handle, moved up the walk and pushed open the front door. "Mama?" he called, closing the door quickly against the glare. "I'm home, Mama."

Silence.

Bubba sighed. It was going to be another one of those days. His mother had become increasingly cranky lately. Nothing suited her, not one thing. She snapped at him, "Why don't you get married?" Then in the very next breath, "Hon? Would you run down to the store and get me another carton of Cokes?" She was touchy to live with—and getting worse. He had suggested travel, a change of scene (and beverages). The two of them had made several trips to Europe and Bubba had absolutely adored it. He observed that his mother had enjoyed herself as well, especially in Italy. She liked both the fountains and the waiters. But lately she wouldn't hear of it. Whenever he mentioned the idea she said no, she wasn't feeling well. Of course she had been the picture of health all winter—not even a cold. Just let his vacation come around and suddenly she wasn't feeling well.

"What's the matter with you?" he had asked, maybe just a tiny bit peeved.

She had glared at him. After endless arguments during which his exasperation verged on explosion and then veered into a whining nag, she had finally consented to pay a visit to Dr. Cartwright. She left the house in a state of silent outrage, was gone for two hours and returned with her lips defiantly sealed.

Bubba met her at the door. "Well, what did he say?"

"Hmpf. We talked about the weather."

"The *weather*?" He drew himself up.

She fixed him with a challenging and mischievous eye. "Need I remind you, Bubba, that Caleb Cartwright and I are the oldest of friends? He delivered *you*. . . . What he and I discuss is nobody's business but our own."

"Well, Lord God! Didn't he even check your heart?"

Fuming, "Well, *of course* he listened to my heart. He *always* listens to my heart. . . ."

"So what did he say?"

"Say? Why he didn't *say* anything! Just gave me a handful of those silly little pink pills. Say? He said I ought to rest more and stay out of this heat. Honestly, Bubba. . . ."

Thoroughly annoyed, Bubba had let the subject drop and resigned himself to a long summer with nothing to break the monotony but watering the lawn and drinking glasses of iced tea. He would never have dreamed of going abroad without her.

"Mama?" he called again. No response. A small twinge of worry began to nag at him. Maybe she was lying down . . . it could be that she really wasn't feeling quite herself . . . he had noticed lately that she was more attentive about taking her pills no matter what she said to the contrary . . . and these last few evenings she had been retiring rather early. . . . Remorse and sentiment swept over him. He tiptoed to her bedroom door and peeped in. She was not there. The blue satin spread was neatly made up and the room dim, dusty with the scent of lavender and lilac. He breathed the air in gently, savoring the quiet and shelter of the place, as if all the hard edges of life could be shuttered out as they were here, filtered to a soft twilight of assured safety. Yet he looked at the bed warily, unable to imagine that he himself had been created there. His mind and gaze bent away from the thought, shunned the shocking tableau.

On the marble-topped table beside the bed were the two items she always kept there—the charming little enamelled clock which he had bought for her in Florence and the gilt-framed picture of his father. Even from behind glass, his father's presence asserted itself, powerful in the dusky room—overbearing, uncompromising, unforgiving. As always, he made the son uneasy in his mother's bedroom, a voyeur at the keyhole witnessing the lives of real men. Even at this age Bubba still had nightmares about his father—a dark, titanic figure who reeked of whiskey and cigars. From the fathoms of Bubba's dreams, his father towered, rose to the stature and wrath of an angered Jehovah. Then with the love of the unconscious mind for the bizarre, his name would glaringly appear in blazing neon, billboard letters stories high—CARTER HOUGHTON. Far below, in the shadow of such unimpeachable grandeur, a small boy backpedaled on his tricycle, gazing up in fear and awe. Carter Houghton—big-time rancher to hear him tell it, last of the Good Old Boys. Killed in a plane crash one sunny afternoon. Wrapped his wings around a peak when the boy was a mere fourteen. And the only memory which the son carried away from the funeral was his own vast and tearful relief.

Bubba backed away from the bedroom door, beyond the range of his father's frown, and went down the hall toward the kitchen. Odd, he thought, that his mother was still so quiet. Usually she . . . One step through the kitchen door he stopped in horror and went cold inside. There she lay, half-sprawled across the kitchen table, her right arm flung forward and the fingers of that hand clenched blue around a wad of money. Her face was partly hidden in the crook of her left arm but her mouth seemed slightly open and Bubba, in rising hysteria, feared that he saw the gleam of an eye. Running slantwise across her neck and up into the fringe of white hair was the unspeakable violation—a long weal, red as proud flesh, mottled purple along the bruised edges. In one corner of his mind, a small picture like a moving film frozen in a single frame, Bubba heard himself thinking, "How very ugly!" Involuntarily, he took a step back. The kitchen was in chaos—mixing bowls over-turned, wooden spoons splayed across the table—a Coke bottle lay in its own brown pool. On the far end of the table, the old green tackle box in which she kept her cash gaped empty, one hinge sprung. Tossed across the kitchen floor like autumn leaves, a few crumpled bills led toward the back screen door, which hung open, slapping gently in the wind.

Bubba took a deep, shuddering breath. "Mama?" His voice was almost a croak. She gave no sign. Gingerly he stepped forward, extended one finger and touched her bare shoulder where the wrapper had slipped off. Sickened, he jerked back his hand and peered in disbelief at this sprawled and scrawny thing with the violent red swelling still rising on its neck. Backing now in terror, he put his hand over his mouth. "Oh, my God! OH, MY GOD!" His shoulder collided painfully with the doorjamb. He turned and ran for the phone.

CHAPTER 3

. . . .

Summoned from his dinner by Bubba's frantic call, Dr. Caleb Cartwright belched softly, consulted his pocket watch and pronounced Augusta Houghton dead. "I'm real sorry, son. She's gone." He then asked politely whether he might use the phone, went into the hall and telephoned the sheriff. J. D. Killion and his deputy, Rowdy Heywood, arrived almost immediately, tires screaming on the hot asphalt. Stepping into the dim front hall, they stood for a moment silhouetted against the glare outside, blinking and straining their eyes. As if on cue, they removed their Stetsons and held them respectfully at belt buckle level. J. D.'s blond hair was dark with sweat where the hat had been, while Rowdy's curls came slowly back to life like bent clover. Wordless, they nodded to Bubba and followed the doctor back to the kitchen. In that broad light, they winced and circled, facing the scene reluctantly. It was not a man's kind of crime. Their eyes went to Gussie and away again, embarrassed. Her disheveled appearance . . . bare legs sticking out from the loose wrapper, her hair a mess and her mouth hanging open in petulant surprise either from the doctor's turning her head like that without leave, or from some kind of assault, or maybe from a simple disbelief in being dead . . . she would never have allowed herself to be seen like that. They, being gentlemen, knew it and looked the other way. Their boots scraped uneasily on the linoleum, their leather gun belts creaked, their hats shifted from one hand to the other.

"Here now," said Dr. Cartwright gruffly. "We got a job to do. Let's get on with it."

Bubba, watching from the doorway, turned white and vanished like a ghost.

J. D. sighed. "Now what in the hell . . . ?" laid his hat on the counter, bent to examine the red mark on Gussie's neck. Rowdy, observing the sheriff carefully, set his hat down, too, but stood back waiting for instructions. He swallowed with nervous excitement and looked around. Boy howdy . . . Gussie herself would have had a fit if she had seen him standing there in her kitchen. She had always maintained that he was the worst kind of choice for a deputy. Within his hearing, too—she didn't care. Told the judge and the district attorney, anybody who would listen. "Boy like that shouldn't even be allowed to *have* a gun," she declared. "Far less paid to carry one!" Hearing her judgment echoing around that kitchen, sensing some kind of triumph, Rowdy spraddled his legs, rocked back on his boot heels. "That kid is nothing but an outlaw with a badge," stated Gussie. Rowdy hooked his thumbs in his gun belt and stared out the back door.

Bubba sat in the living room, stunned. His hands lay limply in his lap. Every so often his fingers would twitch or his thumb would give a little jerk. His mind refused to take in what had happened and fastened instead on all the times he had told her to keep that back door latched. Over and over he had told her. Time and again. She never paid any attention—she had never paid attention to anything he said. Now this . . . this unthinkable thing had happened. Was it her fault for being so stubborn? Or his own failure? A verse from early childhood began nagging at his mind, something his mother used to read to him in rare moments of tenderness—what was it? Something about a little boy who was only three years old and bossed his mother around. An English jingle . . . James James Somebody Somebody . . . he had an impossibly long name. Bubba remembered the monotonous beat of the poem and how impressed he had been with the arrogance of the child. Little James assumed command. He ordered his mother never to go anywhere without him and even kept her on a leash while he rode his tricycle. Bubba couldn't conceive of himself in a position of such authority. The thought of his own mother on a leash was beyond his powers of imagination. Still, if he recalled correctly, the three-year-old's mother didn't fare so well. She hadn't listened to her son either, but had wandered off, slipped the leash and disappeared forever.

With an effort, he forced his mind to focus on the present, on the voices coming from the kitchen. Dr. Cartwright and Sheriff Killion were talking in low tones. J. D. was all right but Bubba had a long-standing grudge against old man Cartwright and consulted his son, Jason, instead. Jason, presently in partnership with his dad, was gradually taking over the practice. "Thank God!" had been Bubba's reaction to the news of the older doctor's eventual retirement. Jason had a so much better manner. His education was certainly more scientific and up-to-date and he treated his patients with a cool, very professional detachment which Bubba admired and found reassuring. Not the old man. Lord no. Old Cartwright would actually ruminate upon a person's complaint. Then he would ask a bunch of highly personal questions, get lost in thought, seem to forget that he even had a patient and wander off in search of some missing object—his stethoscope or his glasses—and leave you sitting there mother naked and surrounded by disorder. His office was filled to the ceiling—leaning towers of dust-quiet books, filing cabinets crammed with yellowing records and a large, lopsided sofa bearing a distasteful stain. The instruments which littered the old doctor's desk were positively medieval—contraptions of heavy iron clearly designed for torture. Bubba had once remarked to his mother that old Cartwright would have made a better vet.

She had let out a snort. "Well! I guess you never *will* forgive him for that business."

What she was referring to (with her usual delicacy and tact) was an utterly mortifying memory for her son. When he had been about twelve or thirteen, he had been pleased to discover certain changes occurring in his body and delighted in the exploration and examination of these new and undeniable developments. Correspondingly, he was equally horrified to find something amiss in that most personal part of his anatomy. (To this very day he would *die* rather than use the word "privates," although at the time his mother and the doctor had tossed the word around with a casualness that was unbearable.) Whatever it was, it itched like hell and hurt at the same time. In his dreams he had visions of the wrathful finger of God pointing directly at him, a sort of shocked and white-lipped Uncle Sam saying, "I want *you!*" Bubba resigned himself to going straight to hell. But the itch kept up, and after some ill-considered doctoring on his own, he had finally gone to his mother, flushed with shame and hopping from one foot to the other. She had given him a long, hard look—like he was somebody she didn't even know—and dragged him off to see Dr. Cartwright.

Bubba never forgot that ride in the pickup. Every cattle guard was forever etched into his biological memory. When they eventually got to town, Dr. Cartwright made a clumsy and perfunctory examination, told Bubba to button up and prescribed the same purple medicine that they used down on the ranch when the horses got cut up by barbed wire. Radiant with fury, Bubba had listened while the doctor explained to his mother that the stuff was as good an antiseptic as any he knew of, and since they no doubt had plenty of it already he saw no reason to prescribe some newfangled salve. Only be messy, cost good money and take twice as long to work. So they made the long drive back. And for two whole weeks Bubba had been forced to suffer the added humiliation of lurid sitz baths in a tin washtub and daily inspections from his mother, who studied him with the same interest she would have granted a bull calf. Forgiveness? For that man?

Bubba's thoughts were jarred rudely back to the present by Rowdy Heywood, who stomped loudly down the hall, yelled something into the telephone, and stomped back to the kitchen. (My God, what were they *doing* in there?) A few minutes later another vehicle pulled up outside. Sig Percy from the funeral home came in. A stretcher was brought. More discussion in the kitchen. Sounds of a scuffle, scraping noises. Then something was carried out on the stretcher, something all sharp angles under a sheet. Then an absolute din of car doors slamming and everyone drove away except Dr. Cartwright. He came into the living room where Bubba was sitting and stood there silently, almost apologetically. Finally, after considerable rummaging and muttering, he located a form of some kind. He sat down in Gussie's favorite chair and wrote out her death certificate on his knee.

Then he left and Bubba was alone. For a while, he simply sat there, he didn't know how long. Eventually he roused himself and telephoned the school secretary, explaining that he would not be in for several days but not saying why. The line hummed with suppressed curiosity. After that, he braced himself and phoned his mother's brother, Beau. Beau was out at his ranch north of town. At first there was only a shocked silence. Bubba could almost see it—little fireworks going off soundlessly in the distance. Then Beau exploded.

"*Well, I'll be a son of a bitch!*" Bubba could hear him yelling for his wife. "Charlene? Hon? Where the hell are you? Godalmighty! Gussie's gone. What? *Where*? She's dead, that's where." He came back on the phone full blast. "*Christ* Almighty!" Bubba cringed, held the phone out at least a foot from his ear. "What the hell happened to her?" Beau roared. "What? You don't *know*? What do you mean you . . . ? You think somebody *hit* her? Who the hell was it? I'll kill the son of a bitch!"

Bubba tried to explain, unaware that he was still holding the phone way out.

"Speak up, boy!" blasted Beau. "I can't hardly hear a word you're sayin'. Did he get you, too?" There were sounds of an argument. Apparently Charlene wrenched the phone away.

"Are you *bleedin'*, Bubba?" she wailed. "Are you bleedin' anywhere? Just get you some ice. Get you some ice and then call the doctor."

It was a good ten minutes before he was able to make them understand. He could hear Beau stamping and shouting in the background. "Je–sus Chi–ri–i–st! My own god-damn sister . . ." Charlene, however, kept a firm grip on the phone.

"Bubba? Honey? You don't want to go and stay in that old house by yourself. Not now. Lord! You come out here and be with us. No, now you just come on. It's not even *safe* in town anymore!"

Few men had ever said no to Charlene. When Bubba finally put down the phone he had a terrible headache.

He leaned back in the chair and closed his eyes. After a time he became gradually aware of the ticking house around him, dim and shuttered against the heat, silent except for the clocks. In the slow backwash of shock and horror, emerging smooth as a shark's fin, his own emotions took shape. Anger and resentment began to rise. What did she mean, going off like that? Without one word of warning and in such a gruesome manner? Why couldn't she have died in bed wearing her lace jacket, hands folded on the counterpane like decent people did?—not be packed off like something for the locker plant. And how was he supposed to manage? Not only the details of this . . . vulgar . . . situation, but the rest of his life? He had always visualized himself in the role of dutiful son—at her elbow during parties, removing or replacing her wraps, anxiously and graciously attending, holding doors . . . . Actually he was more often burdened with cartons of Coke, panting from endless small errands—postage stamps, moleskin, silver polish . . . and here he was now, uneasy in unexpected freedom, adrift, cut loose from the pull of that familiar gravity. Dismay, annoyance and something not far from panic were among his emotions. Grief was not.

*

Dazed, moving like a sleepwalker, he got to his feet and went back to the kitchen. The chair she had been sitting in had fallen over, the table was shoved slightly aside. Carefully he lined up the table and replaced the chair. The screen door still flapped gently in the breeze. Bubba stepped over and latched it, the irony not lost on him—like locking the barn door after the horse . . . He turned back to the table. Bowls and spoons lay scattered. At least nothing was broken. But why was her favorite mixing spoon—that old maple thing—clear across the room, flung into the corner like that? Bubba bent and retrieved it. Then, one by one, he collected the other utensils and carried them over to the sink. There he carefully washed each item and wiped it dry with a tea towel. The towel his mother had used that morning still hung on the little rack, slightly damp. A few crumbs littered the counter. The package of frozen strawberries lay thawing on the edge of the sink. As if she had just stepped out.

CHAPTER 4

. . . .

J. D. and Rowdy skidded to a stop and scattered gravel. Then they made tracks down the length of the courthouse hallway, dust smoking up from under their boot heels every step of the way. Sweat-stained and breathless, they pulled up in the doorway of the D.A.'s office with all the impact and fragrance of a small stampede. Austin Bailey, who was seated quietly at his desk working on a letter and wondering idly if he should run for the legislature, looked up, startled. J. D. sailed his hat for the rack with practiced ease and launched directly into his story. Austin bit off the end of a fresh cigar, which he never lit. Instead he sat back listening, his face slowly tightening, his mouth turning grim. He then dispatched J. D. to the funeral home and sent Rowdy back to the Houghton place equipped with a new notebook, a pencil and old Jessie, who was justice of the peace and who should have been called in the first place. After all that was dispensed with, Austin took a few moments for himself, staring out the window at the courthouse lawn, the red brick jail and the street beyond. It was an ugly business. He would miss Gussie—everybody would. But it might develop into a big case, really turn into something. Might provide him with just the publicity and the political boost that he needed to get on with his

with his good looks and ambitions wanted
:torney in rural West Texas for the rest of
houghtfully Austin turned and looked at
tne telephone. Then he picked up the receiver and called
his wife.

So it was that the bridge club learned of the news before
anybody else, and the very people Gussie had been fixing
to bake a cake for spread the word of her death with amazing speed. The Lone Star Bidders (known in some parts of
town as the Lone Star Biddies) heard about the murder of
their old friend long before the sheriff in El Paso got the
news, a full hour before the radios of the Highway Patrol
started to crackle. They knew all the details and had even
formed certain opinions before the Border Patrol and the
Texas Rangers even picked up the phone. It was remarked
later that they would have had the case solved and the vil-
lain hung that same afternoon if they had been left alone.

In any event, the instant Austin Bailey put down his
phone, all the others in town were picked up. To this
day some people swear that the temperature went up ten
degrees solely in response to the humming of telephone
lines—a grid laid across the whole community, blue-white
and sizzling. Johnnie Mae Spence, for instance, dreaming
fondly of strawberry shortcake and a trump in hearts, had
already left the ranch and was halfway to town when the
news broke. So she never heard the phone next to her
bed all but strangling itself with excitement. She knew
something was up, though, the minute she pulled up outside Amity Longsford's house. Amity was out the door
and down the front walk screeching like a peahen before
Johnnie Mae could even get the car door open. Right about
then, Charlotte Buchanan showed up. There was a breath-

less exchange of news which left Johnnie Mae stunne unbelieving, and then they all rushed inside to call Lady Lynn. Now Lady Lynn—a dreamy person who was often dewy-eyed, frequently found herself reminded of the light, how it fell so golden and rainbowed through the stained glass windows of the Presbyterian church, and of the lilies, how they smelled at Easter—Lady Lynn was vaguely and patiently feeding lunch to her old mother when the phone in their kitchen nearly jangled off the wall. They both jumped at the sound and looked. Her mouth still open in a receiving position, old Mrs. Reeves glared around at the offending instrument. Meanwhile, Lady Lynn, who had to stretch to reach the thing, poked a spoonful of mashed hominy where her mother's mouth had been only moments before. Unfortunately she connected with the old lady's ear and innocent hominy was packed into an opening where it had no business to be. Ada Reeves jerked around, furious. The spoon went flying and mush got sprayed in her hair. At this, old Mrs. Reeves commenced to shout. Lady Lynn, the receiver halfway up, dropped it, leaving it to dangle and bounce with Charlotte Buchanan shouting on the other end. Trapped that way, caught between two shouting women, Lady Lynn thought briefly of running. Running and running . . . over the hills . . . the wind lifting her hair and nothing but birdsong, spring flowers and grass . . . Instead, she made frantic motions toward her mother, grabbed the spinning receiver and listened, gradually turning the color of a wet sheet. She replaced the receiver as if it were made of bone china and sat down in a kitchen chair. Wide-eyed and pallid, she explained to her mother what had happened. Mrs. Reeves gummed over the information with relish and seemed to suffer no loss of appetite. Smacking wetly she wanted to know what else a person could expect? Especially a greedy old goat like

Gussie. This world was headed straight for hell and the sooner the better. That settled, she pushed away the bowl and demanded a washrag for her ear. In contrast, a few blocks away, Sadie Jo Hawkins put down her white phone and fluttered a hand to her breast. Immediately she rushed to her closet to take inventory of her wardrobe. Sadie Jo was sure she would be called upon to sing at the funeral.

As soon as Austin Bailey finished talking with his wife, he put on his hat and strolled around the corner to have a word with his old friend and former law partner, Houston Carr. The two men had often been the butt of what some people considered very clever humor. For example:

"You going to Houston?" (About some land dispute, horse theft or a will.)

"Hell no. It's too far. I reckon I'll settle for Austin." And so on. Very funny the first ten thousand times. The two attorneys, being tolerant men, put up with it. But after Austin had been elected district attorney the joke kind of faded out, surfacing only occasionally at Rotary Club luncheons or big barbecues at the Legion Hall. Of the two, Austin was of course the more politically inclined and he was often in demand to speak at high school commencements and to give lectures on juvenile crime. Not a tall man, he was handsome in a faintly spoiled way. A hint of self-indulgence lingered in his features and gave rise to the overripeness which characterized his corpulent figure. Nevertheless, he had poise and never lacked for self-assurance. He dressed very well indeed and was fond of shooting a cuff if only to smooth the waves of his glossy and still-dark hair. Houston, on the other hand, was tall, big-boned, a shambles of a man who seemed loosely strung together underneath oversized, rumpled suits. He conducted his law business from an office which looked and smelled like the den of some large animal. Everything about Houston was large, worn and comfortable. Leaning back in his old leather chair, he listened to Austin's story without interrupting, his face deeply troubled and the chewed butt of a cold cigar between his motionless fingers. When Austin had finished, the two of them sat in companionable silence for a while.

"Well?" said Austin finally. "What do you make of it?"

Houston wagged a shaggy head. "Bad," he replied. "Real bad. Hell . . . everybody and his dog knew that Gussie kept all that money around the house! Looks to me like it got her in the long run."

Austin sighed. "We sure haven't got much to go on. I guess I better tell J. D. to round up a posse."

"Looks like it."

CHAPTER 5

. . . .

Word went out. Before long, pickups and Chevys, Buicks and station wagons were glinting in the sun all around the rodeo grounds. A haze of dust hung in the air. Men nodded to each other, spat, crowded up in the bars of shade laid down by the slats in the grandstand. Greeting each other in low voices, they chewed, smoked or simply squatted on their heels.

"Otis, you hear what happened?"

"Gene, I'll tell ya. Like to floored me."

"Damnedest thing I ever heard."

"Whadda you figure?"

"They ain't got no idea who done it?"

They shook their heads and passed the time, waiting for the arrival of the sheriff. Hunkered in a scrap of shade, squinting up against the sun, smoking and sweating, they waited, trading opinions. When J. D. finally arrived he didn't have much to tell them that they didn't already know.

"Shoot. That's precious little," summed up one fella.

"All wool and a yard wide," added another.

The sheriff asked if any of them had seen anything unusual or had anything worthwhile to pass on. There was a low rumble in the negative. Hats moved sideways, none of them up and down. Then Chuy Gallego, who was standing toward the back, timidly raised his hand.

"Señor Killion?"

Every head turned and they looked. Their eyes narrowed just a fraction, not because Chuy was standing between them and the sun, either—he wasn't—he was full in it, as a matter of fact. Their eyes beneath their hat brims hardened ever so little, glinted the faintest warning. Nobody made a sound. The wind pushed a dry tumbleweed against the wire fence and then settled back to mess up the grass. There was a hot, sweet smell of grass and dust. Chuy swallowed and prayed for courage. He knew what they were thinking, every last one of them. He could actually hear it—or the echo, since he had been hearing it all his life: Mexican. What does he know? Smart ass Mexican. Messkin. Damnmesskin. Greaser. Messikin. Chuy Gallego was not a Mexican. He was a U.S. citizen just like these men were. He had been born in America and if there had been a war on he would have signed up to prove it. Chuy had never even been to Mexico, not past Ojinaga. And even those few times had not been worth the trip: the Mexican girls had been skinny and listless, the mattresses filthy, the gas had water in it and the guys at Customs gave him one hell of a time. Chuy hated Mexico. But to these men he was a Mexican. Forever. His father had worked for them, doing yard work and hauling trash, and his mother and sisters still did, cleaning the houses for the wives of these men. Chuy had set out to better himself, to improve his position in life. With a kind of head-down determination he had completed high school despite the wine-ripened derision of his brother, Martín, and a sweaty-handed clumsiness with the English language. Chuy had a way of dropping the words like bricks; they landed at his feet and he was always tripping over them. Despite all that, he had graduated (his diploma was framed and hung in the front room of his house). He had a good job. He had gone to work for the highway department and now he held an important position. He bossed a road crew, which was why he had seen what he had seen and why he had to speak. They were waiting . . . these Anglos.

Sweat starting up in his armpits, he began, *concentrating* so that the *i*'s would not sound like double *ee*'s, trying hard not to sing the words off his tongue but lay them out flat and hard the way the Anglos spoke their language. He and his road crew had been working west of town, Chuy reported. About half a dozen of them with picks and shovels, the tar wagon and the gravel truck—working like that. Bad holes on that highway . . . not far from town, just beyond the first underpass . . . perhaps they knew the spot?

Not a flicker, not a sign.

Chuy plunged ahead. Well, he said, they were making lots of noise so they didn't hear anything coming. The flagman shouted out but then he had to run. All of a sudden—out of nowhere!—here came this *beeg*, this *huge* white car. Man! So fast! It nearly knocked them over, threw tar and gravel all over the place. They shouted and shook their shovels. The guy in the tar wagon honked his horn. But he couldn't go nowhere in that thing. . . . Anyway, that car was gone before they knew it. Gone . . . just like that. Washed away in the water that always spreads across the highway in the heat. Only the noise of his horn, that guy in the car, coming back from far away like a bad word . . . or a certain gesture. "You know?"

For a long moment nobody said anything. Then J. D. spat into the dust and hitched at his crotch. "You get the license number, Chuy?"

"But *no*! No, Sheriff, that is what I have been saying. It happened too *fast*! Out of nowhere a beeg white car—ZOOM!—" he stretched his arms wide. "Like that. Then gone."

"Well, what kinda car was it?"

"Like I say, a big one. And he—*it*—have no top. Open."

"Are you trying to say it was a convertible?"

Chuy nodded eagerly. "Yes sir! That was the kind."

"How many folks was in it?"

Chuy was crushed. He should never have spoken. It was no help. He did not know anything of use. These men would never listen to him. "I do not know, Sheriff. Maybe one, maybe more."

One of the men let out a short laugh. "Well, I reckon there was one fella in it leastaways. Otherwise you got yourself a ghost car, Chuy."

General laughter. Then a man wearing a tan suit spoke up. He was a stranger and he made his remarks from the edge of the crowd. He said he'd seen that white car all right, a Caddie convertible fairly smoking up the road. But being as how he was a cattle buyer from El Paso and had to cover a lot of country, he saw cars like that all the time. "Y'all know that stretch just this side of Sierra Blanca, that *long*, empty stretch straight as the aisle on a weddin' day?"

The men grinned and nodded in agreement.

"Well, it was along about in there. That old boy was fairly flying. But then who don't? Only thing you can do through there short of shuttin' your eyes."

Everybody laughed and agreed. Even J. D. had to grin. Chuy Gallego smiled, too, but so stiffly and for so long that he felt his teeth turning dry in the wind.

J. D. spat again and resettled his hat. "Hell," he said. "I don't see why a fella who drives a Cadillac convertible would rob a old woman and beat up on her like that."

The men mumbled agreement and the mood turned more serious. Rowdy showed up along about then and reported that he had combed the back yard and the alley, checked everywhere around Gussie's house and hadn't found a thing. As if acting on some secret signal, the men stood up then. They dusted their hands and hitched their belts. J. D. took off his hat and swiped at the sweat on his forehead. "Well," he said slowly, "that sure don't give us much to go on."

"Well, damn!" said one man, plainly itchy to get going. "What are we gonna *do*?"

"Fan out!" ordered J. D., suddenly inspired. "Fan out! I want three men on every highway leading out of town. You boys with pickups, hit the ranch roads. Rest of you, work a grid across town like this." He squatted down and drew in the dirt. "Guys with horses handy work the rough country . . . hills around, up them canyons. Be sure you're armed and keep your eyes open. This son of a bitch is dangerous." His lips tightened into a thin, white line. "We'll get him. *Whoever* he is and *wherever* he is, we'll get him."

· · ·

In the seclusion of his private office, Lincoln Winters replaced the telephone receiver gently in its cradle. Around him the bank hummed with the usual sedate and smooth efficiency but Lincoln's thoughts were not on business. For several moments he sat perfectly still. Then he picked up his silver pen and drew a row of little stars on the pad in front of him. When he reached the end of the row he stopped and then added a period. That period represented the end of an era. For a long time he had been aware of Gussie's peculiar and devious habit of always marking her bills—every single one that she brought in for deposit—with a small but distinctive Lone Star inked

in the upper right-hand corner. Lincoln had never understood why Gussie did it and of course he never let on that
he knew—not to her, not to anybody. People, as they got
older, were entitled to their eccentricities—or so Lincoln
believed. And everyone was due a certain degree of privacy.
He stared at the neat row of stars a while longer. Then he
picked up the phone again and quietly passed on information which, although remaining odd, could no longer remain privileged. "Austin? Lincoln Winters. I believe there
is something you ought to know. . . ." The district attorney
listened intently.

By that time everybody who wasn't chasing around with
the posse had gathered downtown for a Coke, a cup of
coffee or a long, cool glass of iced tea. Even people who
didn't particularly like coffee or Coke or iced tea, or each
other, and who normally never went out in the afternoon—
they were all there, crowded into the Texas Cafe. The
atmosphere was high with excitement, a little like a re-
union. Folks who hadn't really talked to each other in years
nodded a greeting, sat down, told what they knew and listened. For their part, Spud and Irma Harris, who were the
owners of the place, thanked their lucky stars (not knowing, of course, about Gussie's, or about the conversation
Lincoln and Austin were having at that very moment).
Spud and Irma were more interested in the unexpected
run on cherry pie. Pap Benson, who ran the pool hall, got
into a heated argument with Sadler Williams. It seems Pap
was ready to hang somebody while Sadler favored shooting. Across the room, Cliff and Clay Weyerts, identical
twins who ran a spread way east, listened with pink and
flattering attention to Virginia McCutcheon from the Pilot
Club. Virginia did not mind; it was not often that good-
looking boys of twenty-eight gazed so admiringly upon a

woman of middle age. When Beau and Charlene Merriwether arrived, however, they created an immediate sensation which eclipsed all other dramas. Charlene, as usual,
was got up to the hilt, dressed in a flowery, low-cut thing
hardly suitable for the occasion. Beau was buttoned up in a
brand-new pale blue western shirt. They settled in, the center of attention. Around them, chairs were scraped back,
crockery rattled and the conversation eddied and swelled.
Overhead, the big old ceiling fan flapped mournfully, pad-
dling the heavy air with a kind of hopeless resignation.
Its slow rotation dipped slightly on every southern sweep,
causing a drift of dead flies to stir on the windowsill next
to a pot of yellowing cactus. The only person who noticed
was the waitress, Janelle French, and she was far too busy
to care. It just struck her at the time.

In the private kitchens of town, food was being prepared
feverishly. Presently platters began arriving at Bubba's
door. Startled, he stood back in awe while the entire
local chapter of the Daughters of the Confederacy marched
in determined formation toward the kitchen, their arms
laden with plates and bowls and covered dishes. That same
kitchen—still reeking faintly of violence, as if someone
had struck a match and the sulphur lingered—that kitchen
now took on the appearance of a church supper. Bubba
filled the refrigerator. He loaded the table and both counters. Food continued to arrive: ham, fried chicken, potato
salad, molded salad, an oddly festive dish of cookies—he
had no idea what to do with it all. Assuming an air of dig-
nified sorrow, he thanked the ladies gravely. They paid no
attention to him whatsoever. Instead they shuttled in and
out, speaking to each other in hushed, conspiratorial tones.
Bubba looked at them, bewildered. He had known these
women all his life but all of a sudden some transformation

had taken place. These were not the same women he had greeted yesterday in the grocery store, the ones who played bridge with his mother and who screeched and gossiped, catted and complained . . . no. They had undergone some elemental change, muttered some dark oath never heard by the ears of males, sworn themselves to some ancient sisterhood whose rites he chilled to think about. Annoyed finally, his nerves on edge and made more raw by all this hissing and scuttling, Bubba Houghton raised his voice. He had never done so before. The sound both frightened and pleased him. Aghast, the women stopped and stared. Stopped in their tracks and stared at him like who did he think he was? Clearly they had forgotten he was there.

Life on the larger scale went on as usual. Death made no impression. The surrounding hills turned blue while a trio of buzzards floated lazily in the high dome of limpid twilight. The breeze cooled and the cloudless sky turned gold and then the color of a purple iris. Presently, huge, luminous stars appeared and darkness deepened over the town, settling gently on the mountains, pooling in the live oak canyons, spreading smoothly from the east all the way from the clay banks of the Pecos River and beyond. Meanwhile, several hundred miles to the north, a little night wind sprang up, searching the thorny brush and sandhills, moving smooth along the lonesome highways of New Mexico.

CHAPTER 6

. . . .

*T*wo days later, Augusta Houghton was laid to rest, buried in that same earth she had fought with all her life (and sometimes hated, but nevertheless managed to force a fortune from) and under that same wide, blank sky which had arched over greedy Spaniards and misguided friars alike, also Apache Indians, cavalry troops and river smugglers and, for the time being anyway, was overseeing with equal indifference large ranches of white-faced cattle—that same sky which sometimes granted rain and life and more often did not—in other words, Gussie went back to where she came from, some people meaning one thing by that and some another. Her funeral was to be remembered for years. The church was filled to overflowing. People came from all over, flew in from Chicago and Abilene and even from New York and San Francisco. Flowers were banked down both outside aisles and formed a solid wall behind the altar—sprays of coral, peach and lemon glads, wax-white lilies, wreaths of baby's breath and carnations, roses the color of butter and cream and tiny buds ranging from shades of pastel pink to port wine . . . all exhaling at once so that the air was dense and layered with scent. In somber contrast, the pallbearers lined up in stiff black—solemn, scrubbed and raw-boned men, necks and wrists reddened by the sun and chafed to an even higher color by white collars and cuffs. They were all Gussie's friends, men she had known a lifetime: Jiggs Skinner, Cab Stillwater, Asa (T. D.) Hines, Cliff and Clay Weyerts (in honor of their father) and her special friend and advisor, Houston Carr. The honorary pallbearers sat apart in a row reserved especially for them: former senator Buchanan in a state of deep meditation, his skin smelling faintly of lilac water; next to him slouched Judge Ira Hainsworth, heavy, florid and reeking gently of cigars. Ira Hainsworth was not looking forward to the trial bound to follow on the death of this woman. Nossir. Up until now he had hoped for a routine summer, maybe get in a little fishing down on the lake. Now all that seemed most unlikely. First he would have to gather up the jury, then there would be the lawyers (Judge Hainsworth hated lawyers; he knew all about them) and most likely the press—hell yes, the press, big trial like this one was fixing to be (he hated newspapermen even more than lawyers except during election years)—and all manner of fuss and fumigation. Assuming, of course, that they caught the rascal. Course, they might not catch him . . . they just might not. Not with what passed for law enforcement these days and what with Mexico being so close. . . . He blew out his cheeks in the heat. The lines along his jowls settled back into their familiar folds. Directly behind Judge Hainsworth and right on the aisle, sober as a parson and twice as shiny, sat Gussie's favorite old pal—her foul weather friend she called him—Gus McIntyre. Trussed up in a black worsted suit (obviously recently shaken out and brushed for the occasion, fairly radiating the sharp green odor of camphor), his boots shined up and his hair slicked down, Gus sat quietly, blinking his white eyelashes and staring down at the rough hands spread on his knees.

*

The appearance of old Gus had caused what almost amounted to a breeze in that otherwise stuffy and over-heated church. He had arrived at the door uneasy, hat in his hand but unsure about what to do next. An oily young man had materialized at his elbow, made off with his hat and herded him clear down to the third pew, where he pointed out the only seat left, the one right on the aisle. Gus, who longed for the back row where there was some fresh air and a hope of escape, hunkered down unwillingly. He gave Gussie's casket a quick glance and then kept his eyes on his hands. Nearly every other eye in that church, however, was on him—lined up like a ledger and figuring. Some eyebrows went up in surprise while others were pulled down hard in disapproval. Gus couldn't have cared less. He had come to say so long to Gussie and that was all. He owed her that much. But somehow he had let himself get boxed in down there. A man couldn't breathe, buried under all those flowers like he was.

Gus ranched down along the river—had for over fifty years—hard, lean years and every one of them showed. People who lived in that harsh and intolerant country came to look like the landscape they wrestled with and Gus was no exception; in fact, he was a prime example. He and Gussie had been neighbors but Gussie's ranch was higher up, more rain and more grass. Old Gus had settled down in caliche country and his best crops were greasewood, prickly pear and lizards. If it rained he went out and stood in it. If it filled up his boots, it was a gully-washer; otherwise it was only a sprinkle. He rarely came to town and then only to fill his grub box with flour and coffee and whiskey. Until that day he had never darkened the door of a church, said the only way they'd ever get him in one would be feet first and he figured buzzards could do a better job come to that so just forget the church business altogether. Yet here he was, a living token of his esteem for an old friend and a woman he had deeply admired.

Gus McIntyre spent most of his days leaning back in a cane-bottom chair squinting down the barrels of his shotgun and taking pot shots at anything that moved. As the sun traveled, so did he, dragging that old chair up and down the slope of his sagging porch. He always kept a jug nearby, so as the day wore on the shots became more random and varied in frequency. People were thus understandably cautious and tried not to bother Gus unless they absolutely had to. Not long ago he had winged some geologists who had no business being on his property and nobody dared to speculate on how many wetbacks lay dead or wounded out there in the brush. A sloppy, hand-lettered sign swung in the wind over his cattleguard: GAWDdaMMit. KEEP the HELLout. In his golden years Gus had lost interest in ranching and taken up prospecting, frequently disappearing for weeks at a time into an old abandoned silver mine. When they didn't see him come to town for a month or so, folks figured he had died in there or been buried alive. Since nobody was crazy enough to risk finding out, they just let him lay so to speak. Then one day he would show up again, white with dust and sprouting a bristly two weeks' growth. Angry at the sidewalk for some reason, he would stomp a chalky trail from the feedstore to the liquor store and be gone again.

In the old days, Gus and Gussie had spent many an evening together sitting at her kitchen table in the light of a kerosene lamp and swapping stories or exchanging news about the weather. So when he took up with that Mexican woman Gussie wasn't surprised and it didn't change her feelings toward him one bit. Of course, when the news reached town, there was a shrill outcry from the bridge club. Gussie reared back in her chair and looked them all in the eye. "Well, for Pete's sake! You-all are damnfool silly! What in this blessed world do you think goes on in those bunkhouses, anyway? Gus McIntyre is simply an honest man, he doesn't sneak around like the rest. Do you think I don't know that Carter himself had a taste for dark meat now and then?" There was a collective gasp of dismay followed by a silence as sharp and brittle as ice. Gussie went on. "My Lord! You girls have got your heads in the sand, buried clear to the neck. How come there are so many little blue-eyed and red-headed children over there in Mexican town? Just tell me that before you go passing judgment on a man like Gus. I declare!" The bridge game had ended early that day and Gussie drove home in a state of rare good humor.

So on the day of Gussie's funeral, the eyes of the Lone Star Bidders bored into Gus McIntyre's back like fence-wire staples. Charlotte Buchanan let out such an unladylike snort that her husband, the senator, although several pews away, started up like a man interrupted in the middle of a Sunday after-dinner nap. Next to Charlotte, Mrs. Asa (T. D.) Hines studied Gus in the way of a large country woman slow to make up her mind. Beside her, Amity Longsford fidgeted and re-crossed her knees several times, wondering if her husband had ever had anything to do with a Mexican woman. Susannah Bledsoe fluttered her fan. Susannah and that little Japanese paper fan were inseparable. She carried it with her wherever she went and fluttered it around whenever she became agitated, which was often. Now she waved it rapidly, causing Amity's perfume to waft onto Effie Sue Ethridge, who made up the other side of Susannah, holding her in like a bookend. Effie Sue could not abide perfume. She was a thin, dry person with eyes like shiny buttons, a sharp nose and an equally pointed wit which matched Gussie's own. Effie Sue was not at all offended by Gus's presence at the funeral—she figured Gussie would have wanted him there. Effie Sue was more annoyed by what she considered to be a waste of perfectly good flowers.

The family of the deceased occupied the front pew directly before the casket. First on the aisle the son, Bubba, properly subdued and perhaps a bit pale. He wore a lightweight charcoal suit, a pearl gray shirt and a tie the color of slate. (The choice had surely been unintentional but the satin lining of the casket exactly matched the shade of his tie.) Next came Gussie's brother, Beau, hot and itchy in town clothes, breathing out a succession of low, whiskey belches. Beau's wife, Charlene, was decorated in black lace topped by a slab of very bright red lipstick. Bubba looked at her and shuddered. The phrase which came to his mind describing his aunt-by-marriage was "Señorita Garish." Leave it to Charlene to go to a funeral dressed up like an Ojinaga whore on her way to High Mass.

To everyone's relief, the service was simple. The Reverend Quinn was short-winded and Sadie Jo Hawkins had been persuaded not to sing. The graveside ceremony was hot, dusty and mercifully brief. The big, quiet men of that country picked up the ropes and lowered their sister into the earth as tenderly as if she had been a carton of eggs. The coffin momentarily resisted, scraped unnervingly against rock then reluctantly settled. Everyone breathed a sigh of thanks. A final prayer was intoned and people departed in twos and threes, hushed and thoughtful. Soon only a wavering trail of dust marked their passage back to town. The two Mexican-American men who had been standing discreetly to one side in the shade of a large elm emerged, crossed themselves and picked up their shovels. The first pebbles hit the coffin lid like buckshot.

CHAPTER 7

. . . .

Hell. What are we gonna do, Austin?"

It was the morning after the funeral. Austin Bailey and J. D. Killion were conferring in a dispirited manner in the D.A.'s office. It wasn't that they were grieving for Gussie, the problem was that they didn't know what to do next. Suddenly all eyes in the community had turned upon them, creating a glaring and unwelcome limelight; they were expected to come up with a solution—and soon. A crime had been committed not only against Gussie but against an entire way of life. Everything they stood for had been violated—church, town, community, law. Now people were waiting.

Austin sighed and picked up his pen. He began tapping the yellow legal pad on his desk. Light poured through the tall, arched windows and reflected off the white, stamped-tin ceiling. Austin hated morning light. The truth was, he hated mornings. But morning light was unmerciful. It showed up the streaks of silver in his hair and the diamonds in his ring. With equal impartiality, it revealed every scratch and scrape and dent on his desk and every splinter in the old wood floor. Austin preferred a dimmer light, or at least a more flattering exposure. He was a good-looking man—a little on the heavy side but he had presence. However, he was aware of certain weaknesses within himself—dark, ugly knots which, strung together, made him human if not exactly compassionate and which in this light were in danger of emerging. He sighed again and stared past J. D. at the shelves of law books. "Well, we certainly don't have much to go on. The posse didn't turn up anything at all and that car Chuy says he saw . . ."

"Shoot!" interrupted J. D. "Ain't that a big help! Just how many white Cadillacs you figure there *are* in the state of Texas? Chuy didn't even get the license number. And you know what else? I got on the radio right away—right after I talked to you, I mean directly I got back from the funeral home—and you know what? Those guys in New Mexico? Damnedest thing . . . they said they'd seen that car all right but *they didn't want to talk about it*! You figure that one out. They were *very* reluctant to talk about that car."

Austin frowned. He didn't like this case. It might still turn into something useful politically but there was something disturbing about it, an absurd, random quality which he instinctively mistrusted. Something mocking, almost flippant. He had the feeling that he was confronted with very devious evidence. "Why wouldn't the troopers in New Mexico talk about a speeding car?"

"Beats me."

Austin cleared his throat. "I'll call the chief up there. Meanwhile, the other thing is the money. If Gussie marked it all like Lincoln says she did then that gives us something to go on. The trouble is we don't know how much money there was. Could have been a hundred—or a thousand. Bubba swears he doesn't know, said Gussie never let him touch it."

"Now ain't that a funny thing? Her own son and all?"

"People get peculiar when it comes to money."

"But with their own kin?"

Austin smiled. "Especially with their own kin."

The two men sat in silence for several minutes, each busy with his own thoughts. Austin made a note on the yellow pad. "Did Rowdy find anything over at the house?"

"Not a dadblamed thing. Not even any sign of a break-in. Back gate wasn't even open—the one that leads out into the alley, you know?" J. D. shook his head. "Not a hair on the gatepost."

"Bubba said she must have left the kitchen door unlatched."

"Could be. Everybody around here does. A person doesn't *usually* have to worry." He pulled a packet of cigarette papers from his shirt pocket and shook tobacco into one, making a careful line down the center. Then he gave a practiced twist, placed the product between his lips and returned the makings to his pocket. Austin watched the process, annoyed. Rolling his own was one of J. D.'s earthier traits. Austin did not understand why he hung on to such habits but there was something stubborn and obsolete about the sheriff. Sometimes he was more like an actor in a Saturday western instead of somebody in real life. His washed-out blue eyes searched the district attorney's. "We gotta do something pretty quick, Austin. Folks is gettin' restless. I feel like a bottle lined up for target practice ever' damn time I walk down the street."

Austin replied testily. "Sheriff, there isn't much we *can* do at this point. I've already put out tracers on both the car and the money, contacted law enforcement all over the country. *Somebody somewhere* must have seen *something*. In the meantime I guess we better question some of the local people."

J. D. grinned. "You mean 'suspicious characters'?"

Austin was not amused. He frowned again. "Well, who-ever did this thing obviously knew his way around. Some-body who was aware that Gussie kept all that money at the house and that she was in the habit of counting it every morning."

"Crissake! Everybody knew *that*!"

The D.A. smiled ruefully. "Most of them voted for us, too."

"You got a point there."

"We've got to start somewhere."

J. D. scraped a kitchen match across his boot sole, drew on the homemade cigarette, blew out the match and threw it in the direction of the brass spittoon in the corner. When he finally spoke it was from behind a haze of blue smoke. "Thing is . . . where?"

"How about Martín Gallego?"

"Chuy's brother? Hell. That Messkin is one no good hombre."

Austin agreed. "Not a bit like Chuy. I admire Chuy. He tries, he really tries. Finished high school, got himself a steady job, settled down and raised a family. . . . Chuy is a good man, a fine example for his people."

"You bet. You bet he is. But that Martín—Mar-*teen* he calls himself, like he was some kind of Messkin hair oil— he gets drunk, smokes marijuana, fools around. I hear he's gotten some nice little girls in trouble, too. That boy is a regular s.o.b. Why, one time—leastways this is what I heard—one time Chuy and his wife and the kids went over for a visit, have dinner you know, see the old lady . . . Chuy is real good to his mama. Anyway, that Mar-*teen*, he plumb cleared out. Left the house. Said he didn't want nothing to do with no white Messkins. *White Messkins?* Don't that beat all?"

"He's a mean one."

"Ain't it the truth?" J. D. glared at the toes of his boots. "Okay. Who else?"

Austin considered. "Rubio Márquez. I know he's still got wet feet from wading the river. And Jesús Valenzuela."

J. D. laughed and slapped his thigh. "*Jesús?* You gotta be kidding! Why old Jesús can't even stand up less'n somebody props him. He ain't likely to survive the trip clear acrost town and pop Gussie on the head as well."

Austin became grim. "Sheriff, somebody did this thing. And it's my . . . our . . . job to find out who."

J. D. got to his feet. "Yessir. I'll get right on it."

Back in his own office, the sheriff discovered his deputy hard at work reading a comic book, his feet propped comfortably on the desk. "GIT UP!" roared J. D.

Rowdy showed the whites of his eyes and scrambled. The comic book went one way, his boots another and the chair flat on its back. Rowdy was on his feet. "Yessir!" Yet even with such a remarkable display of obedience there remained just a hint of a smirk on his face. He faced his boss, legs slightly spraddled and a grin already starting up in the corners of his mouth. The silver star shone, pinned neatly to his shirt pocket.

"I wonder just what it is the girls see in him?" thought J. D. to himself.

The girls would have been only too glad to tell him: "He's so *cute*! That curly hair . . . and those big brown eyes! Lord, that boy makes me go hot all over. He may be short . . . but he is *so cute*! Coupled-up and cute!" And they would have gone off giggling.

The sheriff scowled. "I got a job for you. A *man's* job. You remember that white car Chuy talked about? Well, I want you to git your ass out yonder and find out about it. I mean I want to *know* about that *car*!"

"Sure thing!" The deputy grinned widely. "Ain't we got us one humdinger of a case this time, J. D.?" He grabbed his hat and went out. Before he even reached the end of the courthouse corridor he had developed a noticeable swagger. When he pulled out from the curb he burned rubber for half a block.

J. D., watching sourly from the window, said out loud to himself, "Now just where in thunder does he think he's goin'?"

CHAPTER 8

. . . .

*R*owdy had no idea but that didn't stop him. He swarmed all over town, a sort of one-man posse. He drank coffee until his kidneys were fit to bust. He listened until his ears hurt and talked until his tongue got tired. With the ladies, he tilted his chair back on its hind legs, hooked his thumbs in his gun belt and dazzled them all with his most winning crooked grin. With the men, he was manly— serious, thoughtful. He weighed the silences and shook his head, tucking the grin out of sight. He bought a new Stetson but soon regretted it because the old-timers wryly remarked that his hat size must have expanded.

Actually he found out a good deal, all kinds of interesting stuff—gossip, innuendo, wild rumors—but none of it had anything to do with that white car. Apparently nobody but Chuy and the road crew had even seen it. Finally, on a sudden inspiration, Rowdy sauntered down Main Street and proceeded to interrogate the three old Mexican men who always and forever sat on the bench outside the dry goods store. They were fixtures in the town—ancient, weathered philosophers with snowy hair and faces like worn work gloves. They sat out there on that bench every day of the world except Sundays and Christmas and although they often nodded off they never missed a thing. Dozing in the sun, they observed even the most minor events. They knew more than was probably good for their health but since they never spoke to anyone except each other nobody paid them any attention. Rowdy however had a thought: since all Mexicans loved cars and being as how the bench faced the main street, which was also the highway running east and west through town, well, Rowdy figured, maybe, just maybe, they might have noticed something.

So, whistling through his teeth, he approached real casual-like, glancing in the shop windows and touching his hat to people on the street. He slowed down when he reached the bench and squatted down on his boot heels. Pushing his new hat on the back of his head, he grinned up at the men and nodded. "Howdy, señores. Buenos días."

They looked at him from bright, curious eyes. One of them removed a greasy brown hat and placed it carefully on his lap. They all wore old suit pants and dusty, run-over shoes. One sported a silk vest and another had a red bandana knotted around his neck. They regarded Rowdy silently, even sweetly.

The young deputy struggled with his Spanish. "Un carro," he said, reddening. "Muy grande!" He spread his arms out wide. The Mexicans studied him thoughtfully. Dammit. What the hell was the word for *white*? He couldn't remember. That beer . . . that Messkin beer had the word *white* in it. Cerveza? No. Carta . . . Carta . . . Carta Blanca! That was it! "Carta Blanca!" he blurted.

The Mexicans grinned happily. "Sí! Sí, señor! Cerveza. Ay sí! Muy buena!"

"No, now hang on a minute. . . ." Rowdy was starting to sweat. Several people had gathered on the sidewalk and were showing considerable interest. He shifted his weight. "No, now listen. You fellas got it all mixed up. What I mean is un carro. Blanco. Muy grande."

The Mexicans looked at each other, puzzled. Then they jabbered among themselves for a minute or two. Presently the one in the middle—a tall, thin man with long hands and bony wrists—nodded toward a car parked at the curb.

"Un automóvil, señor?"

"Yeah! That's right! Sí! Sí!" exclaimed Rowdy with great relief. "A white car . . . automóvil blanco. Muy grande. She go ZOOM! Like that. Muy rápido." He waved his arms to indicate speed.

The three men studied him with concern.

"Lissen," pleaded Rowdy desperately. "Maybe uno, dos, tres días pasado . . . tres días pasado."

Suddenly smiles lit up their faces. They turned and nodded to each other, explained with their hands and beamed back down at Rowdy.

"Sí, señor! Automóvil muy grande. Abierto . . . how you say?—open. Like that."

"She don't got no top," explained the little man on the far end.

"Zoom!"

"Sí!"

"Ha ha!"

"Muy rápido!"

"Sí!"

"ZOOM!"

"ZOOM!"

Laughing merrily, they confirmed each other's opinions. Any minute now they would begin to relive the whole experience, go over it moment by moment in elaborate detail and endless discussion. By this time they had a pretty good audience.

"How many?" asked Rowdy hastily.

"Cómo?"

"Qué dice?"

"How many hombres? Uno, dos, tres . . . ?" He held up his fingers.

They smiled again. "El puede contar a tres."

"Hi! Hi!"

"Soom! Soom!" said the first man.

Cackling, the tall one in the middle slapped his friend on the back. "No," he laughed. "Solo uno, señor. Un gringo. No más."

"Zoom. Zoooooom!" They all three collapsed in giggles.

"When? Qué hora?" demanded Rowdy hotly.

"Qué dice ahora?"

"Cuando pasó el carro."

"Ahhhh."

"Mediodía?"

"No. A las once. . . ."

"No, amigo. Más tarde. A la una. . . . Quién sabe?"

"El Miércoles. . . ."

"No, no, amigos. Jueves."

An extensive argument developed. There was much gesturing. With grave courtesy each man disagreed completely with the others. Finally, the old man in the middle shrugged. He pointed at the sun, which was about midway, almost directly overhead. "Como ahora, señor. About now. Mediodía."

Rowdy squinted up at the sun. "Okay. Around noon then."

The other two shook their heads firmly. "No, señor."

"Which way was he headed?" Rowdy pointed first one direction and then the other. The Mexicans agreed on that at least. They all three pointed west.

Rowdy took off his hat, wiped off some of the sweat with his forearm, re-set his hat and stood up. "Well, I sure do thank y'all. I really do. Muchas gracias."

They looked up him, smiling.

"De nada, señor."

"Está bien."

"Sí, it was nothing."

Rowdy shifted uneasily from one foot to the other. He couldn't make up his mind whether he ought to shake hands with them or give them some money. Abruptly he turned on his heel and strode back down the sidewalk. The three old men began to laugh soundlessly. Their bright eyes followed him, delighted. Presently the breeze carried the impact of their quiet mirth down the block, where it landed with a soft plop right between his shoulder blades.

From then on, Rowdy became obsessed with that car. He met two preachers from Del Rio who claimed to have seen it. They pulled long, disapproving faces, said it swam up in their rearview mirror like some kind of avenging angel and then streaked past more like the devil hisself. Well, but did they get the license number? Lord, son! What had they just been telling him? Well, could they tell if it was a Texas plate? They were thoughtful over that. After a while one of them declared it might have been a Messkin plate. Either that or Florida. They were the same color—Florida and Chihuahua, was it? or Nuevo León? Green, anyway. The other man opined that it might as well have been from Alaska or even California; the world was full of godless people. Apparently that included the Highway Patrol up in El Paso. Oh yes, they had seen that car. End of discussion. They were as tight-lipped as the bunch in New Mexico had been. What was it about that car? Rowdy, for the life of him, couldn't figure it out. As time went on, the car took on an almost mythical significance. He even dreamed about it . . . driving on and on into the distance . . . a ghost rider in the sky.

CHAPTER 9

. . . .

Crissake, Rowdy! Will you just shut up about that Cadillac? Forget about it for a minute." J. D.'s head was throbbing and he was sick to death of the subject. He thought for a moment, then got to his feet. "Come on, boy. We got us some other catfish to fry. Buckle up that gun belt and let's go catch us some Messkins."

So, jaws set, they drove across town, bumping over the railroad tracks in the white patrol car, hats pulled down low on their foreheads. Their first victim was Martín Gallego. The way they figured, they could always pin something on him, even if it wasn't murder, and that way they'd be doing their duty. The result, however, turned out to be something of an anticlimax.

Martín was sitting right in his own house eating dinner. He hollered for the lawmen to come in and then went right on mopping his plate with torn up slices of white bread. Martín had dark skin, narrow features and a way of squinting like an Indian. He glanced up, nodded at the sheriff and his deputy as if he had been expecting them all morning and returned his full attention to his food. Making one last swab around the bean juice, he pushed the bread into his mouth and shoved the plate away with the side of his hand. He made no motion to get up.

＊

His mother, on the other hand, stood paralyzed by the sink. Suddenly her hands flew to her face. "Santa María!" she gasped, eyes big and staring over the tips of her fingers. Immediately she rushed to the middle of the room and, drying her hands on her apron, dragged out chairs for the visitors. "Buenos días, señores! Buenos días!" Panting, she scraped the heavy wooden chairs across the linoleum, patted the table for them to come. "Siéntense Uds. por favor!" Her black eyes pleaded, darted from them to her son and back again. "Por favor, señores!"

In a gesture of uncharacteristic gallantry, J. D. removed his hat and signaled Rowdy to do the same. The deputy scowled, then angrily yanked off his new Stetson and stood beating it against his thigh. The mother withdrew to a corner where she crouched on a little stool, watching them like a small, dark spider. Martín, with elaborate indolence, struck a match, lit a cigarette with great care and blew the smoke out through his nose.

"Qué pasa, señores?" he inquired with a tiny smile. "What may I do for you?"

J. D. twirled a chair and straddled it. Sitting with his arms folded across the back, he faced Martín. They had just come for a little talk, he said, they were curious as to where Martín might have spent his time on a certain day. Instantly the mother started up, shrill as a startled hen. Martín turned his head, snarled at her in Spanish. She subsided, muttering prayers and the names of saints. J. D. patiently repeated the question. Martín seemed to have trouble remembering dates. Abruptly he got up and went over to a large calendar hanging on the opposite wall. Along with some other gaudy religious pictures it was the only kind of decoration in the room and Rowdy decided that it was the god-awfullest lookin' calendar he had ever seen. Just looking at that thing every morning would be enough to make a person give up on living right then. It was painted up in colors even a whore would be ashamed to wear. Hanging in the middle was a bloody Jesus with a big gap where his ribs should have been and nasty, dripping slashes in his hands and feet. Below him, imploring, kneeled some pale, skinny saint or other with long white hands and green pouches under his eyes. One half of the background was dark with thunderclouds and lightning while the other side was bright with sunshine and birds and flowers. Rowdy couldn't make it out. It looked to him like matters might end in a draw.

Martín concentrated, walking his fingers across the dates. Then he stood back, studied on them and repeated the whole thing. Most of the days were decorated with fancy letters or pictures and the one his finger finally stopped on displayed an angel wearing armor and rising heavenward on the back of a dead dragon. It also happened to be the date of Gussie's death. Martín strolled back to the table, grinning. Holding the cigarette between his thumb and third finger, he threw out his arms in a wide shrug of innocence. "Señores," he said, laughing, "you will never believe it but on that day I was in the church!"

The lawmen received this statement in silence. Rowdy rolled his eyes and studied the ceiling.

"But yes!" Martín insisted. "It is the truth, señores. I swear!" He tapped himself on the chest. "Me! Of all people! A hard thing to believe, I agree! But I was in the church all that day. I swear it before God."

At this, a shrill chattering arose once more from the little mother.

Martín, eyes flashing, spat some very disrespectful Spanish in her direction. Then he turned back and grinned at the sheriff and his deputy as if the three of them were sharing a joke. "Sí. I tell you, that is how it was. I was helping the priest, Father Dominic. That day—the one in which you are interested—it was a feast day. We were getting ready for a celebration, a big party in the parish hall. First there was going to be a big dinner, later some Bingo and then the dance. A little *baile*, you know? Some chindig. And I was there the whole day . . . sweeping, setting the tables, putting the chairs. . . . Ay, Father Dominic, he was whirling around all over the place stirring up the dust with his skirts! Whew! So much dust! I worked so hard I was too tired to go to the dance! Ha! Anyway . . . I was there the whole time." He sat down, smiling.

In the gathering quiet, there was a rasping sound as J. D. rubbed a rough palm over his jaw and up around his eyes. He looked at Martín with weary disgust. "I didn't know you was such a churchgoer. That's somethin' kinda new for you, ain't it?"

The young man widened his grin, spread his arms in another exaggerated shrug of mutual disbelief. "It is good, no? Who can tell about these things? Maybe Our Lady herself was looking after me."

"Madre de Dios!" erupted from the corner. "Nuestra Señora! Ay!" And Martín's mother began crossing herself fervently.

Rowdy stood frowning, chewing on the inside of his cheek. J. D. leaned on his arms, thinking, or maybe just staring into space. Martín tilted back his chair, folded his arms across his chest and waited. There was a long silence which was not entirely friendly. Martín's grin was starting to look like it was pasted on. He looked far from happy; as a matter of fact, behind the smile his eyes were just plain mean. "Sí, señores," he said softly. His words were silky or padded, like somebody sneaking up behind you with maybe a knife. Involuntarily, Rowdy glanced over his shoulder. "Ask the padre," crooned Martín. "He will tell you. Of that I am most certain. Just as certain as I am about where I was on that particular day."

J. D. considered the situation, running his tongue across an eyetooth. Finally, he reached for his hat and climbed out of the chair in one easy motion. Spinning the chair around so that it faced the table again, he gave Martín a long, hard look. "Okay. We'll see what the padre has to say. We'll check on it, don't you worry about that. Meantime, don't you go nowhere, you hear? You make one move to leave town and you're a dead man. Savvy?"

Martín got slowly to his feet. His eyes had gone cold and there were little lines around his mouth. "Chure," he said, drawling it out. "Chure, you bet. I ain't going nowhere, Cheriff. I got nothing to hide." He went to the door, opened it, made an elaborate bow and stood waiting. The minute the door closed, they heard a regular flash flood of high-pitched Spanish erupt from the mother.

"Boy howdy!" sighed the deputy. "Thank the Lord my old lady don't go on like that."

Mildly depressed, they climbed into the hot car.

"Whaddayou reckon, J. D.? Ain't that the wildest bullshit you ever heard? Shoot. I ain't never heard the like. It's downright insultin'."

J. D. was staring moodily at two brown urchins who were clamped to the front bumper, toes hooked over the chrome and sweaty hands leaving a thin spoor of mud on the hood. Bare except for faded shorts, they crouched ready to run, half-scared and grinning around the gaps of missing teeth. Their eyes shone with excitement and the hair stood up off their heads like roached manes, stiff and dusty. His face twisting into a lopsided smile, J. D. reached over and flipped on the siren full blast. *"Jesus Lord God!"* yelped Rowdy. Ecstatic, the children leaped from the car and fled shrieking. Grinning broadly, J. D. watched them as they tore out of sight and disappeared around the wall of an adobe house. "What the flamin' hell did you do that for?" swore the deputy. Still grinning, J. D. shut off the siren, eased the car into gear and pulled out.

He drove on up the hill and parked the patrol car directly in front of the church. They both climbed out and stood screwing their eyes up against the glare. Each of them was familiar with the building—they had been driving by it for years. From downtown, it stood out against the flank of the hill but somehow it was one of those fixtures in a landscape which go unnoticed due to their very familiarity. If it had suddenly vanished, ascended into heaven as its hostess supposedly had, folks on the north side of the tracks would have gaped at the unexpected vacancy on the side of the mountain. Otherwise, they took it for granted, like a lamppost or a fireplug. Naturally neither Rowdy nor the sheriff had ever set foot inside. Now they squinted up at it, surprised that it was so tall and managed to convey an air of being stooped or humble at the same time. Built with loving if inexpert care of native rock stuck together with white mortar and trimmed all around with the same white, it looked more like a fruitcake than a place of serious worship. Still, many people did take it seriously. . . . There was a bell tower and a niche in it up near the top. Everybody knew about the bell tower (again with that almost unconscious awareness) because it clanged every Saturday

evening and every Sunday morning and sometimes in between. But the niche now . . . Rowdy leaned way back and
shaded his eyes in order to see what was in there. It looked
like a life-sized doll to him but it was probably the Virgin
Mary. She appeared to be about the same age as an eleven-
year-old girl—and that didn't seem right. Not a kid that
age. . . . She wore a gold halo behind her head, a long scarf
and a lot of drapery in the form of a white dress and a sky
blue cloak. Her little palms were pressed tight together and
her china blue eyes stared out into the empty air. Actually
she didn't look all that happy.

"Rowdy, you lookin' to get sunstroke?" growled J. D.
"Come on, let's go on inside."

The pair of them tiptoed across the porch, pulled open
the high wooden doors and peeked in. The dim interior
took some getting used to. In the first place it was too dark
to see anything. And there was a permanent smell of cold
stone, candle wax and unwashed feet. Gradually little rows
of lights emerged, tiny points of flame in red cups. A row
of pictures marched down each wall. Above the altar hung
the crucified Christ, a plaster agony of gold and cream. His
head drooped gracefully to one side and there were horrible
wounds painted on his ribs and hands and feet. The thorns
around his head looked real. The church was hushed in a
way that could not be disturbed, not ever, not by anything,
and its silence was even more oppressive than its smell.

"Come *on*, J. D.," whispered Rowdy. "There ain't nobody
here. Not a blamed soul. Let's get outta here before somebody sees us."

The sheriff paused on the way out, taking a cussed long
time to read a little bulletin board advertising a rummage
sale.

*

Back outside, they stood on the steps and waited for their eyes to adjust to the light. J. D. noticed a little house set back from the road and right next to the church. "Let's go see if anybody's home over yonder." They walked over and knocked on the door. A tiny Mexican woman answered. She stood in the doorway and peered up at them, her head tilted to one side and her black eyes snapping. For all the world she looked like a little grasshopper or a cricket made out of brown leather.

"Yes? Yes?" she chirped. "You want something? The father is having his lunch." It was plain that she didn't think he ought to be disturbed at it.

"Well . . . ," rumbled J. D. "Maybe we could just talk to him for a minute or two? It's pretty important. . . ."

Fiercely protective, she hesitated. A voice called out from the back of the house. "Who is it? Who is it, María? Let them come in."

Begrudgingly, she stepped aside, eyeing them with deep distrust. Unexpectedly clumsy all of a sudden, huge and unwelcome, J. D. and Rowdy shuffled dutifully on the scrap of a doormat. As they stepped down the hall, their boot heels rang out a deafening announcement on the highly polished floor.

"But . . . oh my! Oh my goodness!" Father Dominic rose hastily from his meal, grunting slightly from the effort. "I had no idea that it was *you*! Gentlemen! Come! Come in, come in. How pleasant! Sit down." He offered them dainty chairs. "There. Will you have some wine? No? Ah, I see. On duty! Of course. Perhaps some coffee, then? Good. María, please bring these gentlemen coffee. Well, now." Beaming, he lowered himself once more, his bulky, skirted form causing the furniture to squeak alarmingly. "How marvelous! What a surprise! You will forgive me I hope . . . ?" He nodded toward his heaped plate and resumed eating, talking through mouthfuls of food and washing it down with gulps of red wine. Rowdy stared at the padre's plate in amazement—fried chicken, fresh corn, potatoes, peas, huge slices of tomato, rolls and gravy—and his own stomach let out a growl of pure envy. He cleared his throat in an effort to cover up the sound but Father Dominic noticed and nailed him with a twinkling eye. "Ha!" he chuckled, waving his knife good-naturedly at the young man. "Not *all* beneath God's sun is suffering, my boy. I am allowed one good meal a day (except during Lent, of course) and I try to make the most of it."

Rowdy reddened and nodded politely, all the while thinking that, judging by the looks of him, Father Dominic enjoyed a fair number of good meals.

The coffee was brought in on a tray—tiny china cups so old and brittle you could see through them. Placed in the custody of hands used to much wider horizons, they actually tinkled in fear on their saucers. And the saucers were hardly bigger than silver dollars. . . . J. D. and Rowdy looked at the frail china in dismay. There was no way in the world of getting a thumb through one of those handles. And there were also minute silver spoons, a bowl of sugar cubes and some kind of midget tongs to snag them with and a pitcher filled with pure cream. The two lawmen nodded their appreciation to the disapproving María, clamped their legs together and prayed for grace.

"Now," said Father Dominic, wiping a shiny chin. "What may I do for you?" He leaned back, folding his hands comfortably across his stomach, and regarded them kindly. "Or am I to assume that you have come to learn your catechism?"

Trying to balance his cup and keep a weather eye on the napkin all at the same time, J. D. made a valiant effort to explain their visit. Father Dominic listened gravely. He pursed his lips and shook his head slowly from side to side. "A pity," he sighed. "A great pity. An elderly woman like that . . . God rest her soul. Such a terrible thing. God works in ways which are sometimes difficult to understand. . . ." He drifted off into some private study of his own (or a brief nap) and sat for several minutes with his eyes closed. The minutes grew longer and longer. J. D. and Rowdy squirmed on their antique chairs, wrestled with their china and tried to keep from swallowing so loud. Finally, when the priest showed no signs of coming around on his own, J. D. set down his cup and gave a little cough.

"Yes, yes," muttered Father Dominic, rumbling instantly back to life. J. D. found himself wondering if this was the way it was at confession—the good man dozing off during long chronicles of sin, succumbing to the drone of adulteries, lies, missed Masses and unclean speculations, and then rousing himself suddenly, dazed and refreshed, granting the most gentle of penances to surprised and pleased parishioners. "Yes, of course," resumed the father. "You have come to learn about Martín. Martín Gallego, am I right?" He nodded to himself. "Ah, Martín. A good boy basically . . . but wild. A bit wild, I must admit. So many of them are . . . just a little . . . wild." He drifted off again and then roused himself with an effort. "But on the day in question he was with me every minute. Yes, what he has told you is the truth. I realize that his devotion was, well, unusual. . . . Nevertheless, it is true. He was in the parish hall, I can swear to it." He looked at them thoughtfully. "Ah, you ask how can I be so sure?" They ducked their heads modestly. He nodded. "No, it is a valid question. I would ask it myself if I were in your position. So. The reason I can be certain, my friends, is because I was worried." He smiled in reply to their swift glances. "Oh yes. I was quite worried. As soon as I heard about the tragedy of Mrs. Houghton I began to think. I made a little list. I counted on my fingers and I assured myself that I knew where most of my young friends had been on that day. I was most thorough, gentlemen. It is one of the less pleasing aspects of my job. It is sad but true: the little sheep of my flock are inclined to wander now and then. You know what I mean?" He laughed heartily at his own words. "But of course you do! You of all people. Your house with the grilled windows has given them shelter from time to time, eh?" He slapped his broad, draped knee. "Well. Martín now. There is no doubt that Martín can be a difficult boy at times. Very difficult. I admit I was worried. So I made sure. I went over that whole day minute by minute." He smiled. "I may seem absentminded . . . distracted at times . . . but there is little which goes on that I do not know something about. I tell you, gentlemen, I measured that day inch by inch"—he leaned forward earnestly—"and Martín Gallego was with me every minute. From nine in the morning until after three in the afternoon, he was never out of my sight. Not for a moment." He leaned back once again and linked his fingers over his heart.

A moment or so passed. "Yeah. Well . . . uh . . . would you swear to that, Father? On the witness stand, I mean?"

"I would swear it before God."

Glumly they climbed back into the sweltering car. Rowdy burned his arm on the edge of the open window. Cussing under his breath, he slammed the door hard. "D'you believe him, J. D.? You reckon he's tellin' the truth like he says?" The sheriff sighed. He looked tired. "Yeah, I guess. Point is, a jury would. Whew! Let's go get us some dinner."

"Shit," said Rowdy darkly. He jerked his thumb in the direction of the humble parish house. "We ain't likely to find any grub *that* good. Not hardly."

CHAPTER 10

· ·

*T*hey had no trouble locating Rubio Márquez. Word was that he was working down on the O2 Ranch below Goat Mountain so they got in the pickup and drove down there. But the foreman, the rancher himself and even the cook vouched for Rubio. According to the cook, on the day in question they had been stringing fence up "wan somma beetch heel . . . an it was ver hot, you know? Beeg goddamn heel. Man, she go straight up like that!" and he slanted his hand perpendicular. "You sabe?" Anyhow Rubio had been right there the whole time.

"J. D.? You figure them Messkins stick together?"

In a less than optimistic frame of mind they set out to question Jesús Valenzuela. Rowdy personally doubted that Jesús had anything to do with it. It just didn't seem likely since the worst thing old Jesús ever did was to get drunk, in fact, he more or less stayed that way. Whenever they picked him up—which was about once a week—he would smile in a beatific manner (he was just a skinny little guy, bandy-legged) and pat each of them affectionately on the chest. Then he would belch softly, filling the atmosphere with the smell of cheap wine, and whisper confidentially, "Ay, amigos. Yo tengo mucho pulque!"

"Lordy, Jesús," Rowdy would complain, waving a hand in front of his face to ward off the fumes. "That ain't exactly no secret!"

Once settled in his cell—his, by right of habitual occupancy—Jesús would stretch out on the bed and immediately sink into a deep and malodorous sleep which often lasted for as long as twenty-four hours. He was mild, sweet-tempered, and never harmed a fly except once in a mood of rotgut rage he had knifed another man during the Spanish movie on a Thursday night. After spending a little vacation down in Huntsville, he returned unscathed and took up his familiar abodes. Jesús had two other places where he lived when he was not in jail—either the curb in front of the five-and-dime or the old wooden bench outside the Tex-Mex Cafe. He was as reliable in his way as Gussie had been in hers and without a doubt could be found in one place or the other any day of the world.

Jesús, however, had one other fault besides his fondness for wine and when he indulged in it, although it wasn't even a misdemeanor, everybody within earshot declared it a crime. Jesús loved to sing. And as soon as the alcohol had cleared out of his head a little he would stand in the upstairs window of the county jail and warble his heart out. Loud and long he wailed, songs of love and desertion, heartbreak and disappointment. Songs—to judge strictly by the sound of them—of eternal pain and misery. Every person and dog in town knew his voice well. People covered their ears when he started, but the dogs joined in, creating a terrible and mournful din the likes of which was enough to drive others to drink. Folks who lived or worked in the vicinity of the jail learned all the songs by heart whether they wanted to or not. Most people were more or less resigned to the racket and the only person who really complained was Sig Percy over at the funeral home. Sig said he had enough tragedy in his life without having to listen to that. But of course Jesús kept right on and in time he became known as the Tequila Canary.

This time, however, when J. D. and Rowdy went to looking for him he was nowhere to be found. He wasn't slumped on the curb outside the five-and-dime and he wasn't dozing on the bench in front of the Tex-Mex Cafe. Rowdy even went so far as to question his old buddies, the Mexican men who inhabited the bench outside the dry goods store. Delighted to see him again, they gave knowing looks and shrugged.

"Quién sabe, señor?"

"Jesusito? Ay . . ."

" 'Stá borracho."

"Sí. He is probably over there in the jail."

"Al caliche . . ."

"Hi, hi! Jesús ha ido al caliche!"

"Pobrecito . . ."

And they cackled away at their own jokes.

So finally one morning J. D. gave Rowdy a meaningful look.

"I reckon," sighed the deputy. "Seems like we ain't got no other choice."

They set their hats and drove back across town to have a visit with the wife of Jesús Valenzuela. Her name was Celestina and she was one big woman—powerful, in fact—with a hook to her nose that gave her expression all the benevolence of a bald eagle about to land. She had green eyes and a birthmark on one cheek the color of a two-day-old bruise. Among her neighbors Celestina was revered, or at least given a wide berth, due to her unpredictable temper and her attacks of violent anger. It was said that she had made life hell for poor Jesús. On one historic occasion she had become annoyed about something (nobody ever knew what), picked Jesús up and threw him bodily into the middle of the street. He had landed in a kind of personal little dust storm, arms and legs flying. When the dust settled, he lay there for a while and then rearranged himself with solemn dignity, ceremoniously wiping one knee, straightening his shirt with the air of one unjustly injured. He stayed out there in the street all afternoon with his legs sticking straight out in front until finally a car came along and he was forced to move or else be run over. Following that incident, he had never set foot in his house again, but took up residence wherever he happened to be, which was usually the curb, the bench or the jail.

The day Rowdy and J. D. pulled up, Celestina was out sweeping her yard. She looked like she might be in a bad mood. Her yard was as smooth and hard as cement, the house was freshly whitewashed and there were gay pots of geraniums in the windows glowing red against the bright blue frames.

"Mornin', Miz Valenzuela," said J. D., standing respectfully at the gate. "Real nice flowers you got there."

She threw him a black look and went on sweeping with renewed energy.

J. D. shifted his feet around. "Uh . . . I hate to bother you . . . but maybe you could help us?" Silence. Swish, swish, *swish* of the broom. "Thing is, we're lookin for Jesús and we wondered if maybe . . ."

She whirled on them so fast that Rowdy damn near went

for his gun. Flaring her nostrils impressively, she took a mighty breath and spat out words. "Jesús?" she hissed. "Yo no sé! How should I know? He ees not my husban. That one, he ees a worm." And she launched into a truly alarming display of sweeping.

"Well then, I take it you ain't seen him lately," added J. D. lamely.

Her voice rose to a screech. "No, señor! I have not see *heem*! He don't come around here no more, sabe? He, that little hijo de puta . . . he knows I will keel heem if he does. He ees one no-good Mexican." Her hands tightened on the broom handle in a graphic demonstration of what she had in mind.

The two men looked at each other under arched brows. J. D. made one last stab. "Well, you wouldn't happen to have any idea where he might be . . . ?"

"CHINGADO!" She screamed and shook the broom over her head. "I have not see heem since that day I trow him in the street—out there." She pointed threateningly at the road. "He don't come around here no more, gringos. He knows I will keel heem. I sleep with a knife at my side."

"I believe it!" muttered Rowdy.

J. D. was backtracking toward the car. "Yes, ma'am. Okay. Sorry to have bothered you. . . ."

"Pah!" She spat into the packed dirt. "That Mexican, you can have heem. He got brains for nothing. Borracho. All the time borracho. I wish God would send me a *man*, not that little worm." She looked up and pointed at the sky. "With any luck he is out there. Follow the buzzards and you will find heem."

Flushed and wordless, the lawmen climbed back into the car. Rowdy blew out his cheeks and shoved his hat on the back of his head. J. D. drove to the courthouse in silence. By the time they got back to the office both of them had developed a good deal of sympathy for poor old Jesús.

Sympathy, however, didn't help any when it came to finding him. The bartender at the Tex-Mex Cafe smeared his rag around on the scarred counter and shook his head. "No, señores. I have not seen Jesusito for it must be many days now. I don't know . . . as a rule he comes in for a little while and then he goes out there on that bench. Did you look on the bench? Well then, I don't know. . . ."

Everywhere they went it was the same thing. Jesús? Ay, quién sabe? Maybe he was there yesterday. Or the week before. Who could remember?

The situation was becoming serious, not to mention frustrating. Rowdy, at such times, was prone to violence. J. D., on the other hand, became moody and silent. He brooded darkly that evening while his wife, Shonda, dished up supper.

"Whatever is the matter, honey?" inquired Shonda. "You look so mad."

"Oh hell. It's that goddamn Messkin."

"What Messkin? What'd he do?"

"That damnfool Jesús. We can't seem to find him."

Shonda set out a platter of chicken-fried steaks and a bowl of cream gravy. "That lil ol' drunk? The one who sings all the time? I thought he was always in jail." She reached for the green beans.

"Well, he *ain't* in jail just now. That's the trouble. I can't find him and till I do I won't know what he done, that's all."

Shonda chewed in puzzled silence. The finer points of the law had always eluded her.

*

Rowdy, meanwhile, went on down to the The Pit and had himself a plate of ribs and several beers. Then he drove out east of town, floorboarded his car and was going real good until he spotted a jackrabbit crossing the road. He aimed for it, missed, went into a skid and wound up hood deep in Johnson grass, a barbed wire fence balled up in the window. By the time he untangled himself he was in no mood for music. But as he drove by the jail he distinctly heard somebody singing.

The phone in J. D.'s house began to ring.

"Shit," said the sheriff and threw down the paper. "Yeah?"

"J. D.?"

"Yeah."

"This here's Rowdy." There was a long pause.

"Well? What's the trouble?"

"J. D.?"

"What the hell *is it*, Rowdy?"

"Well . . . uh . . . ," he slowed down, stammered and came to a halt. There was another painful pause with only the hum on the wire, Rowdy sweating on one end of it and J. D. steaming on the other.

"Rowdy! For Crissake . . . !"

The deputy broke in hurriedly. "J. D., lissen. I found him. Jesús, I mean."

"You *did*? Sonofabitch! Where?"

"Uh, he's been up yonder in the jail this whole time."

"WHAT?"

Rowdy gave a big sigh. "I reckon you heard me all right. He's been up there these past three days. I guess he musta tied on a good one."

"Jesus Christ."

"Yes sir. He—Jesús, I mean—he's right back in his old room. Singing his damnfool head off."

There was a charged silence. Then J. D. exploded. "For the love of . . . how the hell did he get *in*? We sure didn't put him in there."

"No sir. It was the Highway Patrol. Seems they discovered him passed out, laying in a culvert west of town. At first they thought he was dead but as soon as they nudged him a little he sorta came to life. Smiled at 'em . . . you know how he does. So they brung him on down here. That's where I'm calling from, the jail. Musta been Monday night or maybe Tuesday mornin'. Anyway, he's been in the jail-house ever since."

There was a grinding sound from J. D.'s end of the conversation.

"J. D.? You okay?"

"Why the hell didn't those sons of bitches tell us?"

"They did."

"Bullshit."

"No. They left a report right here on your desk. I just this minute found it. I reckon we ain't been readin' our mail. It was laying there under a pile of other stuff."

There was another long pause.

"J. D.? You still there?"

"Yeah. I'm here." He sounded like maybe he wished he wasn't.

"J. D., that ain't all."

"Ain't all? AIN'T ALL? *What the hell else could there be?*"

Rowdy swallowed noisily. "Well, old Jesús . . . he was in the jail on that day, too. The day Gussie was killed? Don't get het up now . . . hang on, J. D. Jes' hang on. I went over and checked the jail log. He was in there all that day and the one before it and the one after it, too. Till six in the evenin'." The phone had gone dead. Rowdy held it out at the end of the cord and looked at it.

Beyond the open window, from behind the barred window on the second floor of the jail, a thin, quavering voice lifted itself in song. Hesitant at first, fragile, it hung in the evening air like a young bird. After a few tries, it gained courage and launched itself fully, sending waves of unrequited love across the twilit town.

Adiós, mi corazón,
Adiós, mi estrellita, mi esperanza.

Farewell, my beloved,
So long, my little star, my hope.

CHAPTER II

. . . .

*T*hings had come to a standstill. The posse had turned out all but useless, the sheriff couldn't find anybody to arrest and the list of probable suspects had dried up completely. There was an atmosphere of outrage and impatience permeating the community, and Rowdy and J. D. alternately flushed and cussed in that uncomfortable climate but it did them no good whatever, their hands were tied. Austin Bailey maintained an attitude of sober reflection, as if he knew what action to take and was busy planning it out, waiting for the right moment. Of course the truth was that he knew no more than anybody else.

As for the bereaved son, Bubba Houghton, he remained mostly indoors. Exhausted by the *exposure*—the sidelong glances, the pressing of hands, the hearty efforts to cheer him—*bone* weary of the attentions lavished on him by the Daughters of the Confederacy and *sick to death* of telephone calls and food, Bubba preferred to pursue his life quietly. At times he found himself startled by the silence of the house—the arrogance of ticking clocks, the smug self-assurance of *things*. The kitchen still terrified him but he forced himself to face it daily, to latch and unlatch the back screen door. He tried to forget the violence—a lingering

taint which hung in the air like a taste, like gunpowder—
and concentrate instead on the new and pleasing sensation
of peace and almost confidence which seemed to be growing inside himself. Still, there were nights when he would
rear up in bed, wild-eyed and in a sweat. Taking the pearl-
handled revolver which his mother had always kept in the
drawer beside her bed, he would creep into the kitchen and
make himself a cup of cocoa. Gradually the memories of
horror dissolved and the house became more and more a
refuge—cool, shuttered—and his own. Most of all his own.
Still, the presence of his mother tarried, and there were
times when the scent of lavender and cut lilacs would drift
from her room and cause him to gasp and nearly suffocate.

Naturally he had endured questioning along with the
rest, an unpleasant afternoon made bearable by the tact
of Austin Bailey and the massive, rumpled comfort of his
mother's (and now his) attorney, Houston Carr. Austin
had inquired as gently as he could and Bubba had described the details: Yes, he had been at the high school
the entire morning. The secretary, the principal, a banana-
bearing librarian and thirty-six shouting adolescents had
all made this very clear. As a matter of fact, yes, he had
left a moment or two early. Why? Well, because quite
frankly he had been concerned about his mother lately
. . . her health. (Actually, of course, he had been hoping
for a serving of strawberry shortcake before she carted
it all off to that bridge club of hers.) Yes, she had seen
Dr. Cartwright recently and he had found nothing wrong
—nothing serious, that is—but lately, well, she had not
seemed quite herself. It was difficult to explain—rather
easily fatigued, actually *willing* to take her pills! (here the
others suppressed small smiles) but no, not quite herself.
He could not put his finger on it. (*Bitchy* was the word. And

always counting that filthy money. It had probably given her some unspeakable disease.) Oh, about the money. Yes (he sighed) she was always counting it—every morning, as everyone knew. Bubba looked down, embarrassed. He guessed elderly people . . . (The others assumed expressions of sympathy, nodded.) But she counted it other times, too. Often of an evening he would catch her at it, laying out hundred dollar bills like she was playing solitaire. But of course as long as she enjoyed it . . . no, naturally he never interfered. Did he know the amount? How much she kept around the house? Goodness no! Bubba shook his head indulgently. She was a teeny bit eccentric (selfish) about her money. (Kept it in that nasty old tackle box.) The box? She kept that on the top shelf in the pantry. Could anyone have had access to it? He supposed so. (As a matter of fact he had searched that shelf thoroughly himself only two days ago, discovering to his dismay fifteen shoe boxes so stuffed with S&H Green Stamps that their cardboard sides had split. Bubba had patiently, if furtively, carried them out in lots of three, making five separate trips to the trash can in the alley, where he burned them to gray ash. As he lit the match, he had felt uneasily like a priest performing some ritual. Exorcism?) Pardon? No, really he had not the faintest idea how much she stashed in that box. It could have been a thousand—or several times that.

Bubba began perspiring. The day seemed very hot. The men looked thoughtful. Houston Carr cleared his throat. His hoarse phlegm acted as a signal, a release for them all. Austin Bailey got to his feet, reached across his desk and shook Bubba's hand. He expressed thanks and deep sympathy in one easy flow of words. Bubba inclined his head in an attitude which by this time he had perfected. He would naturally feel it his duty to testify at the trial should that prove necessary. He would of course assist in any way he could. Yes, he would be remaining in town for the rest of the summer. And now if they would excuse him? He had a splitting headache.

About a week later Bubba had been summoned to the office of Houston Carr. Prepared for a session of tedious legal advice, he was instead presented with a stack of stunning documents, sheaves of paper which lay heavy in his hands—papers rich as cream, the color of magnolias and jeweled with seals, laced with fine old writing in the blackest ink. The writing, tall and steep as Gothic spires, explained obliquely and at length that he was now the sole heir to a fortune. The assets consisted of land, securities and outright cash.

Stunned, Bubba let the papers slide gently to the floor, where they lay like shards of ivory against the threadbare hunting scene on Houston's old carpet. Disbelieving, he stared down at the scattered pages until Houston's leather chair creaked. Then, very slowly, Bubba reached down and picked them up, one by one. Reverent at their richness, he assembled them in order and silently returned them to Houston—as if they did not belong to him at all but should be reserved for safekeeping, preservation—as if he was unworthy or still not allowed—as if they were too precious.

Houston studied him from under shaggy brows. He grinned, leaned forward and bit off the tip of a fresh cigar. "That set you back some, boy?" He chuckled. "Surprised me, too, at the time. Gussie—your mama—she wrote that thing out herself. Every word of it. On your birthday— exactly one year to the day after you were born. Never looked at it again. Never changed so much as a comma."

Bubba bent his head stiffly and examined the signatures. The will had been witnessed by Lincoln Winters, then only a clerk, and an ambitious young lawyer named Austin Bailey. The notary seal was all but carved into the paper and the document dated and made official by some county clerk long since laid away in tissue and black silk.

Weak, Bubba leaned back, a wild hysteria beginning to build in his blood. "I didn't expect . . . ," he stammered. "I never dreamed. . . ." He stopped, desperately afraid of breaking into a giggle.

Houston rumbled on. "She left you well-off, boy. Mighty comfortable, I'd say. And no strings. It's all yours—except for the part that got away!"

Bubba stood, collected the pages and folded them into the stiff, white envelope which had lain sealed for forty-two years. Suddenly he felt a need for air. "Thank you!" he gasped. And reeling past Houston's extended hand, rushed from the room.

Once home, he locked both doors carefully, changed into his silk pajamas and lay down on the bed. There in the darkened room he gazed long at the ceiling. But of course Bubba was not seeing the ceiling, he was not tracing the cracks in that high cream plaster as he had done for years. No, what Bubba saw were the pages of his checkbook riffling. And in that breeze the resentment he had harbored toward his mother—her dying that way—began to ebb gently away.

CHAPTER 12

. . . .

Several blocks away from Bubba's meditations, Dr. Caleb Cartwright and his son, Jason, discussed the death of Augusta Houghton from a medical point of view.

"Well, what do you think, Dad?" Jason crossed one elegant ankle over the opposite knee. Beneath his crisp white jacket, Jason dressed very well. He was one of the new breed of doctors; suave and suntanned, he wore Italian loafers and drove a foreign car. The two of them were sitting in his father's office during a lull. There were a good many lulls in the senior Dr. Cartwright's practice these days. The old man mumbled, pottered about his desk.

"Now where in the world did Ulabelle put my . . . ?" Removing his glasses, he held them dangling in his left hand, polishing one lense over and over. Jason, impatient by nature, had learned to wait. Cartwright Senior dropped his handkerchief into the wastebasket, let his glasses fall on top of a stack of papers and peered owlishly at his son. Too bad Jason had been out delivering that baby when Bubba's call had come. With the young physician it would have been a routine matter, cut and dried. As it was . . . Caleb Cartwright rumbled, cleared his throat.

*

"I don't know, son," he allowed. "It's a sad thing, that's what I think. A very regrettable thing. And I am deeply troubled by it. Deeply troubled."

"What do you mean?" The young man flicked an imaginary speck off his spotless cuff.

"Auuggh. . . ." An old man's noise, something between a hawk and a growl. "Auggghhh . . . hmm. You want to know what I think as a medical man, a scientist. As a doctor, a scientist, a human being . . . what I think is, it don't make one damn bit of difference." Jason glanced up, surprised. The old man rambled on. "When it's time for folks to die, they die. That's all there is to it. They take a notion and then they look around for some way of doing it that suits 'em. They all find some way to get it over and done with. Oh, I'll admit disease is a devious thing, but just the same. . . . Take Gussie, now. She picked a kind of dramatic method—Gussie would." He mused for a moment. "But it worked, didn't it? Gussie saw to it that it worked. She was never a woman to tolerate loose ends. So she saw to it. What I'm trying to say is, it don't make a damn bit of difference how it happens just so long as it gets the job done." He shook his head slowly. "No, son. Our job is with the living. The dead have got beyond us any way you look at it."

The young man looked annoyed. Like he wondered if maybe his father was losing his grip. Or even talking down to him. He stuck out his chin, yanked at his collar with an index finger. "I don't know what you're talking about," he said.

"No," agreed the old man. "No, I reckon you don't. All I mean is, the important thing is that she is dead. It don't much matter how she got that way."

Jason jumped to his feet. "How can you say that? You, a physician! It violates the oath we took and goes against everything we stand for. What's the use of fighting disease . . . all those years of study and research! . . . if all you're going to do is lie down and give up? My God! We swore to . . ."

Caleb Cartwright held up his hand. "Spare me the rhetoric, Jason. I know all that. Believe me, I know all that." He beetled fiercely from beneath wild, gray eyebrows. "I went to school, too, remember? But I've learned some other things as well—things they don't dare to teach you in medical school."

The younger doctor started to speak, bit it back. His father's voice turned reflective, almost sad. "On the other hand, lately it seems like I haven't learned anything. Like I don't know much after all. Or maybe I know a little bit but it isn't enough. What I need to know isn't there when I go to looking for it. Maybe it never was." He heaved another sigh, let his gaze wander over the dusty shelves of his library. "Take Gussie now. Gussie was my patient for over forty years. I've known her all my life. We grew up together, you might almost say. Learned on each other. She's gone now. Not one damn thing I can do about it. I suspect there never was."

Was his father showing signs of Alzheimer's disease? Jason sat down again and carefully modulated his voice, unaware that the older man instantly heard it for what it was—condescension—and withdrew from the conversation, only keeping the words going out of kindness.

"But, Dad! She was murdered! She didn't just die like that—you saw her yourself. I mean, the sheriff came—you called him—and there was money stolen, and she had that contusion on her head. . . ."

"Head and neck."

"Oh, all right. Head and neck, then. But it's as plain as the nose on your face that somebody killed her!"

"Is it?" the old man shot him a look.

"Well, I mean . . ." Jason stared at his father amazed. "What else could it be? For God's sake, Dad. . . ." He stopped talking but the unspoken words hung in the air. *You're over the hill*, they said. Jason got up, moved restlessly to the window. The old man listened to the unsaid words, thought them over carefully and rejected them. He walked heavily across the room and stood next to Jason at the window, both of them looking out, not seeing.

"Gussie was an old woman, Jason. When folks get old, they die. Their lives are used up. Sometimes I think that's all there is to it."

Jason frowned into the glass, trying to remain calm. "But surely! I mean, in this case there *were* other factors. *Somebody* hit her on the head."

"Oh yes. Yes. I certainly do admit that. Somebody hit her, all right." The old man spoke with a far off sadness, almost as if he felt pity for the unknown assailant.

Jason turned to face him. "Well then. Since she is dead, it's up to us—not only as doctors but as citizens—to find out why and eradicate the cause. Call it a social evil if you will, it is still a disease. For God's sake! You can't just let it go, let somebody get off scot-free, maybe do it again." He paused, then continued with renewed intensity. "Here was your old friend, alive and active one day . . . and the next thing you know she's dead. All because some . . . well, who knows . . . but somebody comes along, beats her up and robs her. A woman you've known all your life. I mean, life is too *precious*. We can't allow it to be stolen like that. Somebody has to pay."

"Pay?" inquired the older man softly. "I wonder. I agree with you that life is a precious thing, mighty precious. But I wonder if it can ever be paid for."

"Well, *some* attempt at restitution," said the son, his frustration mounting. "I don't believe in an eye for an eye but you sure as hell can't just let it go."

"No," agreed the father, still musing. "No, I reckon not." After a moment he raised his hand, clapped his son on the shoulder and let the hand remain, his arm loose across the young man's back. They stood that way in silence, staring down into the yard below, still not seeing, aware only of the war of ideas surrounding them.

"Well now," remarked Caleb after a while. "What I *do* reckon is that you and me had better be getting on home. I expect Ulabelle is waiting dinner."

CHAPTER 13

. . . .

Others among Gussie's old friends found it harder to deal with the fact that she was gone. She had not been loved by all—that much was clear—but there were any number of people whose lives were altered by her passing, people who would miss her more than Bubba ever would, folks whose lives had been woven in with hers during years of daily living. These people found their evenings frayed by worry, and despaired that things could go awry like that, violence ravel their quiet lives and sneak away again, leaving behind a tear in the fabric of peace and order which had seemed God-given and forever.

One of these was Effie Sue Ethridge.

Effie Sue was about the same age as Gussie—whether on the plus or minus side she wasn't saying—and had lived on the same street, two houses down, for years. The two of them had visited almost daily, raised children and flowers together. Only Effie Sue knew how disappointed Gussie had been—annually—over the failure of her lilies. And likewise—though not annually but once and for all—in her marriage. It was Effie Sue who had sat with Gussie after the plane crash that afternoon and who had sat with her that night, too, when the search party returned, the men shaking their heads and slowly removing their hats. And Effie Sue had known it would happen (as Gussie doubtless had, although they never spoke of it). Sure as the world, when a man drives around with a bottle for company on the seat of his pickup—and that bottle near empty most of the time—sure as the world when that man takes up flying as a form of transportation, why it comes as no surprise when one day he wraps his wings around some mountain, in this case, Zopilote Peak. The wreckage hung there to this day, glinting in the sun if you knew where to look.

The offspring of that marriage, too. A terrible disappointment. A son—but not the son that Gussie had hoped for. Not the hard, lean, sun-tanned boy with blue eyes and white teeth and sun-streaked hair, not the laughing, helling son who would go out and bulldog the world, wrestle it to the ground and then look back over his shoulder and grin. Oh no. Far from it. Instead, a pale and pasty boy who ran to fat. Who sat blinking and bewildered when they set him outside to play. A child who burst into tears the first time they loaded him (like heaving a sack of oats, Gussie said) onto the back of a sleepy pony and who clutched at its mane, red-faced and terrified, yelling bloody murder until they hauled him down again. Not exactly the kind of boy who would grow up to run a ranch. And she, Effie Sue, had lost track of all the times she caught Gussie watching her own son with narrow and covetous eyes. Gussie had no use for girls so she paid no attention to Effie Sue's two daughters, smart and pretty as they were. But she watched Harlan. Oh yes, she watched Harlan. And every spring when Harlan paraded his steer into the arena at the stock show, it was always Gussie who placed the highest bid. After that, she would have Harlan load up the trailer and the two of them would ride down to the ranch together, the steer bawling and swaying in the back while Effie Sue and Bubba were left behind, standing on the curb in town.

Now Gussie was gone for good. Effie Sue would miss her and that was the truth. Still, she was mighty thankful that she had such a store of memories to fall back on. Things came to mind. Like now, for instance: Effie Sue was out in her front yard watering her zinnias. Just exactly as she had been doing on the morning Gussie died. At about the same time, too. Today it was hotter, if anything. The plants looked faded, washed out. It was too late in the day to be watering and Effie Sue scolded herself for that. The earth was baked hard and the water simply ran off. She ought to get out earlier or else wait for the cool of evening. But since she had started, she might as well finish.

Effie Sue gave a yank on the heavy hose and moved to the next row of flowers. Her big straw hat made a lattice-work of shade across her face and shoulders but there was no coolness in it. She watched the water curling around the dusty stalks. Out of long habit she glanced up the street to Gussie's house. Catching herself too late, she went on and looked anyway. Silly thing to do, though. Nobody there. Not a soul in sight. Just like it had been on that other morn-ing—the morning Gussie died—a hot, empty street with a few cars parked at the curb, trees hanging listless in the heat . . . yes, just the same. No, wait. Effie Sue frowned, thinking. No, it wasn't quite the same. What was it? Some-thing had been different that day. . . . She squinched her eyes in the noon glare, peering almost painfully through the wavering heat mirage. Yes! Now she remembered! That girl . . . there had been that girl. A stranger. Yes. Effie Sue nodded emphatically, the wide brim of her hat flopping up and down. A tall, skinny girl wearing a wash dress, a sallow girl with long, light brown hair. One of those kids who never ever get enough to eat, spend their whole lives undernourished, starved of everything life has to offer and wind up later, gaunt and grown, their eyes wild with religion. That was the kind. This one, her arms full of magazines or pamphlets of some kind, had been walking slowly down the street, pausing and looking at first one house and then another. She stopped about the time she got to Gussie's front walk and stood there, considering. Like she was trying to make up her mind if that house would be a good prospect for whatever it was she was promoting. Effie Sue could have told her, "You're wasting your time, honey. That door will never open, not right now. The lady you want is way back in the kitchen counting her money and wild horses couldn't drag her away from it. You'd be wise not to bother her at all. Nobody *ever* bothers Gussie at this time of day! Law! It's practically gospel in this town—and you surely are a stranger or you'd know it for a fact." Not knowing, the girl had stood uncertainly on the sidewalk, hopping a little from one foot to the other as if the pavement burned through the soles of her shoes. Effie Sue had studied the girl from under her hat. They remained that way for several minutes—Effie Sue studying the girl and the girl studying Gussie's house while trying to keep a grip on that armful of slippery magazines at the same time.

Suddenly Effie Sue had remembered something Charlotte Buchanan had said. Charlotte complained that lately she had been bothered by a bunch of Jehovah's Witnesses. They all but *moved in* on her front porch, Charlotte said, and she like to never got rid of them. *Talk?* Lord! She was preached to death. They would go on and on, convinced that they knew more about God than anybody. Well, Charlotte didn't think so and she expressed her feelings as loudly and as freely as they did. But she was outnumbered. Finally Charlotte shouted at the top of her lungs that if they didn't get off her porch that very *minute* and leave her in peace, she was going to call the sheriff. Angered, mumbling dire predictions, warning Charlotte that she was headed for hell and waving *Watch Towers* all the way, they departed, taking the vengeance of the Lord with them as their personal possession. And so, on the morning of Gussie's death, Effie Sue, studying that strange girl, had had a premonition of worse things to come. She had abruptly turned off the hose and marched into the house, slamming the door smartly behind her. Such a slam was explicit in that part of the world and she assumed that it would be understood even by strangers. Apparently it was. Later, peeking from behind her venetian blinds, she had seen the girl go on by looking worried and certainly the worse for the midday heat. She looked like a Jehovah's Witness all right.

·   ·   ·

One evening a week or so after Gussie's funeral, Effie Sue was out in her back yard ordering Sabino around. Sabino was her yard man, a slow, heavy, almond-eyed Mexican who always wore khaki work clothes and smelled of onions. He spoke no English and Effie Sue invariably ended up getting flustered and flushed because she found herself shouting at him like you would a deaf person. He had worked for her for many years now, coming faithfully every week (which was more than you could say for most of them). Sabino was maddeningly slow—in fact he took forever—but he was thorough. He wasn't lazy, just methodical. A plodder. That day he had finished mowing and was kneeling with the grass clippers trimming around the edge of the house. Effie Sue was scratching around in her rose bed with the cultivator, pecking at the hard dirt with the little iron claw. She liked to keep the earth soft and loose around the plants but there were times when it seemed that God, the climate and Mother Nature had all conspired against her. There was never enough shade, never enough water. The minute she turned her back the dirt turned to cement. Peck, peck, peck. I feel like a chicken, thought Effie Sue. All of a sudden she spied a candy wrapper at the back of the bed right next to the alley wall. Dratted kids. Rode their bikes down the alley and tossed all their trash over into her yard. Straining forward, she stabbed the wrapper with one prong, triumphantly spearing it. Then she looked again to see if there was more stuff back there that ought to be cleaned up. There was: two gum wrappers, a messy little heap of dirt and twigs and a twenty-dollar bill.

Effie Sue sat back on her heels and stared at the bill. Then she pounced—exactly like a duck on a June bug. The cultivator flashed through the air, snatched the bill and pierced it to the heart. Effie Sue sat back again, held up her prey and examined it doubtfully. It looked good enough—maybe a little dirty—but passable. Just like any other bill except for the hole made by the prong of the cultivator and . . . what was that? Effie Sue held the bill up to her nose and then slowly extended it nearly arm's length in order to get a better look. What in the world? A little star inked in on the upper right-hand corner. Now who would do a thing like that? Land sakes . . . a little Lone Star. Well, it shouldn't affect the value any. But what on earth was a bill like that doing in her flower bed way back there behind the roses? Those darned kids didn't have money like that to throw around . . . well, somebody must have lost it. Effie Sue wondered if maybe she ought not to tell someone . . . ask . . . but on the other hand. . . . Furtively she glanced over to see if Sabino had noticed anything but he was just plodding along as usual, head down, knees in the grass—snip, snip, snip. Effie Sue folded the bill and tucked it away in the pocket of her gardening dress.

For a while she puzzled over the bill but before long she got busy with her gardening and it kind of slipped her mind. Later, however, when she went to pay Sabino, she discovered that she didn't have any cash in her purse. "Oh Christmas!" said Effie Sue. "I'll have to get in that hot old car and drive all the way downtown and cash a check." In the middle of her fussing she suddenly remembered the twenty. She pulled it out of her pocket and looked at it. Her conscience was not entirely easy. What would Reverend Quinn say? she wondered. Or the members of her Bible Study group? On the other hand none of them had to clean the trash out of her flower beds. But really, it was too much, far too much—those Mexicans never had any change—it was a lot more than she usually paid. You couldn't afford to spoil these people. Still . . . she couldn't write Sabino a check because she had never known what his last name was. The thought of trying to find out now gave her a headache. She had heard that his wife had just had another baby. Was it the fifth? Or the sixth? Effie Sue couldn't keep track. What she did know was that she didn't feel like dragging all over town in the heat of the day hunting up change. What she felt like doing was having a long, cool glass of iced tea. Effie Sue gave him the twenty.

Sabino stared at the bill. His lips moved and his eyes widened. He looked anxiously at Effie Sue, worry creeping onto his broad, sweaty face. "Para mí, señora?"

"Yes, yes. You take it. Sí." Effie Sue became nervous herself and replied impatiently.

Sabino pondered the bill earnestly, rubbing his thumb over the numerals. Finally he shook his head, shoved it back at her. "No, señora. Gracias, pero eso es demasiado. Perdóneme, por favor. No tengo cambio."

"No," she insisted, pushing his hand back. "Para usted. You take it. Para los muchachos, el niño poco más." He looked at her, puzzled. Effie Sue was getting flustered. That was all she needed—stand around in the heat trying to convince a darned Mexican that he ought to take more money than he was worth. Honestly . . . she never would understand these people, not as long as she lived.

Sabino stood there perplexed, heavy with earth and sweat, the bill hanging limp from his soiled fingers. Exasperated beyond endurance, Effie Sue raised her voice. Shrill, she shouted: "Para los muchachos! Para usted y la señora! Para frijoles!" she yelled. "Es bueno, sabe?"

Sabino's face broke into a dazzling smile. "Todo, señora? Para mí? Sí! 'Stá muy bueno! Muy bueno." He swept off his old brown hat and held it over his heart. Effie Sue observed how stained it was around the crown. "Muchas gracias, señora! Mil gracias!" He stood there beaming.

"Lands," said Effie Sue. "De nada. De nada." Then to herself she added, *It really is nothing since I found the darn thing.* Absolved, she shooed Sabino off and thought no more about it.

CHAPTER 14

. . . .

*L*ater the following afternoon, Lincoln Winters paid a visit to Austin Bailey. Lincoln, a spare and meticulous man, emitted an atmosphere of cool gray wherever he went. He wore steel-rimmed glasses and wrote with a silver pen. His script was graceful, his figures flawless and very neat. He stood in Austin's scarred and dusty office wearing a pearl gray summer suit and a tie of conservative stripe. Gravely, he reached into his wallet—austere black leather with a silver monogram—and withdrew a twenty-dollar bill. With an air of distaste, he laid the bill carefully on the desk in front of Austin and stepped back with the attitude of someone performing a necessary but unsavory duty.

"What's this?" Austin rocked forward in his chair and picked up the bill, squinting. Then he put on his reading glasses and gave it his full attention. It was a sorry thing—no wonder Lincoln had acted so fussy. Also it had a hole right through the middle of Andrew Jackson like somebody had drilled him one—and up in the right-hand corner was a tiny Lone Star drawn in black ink. "Well!" said Austin. "Well now. This *is* something! Is that the little star you were telling me about? The one Gussie used to mark her money?"

"It is indeed."

"Where did you get this thing?"

The banker sat down, careful of the creases in his trousers. "It came from Joe García's grocery store. Joe brought it in himself. It was part of his regular deposit. He laughed about it as I recall. Said it didn't look like much but he wasn't complaining since he didn't often get many that size, not from his customers. Said he wished he could see more of them . . . twenties, I suppose he meant."

Austin frowned thoughtfully. "When did he bring it in?"

"Only this morning. Naturally I didn't ask him about it. He must have a good many customers."

"Not with twenty-dollar bills. Not this time of the month."

"No." Lincoln crossed his legs with practiced elegance. "Ever since this . . . this business with Gussie . . . I have made it a point to keep an eye on all the incoming cash. Casually, you know. Of course, I have no wish to interfere. . . ."

Austin waved the apology aside.

". . . but fortunately I was present this morning when Joe brought this one in. Then I overheard him joking about it. . . ." Lincoln paused, his eyes on the bill. "It's one of Gussie's, all right. No question about that."

Austin tilted back his leather chair, made a steeple of his fingers. "Well, thank God for a lead of some kind. We've been having a mighty dry run with this case." He considered the tips of his fingers. "But . . . I wonder? Couldn't that bill . . . this one, I mean . . . couldn't it have been floating around anyway? Been around town? Even Gussie must have spent *some* of her money. Had she made any deposits lately?"

Lincoln shook his head no to all questions. "She only occasionally made cash deposits. And to my knowledge

she never spent any of the money she kept in that box—
Carter's tackle box, I mean."

"Not even for gas, groceries, things like that? What did
she do for ready money?"

"Now, Austin, you know that nobody uses real money in
this town—not on *this* side of the tracks. Everybody writes
checks. Or charges it. Even Cokes and ice cream at the
drugstore."

Austin considered. "Well, come to think of it, you're
right. My wife goes through piles of them. Then when the
statement comes there's hell to pay."

Lincoln gave a wintery little smile.

Austin continued. "So Gussie never used her own money,
that money she kept at home? How come, I wonder?"

"I believe that she preferred to use mine, if I may put it
that way."

"But what did she do with it, then? Her cash, I mean?"

Lincoln spread his fine hands in a shrug. "Kept it.
Hoarded it if I may say so. At home."

"*All* of it?"

"Well, I think . . ."

"In that old box?"

"In that box. I don't believe even her own son knew the
amount or that she marked it that way—with that little
star. She told me that she thought Bubba ought to spend
his own money. She put it to me once, like a question. But
she wasn't asking my opinion if you know what I mean."

Austin nodded, smiled.

"The only reason I even know about the money and the
stars is that one day—oh, it's been some years back—she
came into the bank hugging that old tin box in her arms
and commanded me to attend her in my office. Behind
closed doors. Well, Gussie and I have transacted a great
deal of business together over the years, as you can guess,

so I couldn't imagine what she was up to. Well, we entered my office—she made sure the door was shut—and then she pried open that . . . well, that *fishy* box . . . and dumped the contents all over my desk."

Austin laughed in spite of himself. He could just see it: Lincoln in a spotless suit, standing there helpless before his fine antique desk, fully expecting it to be covered in muddy catfish at any moment. "Ha! And what was in it?"

Lincoln looked slightly miffed. "Money, of course. A great deal of money."

"And every single bill marked with that little star?"

Lincoln sighed. "Every last one."

"Every bill?"

Lincoln gave him a fish eye. "As I said—each and every bill was marked with that same little star in the corner. I know because I examined each one thoroughly. She . . . er . . . required that I do so. But I don't think she realized that I noticed the star."

"But why did she ink in all those little stars, anyway?"

Lincoln shrugged again. "Who knows? People sometimes get a little . . . strange . . . about their money."

"God almighty." Austin shook his head. "Well, go on. What did she want you to do with it?"

Lincoln recrossed his legs. "We counted it together—several times—and then she demanded that I put it away for her. Along with her other valuables, her papers and jewelry and so forth. I did my best to explain that we couldn't do that—that it was against the law—that cash could not be placed in a safe-deposit box. She became very . . . well . . . difficult."

"Mad as a wet hen, if I know Gussie."

Lincoln gave a look of surreptitious gratitude. "Something like that. She did raise her voice. Said she didn't know what banks were good for if they couldn't perform a simple service like that. Etcetera. Etcetera. I believe she even threatened to bury her money in the back yard."

"But I don't understand. She had been doing business with you for years, she must have already had several accounts. . . ."

"Exactly what I thought myself. In fact, I mentioned those very facts to her. She was not pleased. That was not what she meant, she said. It seems she wanted me to keep that very money. She wanted *storage* for those very bills," he pointed to the one on Austin's desk. "Said she was running out of space at home. I tried to suggest a savings account and she flew into a rage." He looked at Austin imploringly. "She . . . er . . . *explained* that she already had a drawer full of those 'silly little books' and that she had no use for another one. She ordered me to put her money— those marked bills—in a safe place and keep it until she had a mind to ask for some of it."

Austin grinned broadly. "So what did you do?"

Lincoln shifted uncomfortably. "Well, I made out a *receipt*, actually a deposit slip, set up another savings account for her and assured her that I would keep the money nicely bundled in boxes in the vault. Then the minute she was out the door, I had those bills bound up and put in a sack. The first chance I got, I shipped them out of town and as far away as possible."

Austin was still grinning. "Tell me this. What would you have done if she'd come down and asked for it, for some of those special marked bills?"

Lincoln took out a handkerchief and dabbed at his forehead. "Thank goodness she never did." He glanced again at the bill on the desk. "That's how I know this bill was stolen."

*

The two men sat in silence for a few moments, each busy with his own thoughts. After a while, Austin inquired, "But that was unusual for her, wasn't it? To act that way, I mean? I gather she was quite a businesswoman, shrewd when you come right down to it."

"Oh my yes," replied the banker in tones tinged with envy. "Gussie was an amazing businesswoman. Very astute. *Very* astute in all her dealings. Nobody I've ever known could compare with her. But this money she kept at home was . . . well . . . an eccentricity, I guess. A hobby, almost. Otherwise, Gussie was the sharpest woman I ever dealt with in my life."

Austin picked up the twenty-dollar bill and studied it. "I'll be damned." After a moment, he got to his feet and extended his hand. "Well, many thanks, Lincoln. You've been a great help, a tremendous help. I'll keep in touch with you."

The banker's grip was firm, his fingers cool and dry.

•   •   •

Within an hour, J. D. was over paying a visit to Joe García's Grocery and Meat Market. Joe's little store was a brown stucco building on the corner of Avenue D and South 6th Street over in Mexican Town. It had a screen door with an old metal sign advertising Wonder Bread nailed across the middle. There was no sidewalk, only a packed dirt path and a worn wooden sill. Across the side of the building in faded green letters painted with great flourish was the word *Abacería*. Joe greeted the sheriff wearing a white bib apron and a big smile. His round face was pleased, cheerful and eager to be of assistance. "Allo, Cheriff Keelion!" he said, maybe a little bit too loud. Several customers turned and stared. A tiny girl sat by the door sucking on a sticky candy, most of which seemed to be trickling down her chin. She looked up at J. D. with big eyes. J. D. liked kids and he was just fixing to get out his handkerchief when a thin, dark old woman suddenly snatched up the child and darted out the door. Joe García looked after them, embarrassed. He shrugged as if to say, "What can you do?" Since his handkerchief was on the way out anyway, J. D. blew his nose.

"Howdy, Joe," he said. "How ya doin'?"

"Fine. Fine." Joe nodded eagerly as if he were trying to sell the idea and went to stand expectantly behind the cash register.

"Well, I'll just look around here for a minute if you don't mind. My wife told me to pick up some of that hot sausage you all got. That stuff sure is good. She mixes it in with the scrambled eggs on Sunday mornings . . . man, oh man!"

"Oh chure!" agreed Joe, and he started to hurry back to the meat counter. J. D. held up his hand like he was halting traffic. "No, now. Hang on. I'll just look around and see what else you got."

Joe reluctantly returned to his place behind the cash register. J. D. wandered up and down the aisles marveling at the five-gallon pails of lard, the huge cans of jalapeños and hominy, the sacks of corn husks, strings of red chiles and jars of nopales. He knew that sooner or later his presence would make the other customers scarce. He was right; they paid quickly and left. J. D. didn't want to hurt Joe's business but he figured all those customers and a couple dozen more would come back later anyway to find out what it was the sheriff had wanted. So in that way maybe he was doing Joe a favor. García was a good man, a good father and citizen. He tried hard to overcome the image of "Messkin" but living where he was and doing what he did, there was bound to be a certain ambivalence. Joe clearly perceived

the road signs along the road to success and in that he
imitated his Anglo brothers. Yet there were cultural differ-
ences and demands that could not be overcome that easily.
Joe walked a narrow line trying to please both sides. In
J. D.'s opinion it was like trying to mix oil and water.

As soon as everyone had cleared out, J. D. strolled back
over to the counter. He remarked that he had talked with
Lincoln Winters only recently and that the banker happened to mention that Joe had been in the lobby making
jokes about a twenty-dollar bill he was depositing.

"Yes sir!" beamed Joe. "Chu bet. I don't get very many
that size, you know? Maybe a few here and there . . . but
not so many. It is a pleasure when it happens."

J. D. asked him if he'd noticed anything funny about
the bill.

"Funny, Cheriff? How do you mean?" A V of anxiety
formed between his eyebrows. "I was making a joke, chure,
but . . ."

"No, I mean anything odd or unusual about it."

Joe's face fell. "Oh, you mean it is a bad bill? No good?
Something is wrong with it?"

J. D. assured him that the bill was okay, no problem
about that. It was just that there was something kinda odd
about it, something he, the sheriff, needed to check up on
and he wondered if maybe Joe remembered who had given
it to him. Since he didn't get all that many.

Joe García's eyes reverted to Indian blackness and gave
no hint of what might be going on behind them. He was
walking that narrow line of his. Finally, he dropped his
gaze, fiddled with some items on the counter. As if a team
of mules was dragging the words out of him letter by letter,
he mumbled in a low voice filled with fear and sadness. "It

was Sabino, señor. Sabino Espinosa. He is the one who gave me that bill." He looked up at the sheriff, pleading. "Sabino is a good man, señor. He never done nothing wrong."

"Course not. Well, thanks for your help. 'Preciate it. I'll pick me up some of that chorizo tomorrow. Save me about a pound, will ya? Much obliged."

CHAPTER 15

. . . .

*L*ate that same evening, Sabino was sitting in the sheriff's office. The men had come for him the moment he returned home from the day's work. He was still wearing his khaki work clothes and there had been no time to wash. Sabino laid his earth-stained palms together and sat hugging his hands between his knees. He was thirty-two years old, stocky, with a square build and thick black hair. He was not tall. Many years he had lived in that town and never before had he been inside the office of the sheriff. His almond eyes strayed from the floor, around the walls to the windows and desks, up to the faces of the men and quickly fell again. It was the trouble—he knew that. Bad trouble, maybe. His wife, Consuelo, had grown big eyes when the men came. All four children had gone to her and remained hanging behind her skirts the whole time the men were there. Then the men told him to come with them. His wife did not say anything. The children did not cry. The baby was asleep on the bed. The oldest girl had been setting the plates for supper. Then the men came and took him away with them. The same two men who were there now in the office—the sheriff and his helper, the young man with so much anger in his face. The sheriff was talking on the telephone. The young man stood by the door as if he expected Sabino to escape.

Time passed. Soon the young man moved, opened the door for another, the Señor Bailey. Sabino was acquainted with Señor Bailey. He had worked for him and his wife many times. Sabino started to get to his feet but Señor Bailey motioned for him to remain seated. The three men spoke together. Sabino heard the word "Mexican" several times. He assumed that they were discussing him. He was not a Mexican, however. He was Indian. But these Anglos did not know the difference. To them, all dark-skinned people were Mexicans. And since Sabino had been born in Mexico, that made him one for certain, even though the place of his birth was high in the mountains and very far from here. Sensing that it might be the usual trouble, he reached into his back pocket, fumbled with the worn wallet and produced his immigration papers. The men looked up, surprised. No, they said. That was not it. They did not want papers. Even more worried, Sabino folded the papers carefully and put them away again. He clasped his hands and waited, wondering what it could be, this trouble. It was always coming, never far away for long. He had known trouble before, and now he could hear it, beating its huge black wings in the air. It was coming close. Sabino waited. The men continued to talk in low voices.

Then a lady came. She had blue-white hair piled very tall on her head and high-heeled shoes that went click-click-click. The gentlemen gathered around her immediately. The sheriff, setting a chair for her, made some kind of joke and wiped the seat with his bandana. Señor Bailey talked to her while she took some things out of her handbag, a pad for writing and several pencils. At last she was ready, pad on her knees, pencil waiting. All eyes turned toward Sabino. Who sat up in respectful attention, his back straight against the chair.

Señor Bailey spoke. The lady listened, wrote what he said on the pad, then turned to Sabino and told him in Spanish that whatever he said could be repeated in court. She asked, did he want a lawyer? Frightened, he replied no. He wondered what terrible thing he could have done that required a lawyer. Señor Bailey spoke again. The woman wrote, then translated the question. They wished to know where he had been on a certain day. Sabino did not know. He could not think. His thoughts were a flight of frightened birds. The wings made a wind in his head.

They said the day again, showed it on the calendar, the sheriff pointing with his finger.

Sabino tried very hard. He made an effort to concentrate. But the birds kept flying. Also, he did not think of time in the same way they did. These Anglos, these Norteamericanos, they marked off time in little squares. Like on the paper there, the calendar. They did not go by the depth of the water in the river, the color of the leaf or the angle of shade. He had never been able to understand how they thought about time—it made no sense to him. But having no wish to displease, he had tried to see life with their eyes, to live in the measure of their time. He tried to remember. But it was no use. Over and over the lady asked. She became impatient and recrossed her legs. Her stockings made a shocking sound of cloth and bare skin. Sabino looked away, embarrassed. The sheriff grumbled, pointed again at the calendar. Sabino shook his head. A thousand pardons . . . he could not remember. All he knew was that he must have been working. He worked every day except Sunday. Yes, surely he was working. He did not know the day. He did not know where or for whom. What did it matter? Why was it so important? The sheriff was becoming angry. He slammed his fist down on the desk. It did not help. There were only two kinds of Anglo time which Sabino understood: good and bad. This was a bad time. The black wings were beating at the window, trying to get in.

For a little while nobody said anything. Then the Señor Bailey took some money from his pocket, a bill. He held it for Sabino to see. "Have a close look," he said. "Do you recognize it?" The woman translating spoke the words very slowly, as if she had begun to doubt that he even understood Spanish. Sabino listened intently. He looked carefully at the bill. But he was puzzled by the questions. He was not sure what was expected.

"Sí, señor." It was a twenty-dollar bill, very crumpled and dirty, with a hole in the center. He had not seen so many of those in his life but he knew what they looked like. He nodded eagerly. "Sí, señor!" Hoping to please them at last. But they were not satisfied. They kept on asking. Asking and asking. Had he seen it before? Did it look familiar? Was there something about it that he noticed? Finally, Señor Bailey pointed to a little star painted in the upper corner of the bill. Did he recognize that?

"Ah, sí!" Sabino smiled with relief. He did remember the bill. It was the one the señora had given him.

The men looked at each other happily. "Which señora?" Sabino could never pronounce her name.

They were not happy again. He didn't know her name? He had never been able to say it.

But he worked for her?

Oh, yes. He worked for her all the time.

And she had paid him with that bill?

But yes. He remembered because it was much more than she usually gave.

Why had she given him so much?

He did not know.

Well, what did he do with it? With so much money?

He explained how he had traded it to Joe García for some food and a little beer. The rest he put in a jar in the kitchen.

That made them happier but they still wanted to know who the lady was.

Suddenly Sabino had an inspiration. "It was the lady in the yellow house."

They regarded him doubtfully. Which yellow house?

Well . . .

Did he know where?

Oh, sí. Sí, he knew most certainly. He worked there all the time.

Would he show them?

With much pleasure!

The sheriff parked the car on the opposite side of the street. Sabino sat in the back seat next to Señor Bailey. The lady sat up front beside the sheriff.

"You sure that is the house?" the sheriff wanted to know.

Oh, yes. Sabino was sure. In fact, if they would only look there, where the grass was pale? He had put some manure there only recently. . . .

The sheriff was banging on the steering wheel with the side of his hand and swearing in English. "Christ Almighty!" he said. And something else which the lady did not translate either. But Sabino knew most of the Anglo swear words. Señor Bailey was looking back down the street at another house. He muttered something. Then he got out of the car and walked across the street to the yellow house and knocked on the door.

Sabino waited anxiously. He saw the form of the lady appear behind the screen, her white face and hair floating against the darkness inside the house. She opened the door to Señor Bailey, peering across the street as she did so. Sabino was worried. What if the lady was angry and would not want him to work anymore? It was assuredly not a good thing if she paid him extra money and then he brought trouble to her door. He did not wish to bring trouble to anyone. No, she might not want him anymore. That made him feel sad. Not only the work—he needed the work, that was true—but it was more than that. She was such a sharp, thin lady. She was often sharp with him as well . . . always shouting. But he did not mind. Instead, he felt sorry because she had no husband anymore and no children in the house. It was bad to be like that. All alone. Any person would become dry and bitter. No, it was easy to understand why she was sometimes sharp with her tongue. But she had been generous, too. The money. The money . . . why was it so important? What did it matter where it came from? Had it been against the law, then, for her to pay him so much? Sabino sat far back in the seat, hoping that she would not see him.

Soon the Señor Bailey returned to the car and they went back to the courthouse. The young man with such anger in his face grabbed Sabino by the arm and took him upstairs. There was a room. Inside, a long table with chairs all around. The young man pushed Sabino into a chair and ordered him to stay there. He was insulting. Then he left and Sabino heard the door lock shut. It was very quiet. He heard the deputy's boots on the stairs and then it was very quiet. Outside, beyond the windows, the sun was going down. Sabino would have liked to go over to the tall windows and look out but he was afraid to move from the chair. Up in the corners of the high ceiling shadows were beginning to gather. Black wings were beating there, soundlessly.

.   .   .

"Well! I never! I have *never* in my *entire life* been so *mortified!*" Effie Sue Ethridge sat stiffly on the edge of a chair in Sheriff Killion's office. The air around her positively vibrated with outrage—outrage, injustice and hurt. Rowdy, who had been sent to fetch her, stayed well back near the door and outside her line of vision. He did not care much for that kind of duty. Even though Austin said he had prepared her, that she was ready to come, Rowdy had had misgivings. When he got to her door, he had approached warily, removing his hat respectfully, putting on his Sunday manners. She had glared at him as if his very existence were a flagrant insult and then come quickly, wordlessly, brittle with anger. During the drive to the courthouse, she looked neither left nor right but sat ramrod stiff, staring straight ahead. Now, her cheeks flaming beneath a fresh coat of powder, she drew her lips tight and took a fresh grip on her handbag.

"Now, Effie Sue," began Austin in the caramel-candy voice he usually saved for juries and voters. "Now, Effie Sue, please calm yourself. Are you comfortable?"

Eyes flashing, she jerked around. "Comfortable? *Comfortable—?* Of course I am not comfortable. No human being in his right mind would be comfortable. Have you lost your mind, Austin Bailey? Here I am . . . yanked away from my supper . . . driven all over town by that . . . that . . . *outlaw*! No attempt at tact. None whatsoever. Right there in front of everybody. *Paraded* in plain sight before the entire town. Driven directly by the Reverend Quinn's house, too. I thought the least he could do would be to drive one block out of his way—one measly block! But oh no! That would be asking far too much! And sure enough, there was Hazel Quinn out in her front yard watering her crepe myrtle just like I knew she would be. She took it in. Oh yes indeed, she took it in. Her eyes got as big as the collection plate. By now you may be absolutely certain that the whole town knows that I have been arrested!"

Austin was in the process of opening his mouth to say something when she snapped out like a piano string, discordant, on a higher note.

"I am *angry*, Austin Bailey. I don't mind telling you, I am very angry! Of course, I am willing to help . . . but I most certainly fail to see what this is all about or what any of it has to do with me. I want you to understand that. I am angry, mortified and deeply offended. My reputation is utterly ruined, my life destroyed." Then, as if satisfied that she had sufficiently stated her case, she gave a sniff and settled back in quivering silence.

Austin Bailey sighed deeply. "Now, Effie Sue," he began. "I do believe you exaggerate. No one has arrested you; things are not that bad. Please try to bear with us. You were an old and dear friend to Gussie and I know that you want to assist us in every way you can. . . ."

Sniffing again, she interrupted bitterly, "I still don't see what all this has to do with me. Or why I had to be dragged all the way down here . . . ," her voice rose to a shriek, ". . . *just like a common criminal*!"

Rowdy, behind her, wrapped his arms over his ears.

"Now, now," said Austin in a firm, fatherly voice. "If you will only allow me to explain. There is really nothing to get excited about. We have to question all sorts of people— you'd be surprised. Why, we've talked to some of the most respectable folks in the area."

She looked at him suspiciously.

"Yes. I am telling you the truth. And I am sure that nobody believes for one minute that you had a hand in . . . that you are in any kind of trouble whatsoever."

She responded with a small, ladylike snort.

"And so," continued Austin, beginning to warm up, lifting his head and letting his voice roll out the noble echoes which he enjoyed so much, "and so, the sooner we can conclude this matter, the better." When she did not reply, he dangled the twenty in her face. "Now. Do you recall ever having seen this bill before?"

Effie Sue accepted the bill reluctantly, unclamping one hand from her purse but gripping even more tightly with the other one. "Land sakes, Austin. It's just an old twenty-dollar bill. Is that all you've got to go on? No wonder the world is . . ."

"No, now. Look closely."

Effie Sue peered at the bill, holding it gingerly between her thumb and forefinger. Instinctively, she began to sense that something was catching up, but for the life of her she couldn't figure out what. Not yet. Still, she had a strong sensation of something gaining, something not entirely pleasant. Then she noticed the little star in the corner. Now that did look familiar. Why? What was it about that little star? Silly thing to do, marking up money that way. Only a kid . . . but then not a twenty . . . kids didn't have that kind of money to throw around . . . they just bought worthless stuff anyway . . . candy and gum . . . then they threw the wrappers . . . Ah! That was it! Now it came to her. Of course. She had paid her Mexican with that bill. But why had she given him a twenty? Surely that was too much, what could she have been thinking of?

"Yes, yes," she said impatiently. "I recollect that old bill. I paid my yard man with it the other day. It was too much—I can't imagine why I gave him so much. They get to thinking they deserve it."

"Do you remember how you happened to have this bill, this particular one? Is there something about it that is familiar?"

She gave the district attorney a withering look. "If you are referring to that little old star in the corner, well of course I noticed that. I'm not *blind*."

"But can you recall how it came to be in your possession?"

"I really don't know what you mean, Austin."

"Well, I mean—simply—how did you get it?"

Her cheeks turned a deeper red. The knuckles of her purse hand glowed white. She thrust the bill back at him. "I can't think what you mean. Where does a person get money anyway? At the bank, the market . . . I don't know. Are you trying to suggest that I printed it in my garage?"

Grins sprang out from J. D. and Rowdy but were as quickly squelched. The fury of her gaze swept the room like a spotlight.

"Effie Sue," said Austin patiently. "Please try to understand. I don't mean to embarrass or upset you in any way. And we are all deeply sorry for any . . . inconvenience . . . which we might have caused. Believe me, we are only trying to get at the truth."

"Well now, that is all very noble, Austin. Very noble, I'm sure. But I am frankly at a loss to understand what any of it has to do with me, my Mexican yard man or the money I pay him with. I fail to discover any possible connection. Not the slightest. I believe you can see my point?"

Austin turned wearily away and walked over to the window where he stood looking out into the gathering dusk. Behind him, the other three figures remained motionless, deep in shadow. Abruptly, Austin spun on his heel, switched on the overhead light and took an aggressive stance directly in front of Effie Sue. "Where did you get that twenty-dollar bill?" he demanded in a cold voice.

Like some creature accustomed to darkness and suddenly exposed to light, she shrank away from him, peered up, blinking. There was a lengthy silence during which three cars went by outside and a dog chased a child on a bicycle. Then, unannounced, invisible at first, two tears crept out and slid down her powdered cheeks. These were followed by two more, larger, almost apologetic. Effie Sue made no move to hide them or to turn her head, but sat staring back at Austin, the thin tears welling up and then trickling down her papery cheeks. At last she moved her lips. They trembled, opened barely wide enough to let the words out.

"I . . . I found it."

"You *found* it?" Austin frowned. "Where?"

"In my yard."

"Your *yard*?"

"In my back yard, in the rose bed, right next the wall. Where those kids are forever throwing their candy wrappers."

"You mean along the alley?"

She nodded, her face very thin.

Austin took a deep breath. "This bill here?"

"Yes. That very one. I . . . it got caught on my cultivator. That's why it's got a hole in it. Not only the star. . . ."

"I see. Was this the only one? Or were there more?"

Color flamed in her cheeks once again. "That was the only one. I swear it. Right there at the back of my rose bed, in there with the other trash. I paid Sabino with it simply because I didn't have any cash in the house. I know it wasn't right . . . I shouldn't have kept it. . . ." She gulped back more tears.

Austin loomed over her, gazing down. Under his concentrated frown and the glare from the light, she seemed to shrivel before their eyes. Rowdy chewed on the inside of his cheek. J. D. shifted in the chair, cleared his throat. Then, the frown gone, Austin reached down and slid his hand under her elbow. "That's all right," he murmured softly. "That's all right, now. Never you mind. Everything will be fine. Now . . . may I have the honor of driving you home myself? It would give me great pleasure."

She looked up at him searchingly. Then down. Sniffing, she groped in her bag for a handkerchief. Blew. Leaning on Austin's arm, she rose unsteadily. J. D. got awkwardly to his feet. Rowdy moved swiftly away, opened the door. As Austin escorted her out, she said in a small, shaky voice, "I don't know that I shall ever be able to forgive you, Austin Bailey. I just don't know how I can find it in my heart. I guess I will have to pray to the Lord Jesus to help me."

.   .   .

Upstairs, the room had grown dark. Sabino had fallen asleep with his head on his arms. Suddenly the door banged open, light exploded and he started up, terrified, his eyes hurting from the brightness.

"Come on!" commanded the deputy harshly. "Let's get a move on. Vámonos!" Sabino scrambled to his feet confused, and followed, stumbling half-blind down the stairs. The young man drove him back to his house, ordered him out and then roared off leaving a cloud of dust. Sabino stood in the backwash, puzzled and afraid. He was home again . . . that much was good. But what did it mean? A bar of light fell across the yard as Consuelo opened the door and looked out. She had heard the car. Neighbors and friends had also heard the car. Bars and squares of yellow light appeared, changed shape and went away. Quietly the friends and neighbors, the relatives, all came and stood in the little yard waiting. Sabino went inside and they all followed. They pulled up chairs and sat around the kitchen table in the yellow light. Consuelo brought a plate of food. Someone else contributed cold beer. Sabino opened the beer and took a long, thirsty pull. Still no one said anything. His wife watched him, fear crouching in her eyes like a little animal. The others were silent, waiting.

Sabino ate. Later he tried to explain. He said it was about the money. He told about the little star. He described how it had been at the sheriff's office—the lady with the blue hair, the three men. He told how they had gone to the yellow house. Then about the room upstairs in the courthouse. "Quién sabe?" he said. "I do not know what they wanted. It was something about the money . . . they did not want my papers. Yes it is trouble . . . of that there can be no doubt. But as to what kind . . . I do not know." They sat silent, far into the night, thinking about the trouble.

Part II

. . . .

CHAPTER 16

*T*he hell you say!" J. D. yelled directly into the telephone.

Rowdy, who had been resting his boots on the other desk,
lowered them and sat up to listen. It was midmorning, a
day or two after Effie Sue and Sabino had been questioned
and the only time the phone had even rung so far that day.

"*Where?*" shouted J. D.

Rowdy felt sorry for whoever it was on the other end
of that line. The guy's eardrum was probably busted to
fragments.

"San *Diego*? You mean *California*? Well, I'll be a . . ."
There was a long, quiet spell during which J. D. listened
to the deaf person on the other end. Then, "The hell you
say!" again.

By this time Rowdy was all ears.

"Yeah?" continued J. D. "That's right." Another pause.
"Well, I'll be a son of a gun."

Rowdy fidgeted.

"Sure thing!" boomed the sheriff. "That'll be fine. Oh,
we'll be waitin' for him. Yeah. You bet." He put the phone
down and stared off blank like he couldn't believe what he
had heard. Then he turned to the deputy. "I'll be a son of a
gun," he said again. "You know what? They got a boy out

yonder in custody—all the way out there in California—a sixteen-year-old kid. And would you believe it? Guess what they found in his stuff?"

Rowdy shook his head.

"A whole goddamn *wad* of money . . . and ever single bill with a little ole star in the upper right-hand corner!"

It was Rowdy's turn to get excited. He whistled through his teeth. "Well, I'll be goddamned! Now ain't *that* somethin'!"

"Sure as hell is!"

"What are they gonna do with him?"

J. D. grinned triumphantly. "I'll tell ya what they're gonna do: they're gonna put him on a train and send him to us. He ought to be here . . . ," he stabbed at the calendar with a pencil, ". . . let's see . . . day after tomorrow."

"Well now. Ain't that *somethin'*!"

"You better believe it! They're sending a special deputy and everything." J. D. grabbed his hat. "Come on! Let's tell Austin. Then we'll go get ourselves a cup of coffee. I think we've earned a little rest."

"That's a fact!"

.   .   .

On the morning that the train bearing the boy and the special deputy was due to arrive, the two lawmen were down at the station early. Rowdy paced up and down in a regular lather. J. D., being more experienced, squatted in the shade and rolled himself a smoke. Still, it seemed like that train was never going to come. They both kept looking but the tracks stretched empty off to the west, shining and quiet. Not even a hum in the rails. Across the tracks from the depot—over on the Mexican side of town—some tinny little music spilled out of the doorway of the Tex-Mex Cafe. Rowdy glanced over to see if maybe Jesús was there and then remembered that he was back in jail again. Zeb Starnes, the station master, came out and thumped a big sack of mail down on a cart. He nodded to the sheriff and the deputy and went on about his business. The steel rails gleamed, the smell of creosote was sharp. The morning ticked on like it would never end. Just as they were convinced that that was the case, that some catastrophe had taken place, that the train had been wrecked east of Tucson and the boy had escaped to Mexico—but not before he had held up the passengers and made off with thousands of dollars—just about then—*whoooo–eee!*—a far off whistle from way down the tracks. In a matter of minutes the train appeared, grew large and rumbled into the station, screeching and grating to a halt. J. D. got to his feet, ground his cigarette under his heel and stepped forward. Only two passengers got down—a thin, dark boy in handcuffs and the special deputy from California.

"Howdy!" said J. D., sticking out his hand. "I'm Sheriff Killion. Boy, are we ever glad to see *you*!"

The special deputy, a tall, freckled man with a humorless mouth, shook the hand limply. "Right," he said. "I'm Guy Jenkins, SDSO."

"You bet," agreed J. D., trying to work out what the letters meant. "This here's my deputy, Rowdy Heywood."

"Mighty pleased to meetcha!" grinned Rowdy, crowding up.

The special deputy looked away coldly, turned to the prisoner. "I guess this is the guy you've been waiting for. You're welcome to him."

They all three looked at the boy. He glanced up in surprise, then quickly ducked his head and stared hard at the ground. A piece of lank, black hair fell across his forehead and over his eyes. He was a skinny kid and none too clean. Red pimples spotted the back of his neck and his elbows were permanently rusted. He wore a gray-white T-shirt, faded jeans and scuffed black shoes.

"Well," said J. D., "let's get a move on, then." And they all started toward the sheriff's car. The boy tossed his hair back once and then walked, head down, between the sheriff and the special deputy. Immediately the hair fell forward again, covering thick, dark brows, falling into his eyes. His hands were cuffed in front and he walked stiffly, looking very slight between the two men.

They all climbed into the car and the boy, the murderer, was driven to the jail. But what a small jail—nothing but a two-story, red-brick building—not at all like the huge, noisy prison he had come from, not one bit. Nothing but a one-horse jail to go with a one-horse town. The boy curled his lip and appraised the windows. They were set deep and planted with heavy iron bars which looked like they'd been there a hundred years. Outside the bars was a heavy mesh screen. Somebody poked him in the back and the four of them went up some steps, across a porch and through a sagging screen door into a room which looked like somebody's kitchen. Inside the room there were two people, a man and his wife most likely. Foreigners. They acted like the jail was their home and the room served as their kitchen. The sheriff—a sandy, sunburned guy—introduced them to Jenkins as Horst and Anna. The man was grizzled and barrel-chested. The woman sat in a wicker chair behind a table heaped with cloth and sewing paraphernalia. She was stitching by hand and her lips were all puckered up around a bunch of pins. Peering over the tops of her glasses, she gave the boy a long, steady look. It was not an unkind look but you might say it was thorough. The boy glanced away and down at the linoleum floor. The pattern was almost familiar—green squares with black borders and circles and flowers inside. In a number of places—in front of the sink and before the screen door—the pattern was worn through to the gray. The room smelled familiar, too, almost homey. Like old people, old things. Everything in it had been used a lot.

"Vell, now," said the man named Horst. "So. This is the von, eh? Vell, vell."

The woman continued looking steadily over her glasses. Jenkins reached over and unsnapped the handcuffs. Horst took down a bunch of keys from a big hook and tossed them to the sheriff's deputy, a young guy, not much older than the boy himself. The deputy caught the keys easily, like somebody who was good at sports. Backfield, most likely. He wore real tight jeans, high-heeled boots, and walked with a swagger.

"All right, buddy. Let's go," he said and gave the boy a shove.

"Hold on," ordered J. D. "You got some papers to hand over? What's this kid's name, anyway?"

The special deputy's composure slipped just a fraction. He reached in his jacket pocket and produced an envelope. "Cantwell," he muttered. "Jewell Ray Cantwell." He shook his head and reddened slightly.

"Well, come on then, Sapphire. Or is it Pearl?" Rowdy shoved even harder. The boy stumbled through a door and up a flight of metal stairs to the second floor. Up there it wasn't nearly so homey. Just rows of cells, iron bars and grates over all the windows. They went down to the very last cell, next to one filled with Mexicans, who peered out with great interest. The deputy prodded the boy into a solitary cell, slammed the bars shut and turned the key. After that he stood on the outside grinning, legs spraddled wide apart.

"Well, there you are, fella," he said. "Make yourself right

at home. I reckon you got that room reserved special for quite a spell." Still grinning, he turned and left, the door at the top of the stairs clanging, his boots ringing every step of the way down.

The boy looked around the cell. It had iron bars all across the front, a little window at the back and brick walls on either side. There was a cot along one wall, a toilet and washbasin in the corner of the other. The boy sat down on the cot. He sat there for a long time without moving. After a while, the woman brought him a plate of food and some coffee. He ate, still sitting on the edge of his bunk. Then she came and took away the tin plate and cup and he was left alone once again. Later, the shadows in the cell began to deepen and the sky turned gold. He heard women's voices outside so he got up and went over to the window. Several Mexican women were standing just below. They were shouting and calling up to the prisoners in the next cell. The men were shouting back and laughing. Since everything was being said in Spanish, Jewell Ray couldn't understand a word. Still, he stood at the window listening and watching the women. Sometimes they seemed very angry with the men. They went to cussing and screeching and making what sounded like terrible threats. Then the men would reply in soft, sing-song, sly and easy voices and the women would forget they were mad and scream with laughter. They would all laugh together and then engage in an exchange of jokes and insults of an obviously sexual nature. Jewell Ray wished like anything that he could understand Spanish. Those people sure seemed to be having a good time, especially considering the circumstances.

The women stayed until it began to get dark. When they finally left, it was as if they took the light with them, leaving behind a fading trail of threats, complaints, promises and laughter. Jewell Ray could hear the men next to him laughing, too. Laughing softly and talking among themselves in low, musical voices. He stood at the window listening and watching the huge stars come out over the little town. Presently the men ceased their talk and all was quiet. Somewhere a dog barked. Suddenly a very strange noise started up on the other side of the jail—a godawful sound like a lovesick animal or maybe something devilish being slowly strangled. Jewell Ray couldn't make it out at all. Finally it dawned on him that it was somebody singing, or trying to. But it was not like any singing he'd ever heard before. In fact, you couldn't call it singing at all, it was more like a long, drawn-out sob. Whoever was doing it must be mighty unhappy. Jewell Ray tried to make out the words. But long about then the men in the cell next door to him started to yell and beat on the bars. They plainly wanted the singer to shut up. You didn't need to know Spanish to figure that out. But the singer, far from being discouraged, wailed with renewed strength. It was long, quavery and very sad but Jewell Ray kind of liked it. The men next door, however, cursed and kicked the wall. The singer seemed not to hear, and the sad, frail notes drifted out over the sleeping town like a flimsy curtain blowing gently from an upstairs window.

CHAPTER 17

. . . .

*P*eople in town were shocked to learn that Judge Hainsworth had appointed Joel Ferris to defend the boy in court.

"Joel Ferris? *Joel Ferris?*"

"My God!"

"Hell, maybe he ought to retire."

"Who? Ferris?"

"No, Hainsworth."

"Well, he probably couldn't get anybody else to take the case."

Austin Bailey was especially disappointed in the choice. Austin had been looking forward to a real challenge, a good courtroom drama with plenty of publicity. Murder cases didn't come along all that often, especially ones involving old families with lots of money. Winning a case like this one could have been made into a substantial political gain. But not with Joel Ferris on the defending side.

"Tough luck," sympathized his old law partner, Houston Carr.

"Well," muttered Austin moodily, "I had been hoping for a more worthy opponent."

Joel Ferris was the kind of lawyer usually referred to as an ambulance chaser. He took any and all legal work he could get, dispatching each case with the world-weary air of a ticket collector at a traveling carnival. His arguments for cattle rustlers or against cheating husbands were ground out with the same dry, humdrum despair, his only interest plainly being in pocketing the fee and then moving on. He was a small, sharp-faced man, his complexion as colorless as the food in the two-bit diners where he habitually hung out and which, over the years, had given his demeanor and even his philosophy the same lifeless cast. Overall, his appearance was seedy, down at heel and, win or lose, the expression on his face never changed. He practiced law from an old battered trailer which he hauled from town to town in the wake of his dusty Buick. During a trial, he lived in the trailer until his business was completed and then, with a raucous complaint of old metal and a modest cloud of dust, he would move on. Nobody knew where he came from but it was rumored that his daddy had been a traveling salesman dealing in patent medicines. And there was this: wherever he happened to be, there was always the faint but distinctive aroma of liniment and witch hazel.

That scent—a mixture of cloves, eucalyptus, camphor and rubbing alcohol—prevailed even among the rich and riper flavors of the second floor of the county jail as he sat and had a look at the boy he was being paid to defend. It was hard to tell what he might have been thinking just then—the only possible clue was the activity of his ever-present toothpick. Joel Ferris worked the toothpick over to the right of his mouth and then back down to the left. It shifted, rode a steady, thoughtful gait, switched back once again and settled in the corner of his lips. He sat staring at the boy across the table. The boy did not look at him but hung his head, sullen. A piece of long, lank hair fell across his eyes. Shoulder bones stuck up beneath his T-shirt pointy as plucked chicken wings. He was hunched over, picking at the already scarred wood with a grubby and severely bitten thumbnail. A narrow, barred window set in the wall just above admitted a kind of glare but the light outside was so big and so white that it mostly stayed outside, too big to squeeze itself into so cramped and grilled a space. The afternoon was loud with locusts.

"Lissen here, boy," said Joel Ferris, taking the toothpick from the corner of his mouth. "Have you ever heard of the eee–lek-trick chair?"

The boy jerked up, face gone white and eyes staring.

Ferris grunted, nodded to himself. "Yeah. Well, I kinda figured you had. Most kids headed in your direction think about it now and again. They figure it don't apply to them. But you know what? You're gonna go there *pronto* if you don't cooperate with me. Yessir. Right on down to Hunts-ville and fry. When they're done with you, you won't even make a decent cracklin'."

The boy took in a huge, dry gulp of air.

"Yessir," went on Ferris matter-of-factly. "You can bet your boots that's the way it's gonna be. Unless . . . ," and here he suddenly slammed his fist down on the table so hard that dust which had been resting peacefully for decades exploded violently into the atmosphere.

The boy jumped up like a jackrabbit fixing to run. If he had been any thinner or scareder he would have simply melted between the bars. Been gone.

". . . UNLESS YOU TELL ME EVER GODDAMN THING YOU KNOW! SET DOWN!"

The boy sat, quivering.

Ferris took a fresh toothpick out of his coat pocket, studied the boy over the tip of it. "You savvy, son? You hear what I'm sayin'? Folks in this here town are fairly itching for a hanging. That failing, they'll settle for a fried shrimp. That old lady was what amounts to *royalty* in this country. She was a *queen*. It don't matter whether she was a good one or not . . . ain't nobody even gonna inquire about that now. Thing is, she was rich. Hooo-boy! Was she ever rich! And she was old. She had been around, she had power. And she had lasted long enough to make quite an impression. She *mattered* to the folks around here, she represented something they set a lot of store by. And since these people are used to taking matters into their own hands . . . well, you're damn lucky you even got here alive."

The boy, who by this time had turned almost blue-white, rubbed a shaky hand across his mouth. "I ain't done nothin'," he muttered. "I ain't never killed nobody."

Ferris went on as if he hadn't heard.

"Now lissen, the judge says I'm your lawyer. That means it's my job to get you off . . . or as near to it as possible." He shook his head. "It ain't gonna be easy. And I sure as hell can't do anything unless you tell me the truth. The truth, the whole truth and nothin' but the truth." He grinned, showing a row of tobacco-stained teeth.

The boy was not cheered.

Ferris didn't notice, went on. "Now. Thing is, you're sixteen years old and you're charged with murder in the first degree—that's the very worst kind—which means that in the State of Texas you have to be tried as a *a*-dult. As a man, you understand? None of that namby-pamby stuff they gave you out in California."

Here the boy scowled. His heavy eyebrows plunged together and the limp wedge of hair fell even farther forward.

Joel Ferris continued in his dry voice. "This here trial . . . it's gonna commence in about two weeks near as I can figure. Soon as we cut out a jury. What that means is that me and you got that same amount of time, more or less, to come up with a way to save your hide. Otherwise . . . *other-wise*, these folks here are gonna cure it, nail it to the *ho*-tel wall and show it off as a goddamn tourist attraction. Like some of them snakeskins they got hanging there already. You get it, fella? This here's for real. Me and you got to work together and we ain't got very much time. So we're gonna have to work hard and fast." He tilted his chair back on two legs, shifted the toothpick, squinted at the boy. "It don't make no difference whether we like each other or not," he said softly.

The boy darted him a look.

"Main thing is," Ferris went on, leaning forward once more, "we got to be candid. I know what your chances are . . . they ain't worth cow flop and I'll tell you so. And if you don't level with me, they ain't even worth that. We can't have no secrets from each other. Personally, I don't care what you done, whether you killed that old lady or not. I mean, it don't make me no never mind. I ain't inter-ested—*except as your attorney*. You understand? I am the only thing standing between you and the Chair," he nar-rowed his eyes, watched the boy closely, "and since that is the case, I got to know everything about you. *Ever-damn-thing*. I want to hear about *every minute* since the time you left Dixie until you was picked up in San Diego." He leaned forward, eyes intense, and looked hard into the boy's face. Then, just when the air seemed about to snap like a steel wire, he scraped back the chair and got swiftly to his feet.

The boy stared up, wide-eyed, a thin two days' growth shading his pale cheeks.

"You think on it, boy. I'll be back in the mornin'."

CHAPTER 18

. . . .

We come along this way," mumbled Jewell Ray, tracing a red line on the road map spread out across the table. He would not look at the attorney but sat head down, shoulders peaked under the T-shirt. Across from him, Joel Ferris sat, his mind working like a deck of cards—shuffling, stacking, taking a draw and discarding. He stopped the minute he heard the word "we."

"WE?" he said. "Who's *we*?"

The boy looked up. "Me and Sherrylee."

"Well, who the hell is Sherrylee?"

Jewell Ray squared his shoulders. "My wife."

Ferris spat the toothpick clean out of his mouth. "Your *wife*? Christ Almighty, son. Couldn't you have waited to get yourself into only one kind of trouble at a time? A wife now . . . Je-sus." He contemplated this new development blackly. "Good Lord. Well, where in the world is *she*?"

Jewell Ray looked uncomfortable. "I . . . I don't know."

"You don't *know*? The woman's your wife and you don't even know where she *is*?"

The boy squirmed. "Well, it was like this, see: First off, she was in the same ju-ve-nile home where I was. Them po-lice took us both there together. But after a while— two, three weeks maybe—they put me down in that big ole jail. Then I didn't see her no more." He dug a jagged thumbnail into the scarred surface of the table. "I reckon she maybe went on back home."

"Home," repeated Ferris bleakly. Unlike most lawyers, he carried no yellow pads and took no notes. At that moment his dun brown eyes settled on the boy like leaves in the fall getting ready for a long, hard winter. "But you was really married? Legal, I mean?"

The boy nodded. "Yes sir. We got hitched back yonder in Arkansas. Went to the courthouse, signed a paper. Cost me five dollars."

"But she went on back home? Leaving you to take the rap?" When the boy did not reply, Ferris continued anyway. "Tell me, now. Tell me the truth. She helped you out, didn't she? She helped you get that money? I mean, she was in it every bit as much as you was."

The boy, very pale that morning, hung his head even lower, so that the dark hair dangling over his forehead grazed the tabletop. Slowly he shook his head, still digging at the table with his thumb. "Aw, it don't matter," he mumbled. "She's only a girl."

The attorney grunted. "Yeah. Well, where were we? All right. You say you come along this way . . . ?"

Slowly they traced the route together, Jewell Ray sweating it out all over again, making false moves where he forgot and smudges on the map with his grimy finger, and Ferris clinging to him like a leech, drawing out the last drops of truth until the boy was sucked dry and sat panting, the skin drawn up tight over his bones.

Ferris gazed out the window, whistling softly through his teeth. "Tell me something, son. Did you ever have a gun?"

"I . . . yeah. I did, but I done lost it."

"*Lost* it? How in hell . . . ?"

Jewell Ray explained in a confused rush about a freight car and some men coming after them and how they had to jump out the other side and run. How it was too dark to see where he had left the gun and they were in too much of a hurry. So he had to leave it behind.

"Well, that was probably the smartest thing you ever done," remarked Ferris drily. He shuffled the pack and drew. Leaned forward. "All right. So how about this here town? Tell me about that, how you happened to come through here. And what happened while you was acceptin' our hospitality." He sounded offhand but his voice had a crouch in it, like it was fixing to spring.

For a long moment the boy sat silent. Then he swallowed and began. "We got us a ride with a man and his wife. They was just settin' out on their vacation. They was friends of some people we had met back there," he made a little stab at the map with his finger, "and since they was comin' this way they said for us to hop in and go, too. They was comin' out here to attend one of them Bible get-togethers—a camp meetin', you know?" He glanced up inquiringly. Ferris nodded. Jewell Ray continued. "I guess they got a real good one around here. . . . Anyway, soon as these folks made sure we was legally married, they offered us a ride. Well, me and Sherrylee, we was real tickled—*at first*—because we was tired of trying to hitch rides and being chased off trains and all that. We figured we had us a good deal. But we no sooner got in the car and pulled out on the highway than they started right in to save our souls. Lord, I thought. Seven hundred miles of this? That lady goin' on and on about Jesus and especially about sinnin', and the man chiming in . . . they like to never let up. On and on . . . I thought if I heard one more word about how good Jesus was and how much he loved me, I'd buy me a one-way ticket to hell just to get shed of him. Sherrylee even went and locked herself in a restroom just to get a few minutes' peace. But that lady stood right outside the door the whole time prayin' in a loud voice. Smoked Sherrylee plumb out of there. Yessir. Them folks sure did go on. I guess they was gettin' all warmed up for camp meetin'.

"So anyhow, we pulled in here 'bout the middle of the mornin'. It was a mornin' like this one—hot, glary—and I asked if maybe we could stop so as to get us a cold drink of some kind. (The truth was, Mr. Ferris, I was afraid they was goin' to pack us off to that Bible get-together and then we wouldn't have a chance. . . .) The lady, she nodded real wise and said she'd seen it comin'. I asked her just what exactly it was that she had seen comin' and she said the fires of hell consuming our souls. So I said maybe some water would help put out them fires and she said oh no! And threw her arms in the air and waved around. According to her, the only thing that would quench our thirst (our thirst for salvation, you understand) would be to get out that very minute, kneel down on the flamin' pavement and beg Jesus Christ to come into our hearts. Well, I didn't pay her no mind at all and even her husband looked a little worried. Then Sherrylee! I swear—! I thought she'd gone and lost her mind what with all that heat and prayin' . . . you know how women are about religion, Mr. Ferris. It gets 'em right feverish."

Covering his mouth with one hand, the lawyer nodded.

Jewell Ray continued. "Well, Sherrylee! She ups and says *yes*! Just like that. Says she thinks that's sure enough what we all ought to be doing, ever last one of us burning our kneecaps off out yonder in the street. Well, I'll tell you, I *stared* at her. My head swiveled around like a ball bearing in a fresh-greased socket. And the lady, too. She stops cold and stares, like she couldn't believe her ears. Then she throws up her arms again and goes to screamin'. Like to scared her husband to death. He damn near drove into a ditch. And all the time Sherrylee sitting there sweet as a lamb. I tried ever which way to signal her but she wouldn't even look at me. And that woman all the time screechin' and moanin' . . . Lord. Finally, the man got fed up with all the commotion and he hauled that car off the road like he'd had a grudge against it for years. Ran up over the curb and stopped on the sidewalk just shy of a rock wall. Stalled the engine, too . . . and I reckon that's what done it because he turned bright purple and started in yelling at the lady. She yelled back and they went at it. Meantime, Sherrylee gave me a wink. We grabbed our stuff and eased on out of there and ran like hell. Hid under a grandstand until we figured they was long gone."

He sat silent for a moment. "Whew boy! I sure was glad to be rid of *them*!"

Ferris extracted a fresh toothpick from his coat pocket. "That was in this town here?"

"Yes sir."

"What did you do then?"

"Well, *first* thing, we found us a water fountain and had a long drink. Then we went to a gas station, changed our clothes and washed up. Since we didn't have no money, we went right to work."

"Tell me about that," shifting the toothpick.

"Well . . . ," the boy looked up at the lawyer, his eyes wary under the dark, heavy brows.

"Go on."

"Well . . . Sherrylee, she had all these magazines and pamphlets and stuff . . . ," he fidgeted.

"Well?"

"I got to go to the bathroom."

"Oh hell. Go on, then. But don't be all day at it."

Presently the boy returned. Joel Ferris cut his cards, considered. "All right, now."

Jewell Ray stared out the window, then edged into his chair and resumed his story. "We drifted around for a while kinda lookin' for the right street. Sherrylee—she always picked the street. But I didn't much like the one she settled on. It was real bare—not many trees or bushes or anything—no cover. I got to have good cover for my getaway." He glanced up as if seeking professional approval. Ferris made no comment, so Jewell Ray continued. "This here street was broad and open, didn't have much cover like I say, but it did have a alley runnin' along behind of it. So I said okay, a alley was all right. We split up as usual. She gets herself all arranged, gathers up her magazines and goes traipsing down the sidewalk, real prissy, you know? Just like the Avon lady."

Joel Ferris nodded wearily.

The boy went on. "Well, I got myself set, too, went sneakin' down that alley, stickin' my head up every few feet tryin' to keep Sherrylee in sight—so as to spot which house she picked, you understand. We went along like that for some while, me bobbin' up and down, peekin' over the wall and her sailin' along smooth as a ship. Finally, long about the time I'm fixin' to drown in my own sweat, she turns up a walk and rings the doorbell."

"Yeah?" said Ferris, leaning forward.

The boy sat for a minute, chewing on the back of his hand. Then he laid both hands flat on the table and stared at them while he talked. His voice dropped, became nearly a whisper. "I jumped up on that wall and landed in the yard

soft as a cat. Then I edged along till I got to the back door.
It was just a plain ole screen door, I tried it and it was open,
so I crept in, real easy. And there I was in a kitchen. With
a old lady settin' in there, her back to the door. She was
settin' at the table—big, ole kitchen table—but that *table*!
Mr. Ferris, you'll never believe it, but that table was all-
over money. Jesus Christ! Money all over the damn place.
Ever' kind—bills, I mean. Ever' domination. My eyes like
to jumped right outta my head."

Ferris noted that they grew big with the telling of it,
glowed with the memory.

The boy went on, his voice higher. "Well, I just stood
there starin' at all that money. I couldn't believe it . . .
Lord, I'd never seen such. But I musta made some kind
of a noise 'cause all of a sudden the old lady she spun
around and seen me. I don't know how come she didn't
hear Sherrylee at the front door. . . . I could hear that
bell ringin' and ringin'. It was like a regular alarm clock,
but that old lady she didn't pay no attention. Anyhow, she
whipped around and drew a bead on me. She didn't have
no gun or nothin'—it was just her eyes. You know? 'What
do *you* want?' she said. She had a voice just like iron fil-
ings. I said, 'Just hand over that money and don't make no
fuss.'" He paused, picked at a scab on his arm. "But you
know what she did, Mr. Ferris?"

The lawyer shook his head.

Jewell Ray spoke in a small, tight voice, high and almost
hissing. "She *laughed*! Mr. Ferris, she laughed at me! Jes'
set right there big as you please and laughed her damn head
off. 'Hand over my money?' she said. 'To you and who else?'
Well, I jes' walked on over to the table. 'Hold still,' I said.
'And you won't get hurt.' Well, she really fell out laughin'
then. Sputterin'. Was I man enough to do it? she said. Went
on making fun, said not only was my feet mighty tender

but my horns was right green. Said she left things like me in the pasture to flesh out and that a feedlot wouldn't even let me in. Bunch of stuff like that. Well, it ticked me off, I'll tell you. So I just reached over and grabbed me a handful of that money. Well! She come *unglued*. Grabbed aholt of my arm"—he clamped his right hand around his left wrist—"hard—like that—and hung on. Then with her other hand, she cracked me—whack!—acrost the knuckles with one of them there wooden spoons."

Joel Ferris shifted in his chair, the toothpick darted to the other side of his mouth. "Hold on. Just a minute. I thought you said the table was covered with money. Now all of a sudden you go to throwing wooden spoons around. Where'd they come from?"

"It was." Jewell Ray nodded emphatically. "More money than you ever saw. That deep and I ain't a-wolfin'." He held his hands about a foot apart. Ignoring the lawyer's raised eyebrows, he plunged on. "I ain't pulling your leg, Mr. Ferris. That table looked like a corn shuckin'. But off on one end there was all these bowls and spoons and things . . . like maybe she was fixin' to make a cake or somethin'. She grabbed one of them. One of them spoons. Them things *hurt*, let me tell you. Them spoons. They pack a right smart sting." He rubbed his thumb over his knuckles thoughtfully. "Well, she was haulin' back, fixin' to let me have it again, had her arm way up in the air . . . so I reached out and grabbed aholt of *her* wrist . . . and I guess we both kinda got off balance. Anyway, she latched onto the front of my shirt and tried to pull herself up—or me down, I don't know which—but I was busy trying to back up, trying to shake loose, when all of a sudden her face went all funny. . . ."

Ferris pounced. "Funny? What do you mean, 'funny'?"

The boy looked puzzled. "I don't know. Funny. Strange-like. Pulled up tight at the corners. Then, well right off, she went limp, limp as a gunnysack with all the oats drained out. Just slumped over in her chair."

Ferris was crouched low over the table, listening with every pore.

Jewell Ray rubbed his palms together, wiped them on his thighs. "I . . . I done let go of her arm and it just fell—*thump*—on the table." He relaxed his own arm at the elbow and let it drop on the little interviewing table. The thud was somewhat unnerving. "Like that." Jewell Ray looked at his arm. "After that she didn't move no more."

"What about the hand she had holding your shirt?"

The boy turned even paler. "That. I . . . well, I . . . I had to *pry* it off. *I had to pry it offa me, Mr. Ferris! It was hanging in there like a claw!*" His voice rose to a high, tearful pitch.

"All right. Calm down. What happened then?"

He swallowed like he might have been close to throwing up. "I jes' stood there, I guess. I . . . I think I kinda froze. I couldn't understand what had gone on. Didn't make no sense to me. I guess I was kinda scared. Her fingers all stiff and snagged up in my shirt like that. . . . Then she just flopped over on the table. I realized that I better get outta there. So I grabbed a armful of that money and ran."

Joel Ferris sat working the toothpick back and forth. In his mind, he shuffled and cut, shuffled and cut. The boy looked exhausted, all hunched over, nibbling on his nails. Then the attorney made him tell the whole story again, not once, but three times. Over and over he asked, "Did you hit her?"

The boy denied it violently. "*No!* No, I never!"

"How many times did you hit that old lady?"

"I never! I swear to God! I never did!"

"What'd you hit her with?"

"*Nothin'*! I'm tellin' you . . . !"

"Well, then she must have fallen, hit her head on something?"

The boy was surprised. "No. That ain't how it was. She just kinda collapsed. Gave out, like somethin' you let the air out of. She didn't fall nowhere—jes' sorta sank."

"Was that after you hit her?"

And on and on until the boy was on his feet screaming. "NO! I NEVER! I NEVER HIT HER. I AIN'T DONE NOTHIN'. LEAVE ME BE!"

Curious, the other prisoners came to the doors of their cells and looked out, their faces moving like dim moons in the dusky interior of the jail. They exchanged a few quiet comments but mostly they were silent. It was difficult to tell whether they understood or not.

Without another word, the lawyer scraped back his chair, threw away the toothpick and went on down the stairs. Left alone, the boy stood, arms and head hanging, breathing in deep, shuddering sobs. Then the jailer came, jangling his keys, and locked the boy up again, where he fell face down on his bunk.

. . . .

CHAPTER 19

*M*eanwhile, the arrival of that boy had piqued the interest of the whole town like a dose of Spud and Irma's chow-chow—stuff hot enough to tenderize the tail end of a rattlesnake. Everybody's senses were heightened and life took on a refreshing new flavor.

Teenagers took to cruising by the jailhouse of an evening, craning their necks and gunning their engines in hopes of getting a glimpse of the criminal. But he was as retiring as a monk, avoiding his window with such scrupulous attention that they began to wonder if anything was even living in there. Those people who walked their dogs suddenly noticed the courthouse lawn and hauled back on the straining leashes hoping to catch a glimpse, too. The county groundskeepers, however, complained about this new traffic for a number of reasons. When nobody listened, they simply changed the watering schedule and set the sprinklers going at the time when dog walking was at its peak.

Rumors flew around the tables at the bridge club and there was an ugly new edge to the competition. Interest had shifted from cards to information. As for the main actors in the drama, J. D. assumed the air of a man who has done his duty. Rowdy was both smug and secretive, pretending to know a whole lot more than he actually did. Austin Bailey, as district attorney, behaved like a man with heavy burdens, deep in thought. Judge Hainsworth and Senator Buchanan went on as if nothing had happened, enjoying good whiskey, barbecued steak and a well-played hand of poker.

Bubba Houghton, for one, was vastly relieved when they found that boy. People had remained cordial, of course; they respected his grief. But out of the corner of his eye he had caught any number of them taking sideways looks. For the barest fraction of a second their thoughts had snagged on suspicion, or merely a question. Maybe only curiosity. Whatever it was, it was unpleasant and although he maintained an outward appearance of calm, his palms perspired every time he made out a check.

Beau Merriwether, Gussie's brother, took to packing a gun in plain sight.

Two houses down the street from Bubba's meditations and private jubilation, Effie Sue Ethridge rested in her darkened bedroom, a damp cloth pressed to her eyes. The world had suddenly become a very upsetting place for Effie Sue—very upsetting indeed—and she didn't even want to look at it anymore. Ever since that . . . well, that *inquisition* . . . that nightmare of an evening spent with Austin Bailey and the sheriff down at the courthouse . . . that rude young man driving her right by Hazel Quinn's house . . . ever since then she had hardly gone out at all. Contrary to her usual pattern, she shopped early, darting furtively to the market and back before the usual crowd was out. She ordered her prescriptions delivered to her home, cancelled all social engagements and turned her face to the wall. But of course she had no sooner done so than the telephone started to ring.

It was Charlotte. "Effie Sue? Effie Sue, are you all right?"

Faintly, "Yes. Yes, I think so. Thank you."

"Well, are you sick?"

"No. No . . . I am not sick. . . ."

Well, did she need anything? Charlotte was just getting ready to go out. Something from the library? Effie Sue shuddered. Charlotte's taste in books was deplorable. She read anything with a pretty cover. Well, would she be at Amity's for bridge tomorrow? Effie Sue didn't believe so; she wasn't really feeling up to it.

"Well, for Pete's sake! What *ails* you, Effie Sue?"

The minute she put the phone down it rang again. This time it was Amity. Breathless. She told that the prisoner, that boy, was married. "He has a wife! Can you *imagine*?"

"Uh-huh," said Effie Sue, who didn't care a fig.

Amity rattled on. Said Susannah had her feelings hurt about something. (Nothing new about that.) Miz Asa (T. D.) Hines was going on a revolutionary diet—broiled chicken and bananas. Fine, said Effie Sue. Amity reported that Charlotte had gotten into an awful fight with Rose at the Cut 'N Curl. Apparently Rose had left the permanent wave solution on too long and now Charlotte looked just like a Zulu. Effie Sue tried to picture it and failed. *Yakety, yakety, yak*, thought Effie Sue.

Then Susannah called, sniffing and twittering and (Effie Sue suspected) thoroughly enjoying herself. "What is the matter with me?" Effie Sue asked herself. "These people are my friends. What has become of my charity and Christian love?" She wished she could discuss the matter with her pastor, Reverend Quinn. And that very moment, as if touched by the finger of God, nudged into action, Hazel called and said she was on her way over with a pie.

"Pie?" said Effie Sue. "Pie won't help." And hung up.

And ached because she knew that she would never darken the doors of that church again. Christians preached forgiveness but they didn't mean it. Curiosity and a love for the delicious always won out. No, they might pretend otherwise but they all knew, every last one of them, that she had been arrested and dragged down to the courthouse like any common criminal. They might not know *why*—and to this day, Effie Sue herself was not altogether sure—but they knew. The moment she entered church, they would all discreetly stare and whisper. Effie Sue could not abide a whisper. Oh, they would smile and wave— white-gloved fingers twinkling up near their hats—but they would be staring all the while. And around every dinner table that noon Effie Sue and her transgressions would be served up. Oh, the *shame* . . . the shame of it was simply more than a body could bear. When she got to feeling better she might go and visit her sister in Harlingen for a while.

Effie Sue dipped her washrag into a little bowl of ice water and replaced it across her eyes. Then she concentrated, wishing darkness for herself and death to her next-door neighbor whose power mower was whining and spitting directly underneath her bedroom window. Silly fool, mowing his lawn in the middle of the day. Give himself heatstroke. Deserved it, too. No right to disturb other people, disrupt their rest that way. He had offered to cut her lawn as well but she had drawn herself up, said no, thank you kindly, she would see to it herself. She was certain that the only reason he offered was because her grass was getting long, going to seed and creeping over into his flower bed. If only Gussie had been there. Gussie would have sent her Mexican over in a jiffy. And never asked a bunch of questions, either. Gussie now . . . Gussie had been a real neighbor.

As for her own yard man, that Sabino . . . worthless just like all of them. Had never showed his face again after she gave him that twenty-dollar bill. Just goes to prove it . . . you can't afford to spoil these people.

CHAPTER 20

. . . .

Only a few days before the trial was scheduled to begin, the Continental Trailways bus pulled into the station as usual. The door wheezed open and a tall, pale girl climbed down and then reached back to drag an old metal suitcase after her. She stood there in the hot afternoon sunlight as if surprised by her own arrival. She was thin, flat-chested, and her long, light brown hair framed a face which was sallow with fatigue. But even though she was faded, washed out to the point of seeming almost colorless, her eyes were deep-set and dark green and there was a peculiar strength about her that was hard to pin down. As if she planned to endure. It showed in the slightly defiant lift of her chin and in the way her eyes had of not expecting much.

She stood for a few moments squinting her eyes against the glare of the parking lot. Then she picked up the suitcase and lugged it into the square cinder block building which served as the station waiting room. Once inside, she walked partway across the gritty cement floor then stopped and looked around. Old travel posters curled from the walls. Facing her was a row of chrome chairs with marble-pattern green plastic seats. Most of the seats had split open, burst the plastic so that the stuffing bulged out. A feeble attempt had been made to mend the seats with black tape but now even the tape had begun to peel off and turn gray. That row of chairs reminded the girl of a cottonmouth water moccasin and she wouldn't have sat in one of them for the world.

Across one end of the building was a cheaply panelled counter piled high with grimy ledgers and years of Sears Roebuck catalogs. A large woman was sitting behind the counter reading an old movie magazine. She looked up at the girl, apparently didn't care for what she saw and said in a hard, flat voice, "N'I hep ya?"

The girl hesitated. Pointing out the door, she asked, "Is that the courthouse over yonder?"

The woman's interest perked up. "Yep. That's it." She eyed the girl more closely. "You're from the South, ain't cha?"

The girl did not answer but stood gazing out the door in the direction of the courthouse. After a while she said, "Can I leave my suitcase here?"

The woman considered. "Well . . ."

"Just for a little while?"

The woman was fat and pallid, like a person who stays indoors all the time and lives on greasy food. She had oily, iron-colored hair and a big mole on her chin. She rubbed a plump finger across the mole.

"Well, I guess," she allowed begrudgingly. Then added quickly, "But we close up right at five. And we ain't re-sponsible."

The girl nodded and stood waiting.

"You can set it over there," the woman gestured toward the end of the counter.

Keeping her distance from the row of green chairs and their waddy cotton, the girl thumped the suitcase down and moved to the door. "I'll be back before five," she said, and went on out.

As soon as she was gone, the woman heaved herself up, went over to the door and looked out in the direction the girl had taken.

The girl made her way up a wide sidewalk shaded by locust trees, climbed granite steps and paused at the double doors which stood open at the entrance to the courthouse. At the opposite end of the building, identical doors also stood open, admitting a dazzling square of westering sun. In between, the hallway stretched dim and silent except for a typewriter tapping way off somewhere. Dust motes floated in the light. The girl took a few tentative steps inside and peered up at the signs lettered over the doors. Down at the far end of the hall a door slammed and a figure detached itself from the gloom of old wood. At first it was hard to make him out because of the light being behind him, but as he came closer, she saw that he was small and wiry with a face that put her in mind of a ferret. He wore a shabby suit, a tie which fairly shouted, run-over shoes and a cowboy hat. As he went by, he nodded to her and went on out the doors. She moved on and was reading "Justice of the Peace" when he suddenly showed up again right at her elbow and gave her a start. He took off his hat.

"Howdy, little lady." He smiled, showing a row of tobacco-stained teeth. "Is there somethin' I maybe could help you with?"

She backed up a step. She didn't much like the looks of him. He made her think of the sly-eyed men who sold tickets at cheap carnivals. And he smelled like liniment. Still . . . she had to find out. And there wasn't much he could do to her in a courthouse. . . .

"I reckon I'm lookin' for the jail."

His eyebrows shot up. Then they came back down and crouched over crafty, dun-colored eyes. He fished in his jacket pocket, took out a toothpick and began to work it between his lips.

"The jail? Now what in Sam Hill does a young lady like you want with the jail?"

She replied evenly, "I'm looking for my husband."

His jaw stopped in mid-chew, grew slack. Then, in one amazing, swift motion, he grabbed hold of the toothpick, tossed it away, took a firm grip on her arm and propelled her down the hall and into an empty office. Still holding her by the elbow, he kicked the door shut, pulled a chair forward with his free hand and stood back breathing hard and looking at her.

"Set down, little lady," he said. "Set down." He dragged another chair over, planted one foot on the seat and leaned on his arms across his bent knee. All the time staring at her like he couldn't believe his eyes.

She sat down very demurely on the edge of the chair.

He took out a fresh toothpick and went to work on it.

"Who are you?" he asked in a sandpapery voice.

She returned his look steadily. "Who are *you*?"

He grinned, shook his head. "I mighta known you'd be the feisty one." Suddenly serious, he twirled the chair around and sat facing her, his arms folded across the back. "My name is Joel Ferris. I'm a lawyer. At the moment I am occupied with trying to defend a young man who is charged with the murder of a old lady. Seems he beat her up, took her money and made off for California." He observed closely, saw her turn even paler than she already was, watched her tighten her long, thin hands and twist them in her lap. Then he continued, very softly. "Would that by any chance be the young feller you was lookin' for?"

She regarded him suspiciously. "How do I know you're what you say?"

He narrowed his eyes. "Your name's Sherrylee, ain't it? I thought so. When I first seen you standing out there something told me, 'Whoa there! Go on back now and have a word with that little lady. She looks like somebody who deserves attention.' And I was right, wasn't I?" He shook his head again. "Sure enough. Ain't it a small world?" He mused on that thought for a moment, then abruptly uncoiled himself from the chair and reached for his hat. "Come on then, honey. I'll take you on over to the jail." He opened the door for her, grinning. "Man, is he gonna be surprised! Yes sir! *Mighty* surprised!"

The two of them crossed the lawn, sun-scorched grass crunching under their shoes, and went up the steps to the jail. Ferris held open a screen door and they stepped into a large kitchen. There was a woman at the kitchen table, her hands deep in a mixing bowl. Beside her on the table lay two sheets of biscuits already cut out and set to go in the oven. Ferris nodded to her and aimed his hat for the rack.

"Howdy, Anna. Mind if we go on up? I got a visitor for that boy up yonder." He reached for a ring of keys hanging on a nail by the stairs. Anna looked at Sherrylee, her eyes a mixture of curiosity and sympathy. She lifted hands thickly crusted with dough.

"Ya? Ya? Vell . . . I guess it is all right. You be responsible, Mr. Ferris?" She looked at him, then back at Sherrylee doubtfully.

"Yes ma'am," he replied wearily. "I'm responsible."

Sherrylee waited at a little wooden table while the lawyer went to get Jewell Ray. There were steel bars everywhere, and empty cells. One cell had some men in it, down near where Mr. Ferris had gone. Sherrylee's heart was pounding fit to beat Jesus. She tried every way she knew not to look down that corridor but somehow her head just naturally turned that direction and her eyes wouldn't go anywhere else. She watched a slim figure emerge from between the stripes of steel, only a silhouette at first because it was dim up there and all the light seemed to stay outside. It was a boy and he looked smaller than she remembered. When the light from the little window beside the table finally reached him, she could see it was Jewell Ray all right—pale as pie dough, big-eyed and skinny, every living part of him either a bone sticking out or a hollow going in. The minute he saw her, he stopped dead in his tracks.

"Christ Almighty!" he gasped. And glanced around desperately like he wanted in the worst way to make a run for it.

The lawyer, coming along behind, gave him a push. "Come on here, now. What's the matter with you?"

Jewell Ray stood there spraddle-legged and swaying, staring wild-eyed at Sherrylee.

Ferris gave him another prod. "Git on now!"

At last he came, never taking his eyes off her face. He slid into the chair across from her, his eyebrows working for all they were worth. A long, lank piece of hair shifted and fell forward over his eyes. They looked at each other.

The very first thing Sherrylee said was "Looks to me like you need a haircut."

Jewell Ray covered his eyes with his hands. Sherrylee saw that the nails were bitten down to the quick and that the ragged edges were as black as ever. She sat very straight, waiting. Joel Ferris unobtrusively pulled up a chair to one side and sat watching.

After a while she said, "Jewell Ray? Ain't you even glad to see me?"

Slowly he lowered his hands. The eyes which looked

back at her were dark, accusing, and old for his face. When he finally spoke, his voice was cracked and grainy like he had gotten out of the habit of talking.

"How come you never even wrote to me, Sherrylee?"

"Jewell Ray, is your mind gone? I didn't know where you was." Sighing, she sat back. "And there were other reasons. One was . . . I didn't have no money. I reckon you know about *that* part." She waited while he flinched and glanced away. Then she continued. "The other was . . . ," here she stopped, gave Ferris a sidelong look, seemed to make a decision, went on, ". . . the other was that I didn't want them to know where I was."

"Who?"

"Them people in San Diego. Them P.O.'s, you know? I was supposed to go on back home—they bought me a airplane ticket and ever'thing. But I only went part way, then I got off."

"They bought you a *airplane* ticket? And you got *off?*"

"Well, the plane landed."

"Where?"

"Jewell Ray, for somebody who done what you done, you're sure all-fired nosy."

He looked away again.

She paused for a moment before continuing. "Anyway, I couldn't very well write to you or they would of found out and come after me sure as the world. That judge—he told me to go home. He meant it, too."

Jewell Ray nodded, remembering the judge himself. "Yeah. But then how'd you find out I was here?"

"I done read it in the paper."

His face was a study. She could tell that he was fascinated and maybe even flattered. "In a *newspaper?* Lord, what did it say? Did it have my picture?"

"It didn't say much at all and there wasn't no picture.

Just a little ole paragraph about some kid being shipped out from California and maybe blamed for the murder of a old lady. Thing was: it said your name, where you was from and the name of this here little town. So I knowed it was you."

"And you just come right on?"

She tossed her head. "Well, not exactly right on, no. I did me some studying on it first. I come close to goin' on home anyways. My feelings for you wasn't at what you'd call an all-time high."

Joel Ferris sat over to one side, fascinated.

After a while, the boy said in a puny voice—like he meant it but was scared to say it right out—"I am awful glad you come, Sherrylee."

She made no comment but sat watching while he chewed off what was left of his thumbnail. Presently, she asked, "But what about you? How come they caught up with you?" Then, interrupting herself, she glanced toward Ferris. "Who is this guy? Is he okay?"

Jewell Ray seemed to have forgotten that the attorney was there. "Oh, him. Yeah, he's okay, I guess. He's my lawyer."

"Oh."

"Yeah, it's okay. You can say anything you want to in front of him."

Sherrylee didn't look convinced.

Jewell Ray went on. He looked up at her, kind of sheepish, and ran the back of his hand across his mouth. "It was that there money, Sherrylee. You know? Sure was a lucky thing I had it instead of you."

She lifted her eyebrows.

He continued doggedly. "Yeah, sure was. Them coaches

. . . those guys at Juvy? They found it in with my stuff. Or maybe it was the po-lice. Anyhow, somebody got wind of it and the next thing I know I'm livin' down at the jail. I don't rightly understand it myself. Guess they thought it was too much money for a guy like me to be carrying around. Or maybe . . . ," he glanced inquiringly at Ferris. "Maybe it was marked in some way. Anyhow, they done traced it back here to that old lady, figured I'd took it off her." He shrugged. "So here I am."

Sherrylee digested this information. Presently she asked, "But Jewell Ray? The paper said you was charged with a killin'. Ain't that what they got you in here for? For killin' that old woman? Not only stealin' . . . ."

"Shit," he said. "I never. They're tryin' to claim I did, but I never. I never done nothing like that, I swear. Like I said, I just took the money."

Sherrylee looked at him thoughtfully. Joel Ferris watched Sherrylee like he was trying to hear what her *glands* were saying to each other.

Suddenly a monstrous clatter started up on the stairs— as if a whole football team wearing cleats was on its way. Rowdy charged through the door and glared at the three of them. "What the *hell* . . . ?" he sputtered. Furious, he scowled at Joel Ferris. "What the hell's goin' on here? You know you ain't got no right to let visitors in here without the sheriff's permission!"

Ferris got calmly to his feet. "Simmer down, Rowdy. No cause to get all het up. This here's the prisoner's wife. She just this afternoon arrived in town and I'm letting them have a little chat, that's all. Any man is entitled to a visit with his wife when he's incarcerated. That's the law."

Fuming, Rowdy turned from Ferris, gaped at Sherrylee instead. "His *wife*? Jesus God . . . !"

Sherrylee gazed back at him coolly. Joel Ferris stifled a grin. "Just settle down, now," he said mildly. "It's all right. We was just fixin' to break for supper anyway."

Rowdy was still steaming. "But J. D. . . . ."

Ferris held up a hand. "Never you mind now. I'll fix it with J. D." He turned to Jewell Ray. "We'll see you tomorrow."

The boy got up and stood looking at the girl, wiping the palms of his hands down his thighs. Then she, too, stood up and the two of them looked at each other for a long moment without speaking. At last, Ferris reached over and gently took hold of the girl's elbow.

"Come along, now," he said softly. "Miz Cantwell? I'd be glad to drive you wherever you might be wantin' to go. It would be my pleasure, ma'am."

. . .

Ferris made a phone call while Sherrylee went and got her suitcase from the bus station. The woman behind the counter didn't say a word, just grunted when Sherrylee thanked her. But she followed to the door and watched as Sherrylee went across the street and got into the lawyer's car. Ferris drove her to a rooming house and fixed things up for a week. After that he took her to dinner. They went over the railroad tracks and down some dirt streets to a cafe that served Mexican food and played Mexican music on the jukebox. Ferris ordered a steak and insisted that she have one, too—along with french fries, salad, the works. Sherrylee would rather have had a hamburger with lots of pickles but she guessed they didn't make them in Mexican places. So she gave in and hacked her way through about half the meal—meat overdone and dry as shoe leather, french fries as big as lemon wedges and a two-day-old salad. Despite the liberal use of catsup and salt, she had to give up early. Ferris, on the other hand, cleaned up every scrap and even gave his plate a final polish with a piece of bread. "Like my steak well-done, don't you? Can't stand it when they bring it to the table still bleedin'." He tilted his chair back on two legs, ordered coffee for them both and began picking his teeth.

"All right, now," he said. "Just what were you and that boy up to? And where you been all this time?"

Sherrylee wished that just for once in her life she would get to ask the questions for a change. As it was, everybody and his dog seemed determined to pry and poke into her private life. Still, he was Jewell Ray's lawyer. And he had been real nice to her. She wasn't sure she liked him, though. He wasn't her idea of a lawyer at all. She pictured a much older man, distinguished. A man graying at the temples who wore dark, expensive suits and smelled of shaving lotion. She looked across the table at Joel Ferris picking his teeth and sighed.

"I reckon it's a long story."

"I got all night. Tomorrow, too, if need be."

CHAPTER 21

. . . .

*R*etelling it made it seem a long story, like the unfolding of a fan pleat by pleat so he could see it while the pattern remained whole and open in her own mind. And then, too, it was not easy, because what she remembered most was not possible to tell. So she had to edit as she went along, telling what she could and keeping the rest back. What she told made up the spines of the fan. The rest flowed by only inside her mind, filling in the spaces and flaring out, silent, like scenery.

How could she explain to anybody else how it had been? It was like she somehow had to account for her whole life up to that point in order to make things clear because no matter what anyone said one thing always led to another. All the events were connected in some way: Sherrylee didn't worry about how or why, she simply knew that it was so. Then where should she begin? With the trip across the country? They had had a fine time for a while, that was for sure, her and Jewell Ray. They hitched rides and lived off the land. Sometimes the living was high and other times not so good. But it was an adventure, nobody could deny that. And after she figured out their "system" (and make no mistake about that, it had been her idea:

she conceived the whole thing, figured out how best to make it work and then made him pay attention and practice until he had it down), why then, it had been easy as pie. He learned fast and once he got the idea he was as swift and cunning as a cat, clean away long before she ever finished her part. The system worked. Oh my, how it worked! Them all the time feeling more professional and Jewell Ray shaking his head with admiration, his eyes full of praise for her. Yessir, it had worked out fine for a while. What went wrong, she never had been sure. Somehow he went and messed it up. Somewhere—maybe here, maybe in San Diego—his eyes had gotten too big for his stomach. A mite of greed had touched him—or else he got careless— or maybe just plain stupid. Maybe all three.

Greedy—or could be scared—to grab all that money and then hit the old lady as well. Sherrylee had worried some about that. Oh sure, he swore up and down—first that he didn't hit her and then later that he didn't hit her hard. Why he hit her he never would say. But Sherrylee worried. That was why when she saw that little article in the paper she wasn't too surprised. With old folks, brittle as they were and dry, it didn't take much. Just a little shove and they were gone, off in the other direction and no way in this world to call them back. Funny how they were. You couldn't never tell. Sometimes they just dropped down right there in front of you, collapsed like a heap of sticks or a puffball caving in, heaving out a little sigh of dry air. She had seen them do that plenty of times in the fields. Mostly black folks, but white folks, too. There they'd be— cloth bags slung over one shoulder, rags wrapped around their heads—bending and picking, bending and picking— maybe singing even—then *poof*! They were gone, just like that. A pile of dry sticks and a little puff of dust where they landed. It was always the women, never the men. The women worked to the very end and never even looked up, just like they'd been doing all their lives. But the men . . . the men felt it coming and had sense enough to go home and die in their beds. Some even lay there for years, waiting for it, refusing to go out.

It was the sun that did it. Back home, people stayed indoors or sat in the shade whenever they could. Privileged ladies went around in big straw hats. Field women shaded their eyes with one hand, squinted. Even so, the sun sucked at their skins and withered their souls, burning them dark and bitter. The poor old earth suffered, too. It dried and caked under that sun, turned into cement hot as a griddle, cement which gave off a talc of fine, gray dust upon which no water would rest. That dust settled on everything, like misery or poverty. They gritted it down with their food and coughed it out at the end in the unyielding fields. Sherrylee knew all this because she had worked in the fields, too. Every summer since she was ten. And also because every time a car came by their house, it left a layer of that dust to settle on her and her family. They lived out on the edge of town and people said they were white trash. They weren't white, they were gray.

When Sherrylee was fourteen years old she had wanted a radio so bad she could taste it. "A radio?" her mother had said. "We got us a radio." And it was true. A cream-colored plastic one sat on a doily on the end table in the living room. "How many radios you gonna lissen to?" But Sherrylee wanted one all her own. So one morning she ironed a clean dress and went down to the dime store to see about a job. She went right in and asked to see the manager. He was a sour, waxy man with blue pouches under his eyes.

While she explained what it was she wanted he looked off to one side like his mind was busy with something more important. Then his mouth drooped in what might have been a smile but on him it looked mean. He had her to follow him to the back of the store, where he stopped in front of a door which she figured must lead to his office. He told her to go in and wait. As soon as she opened the door, he crowded right behind her and pushed. Then he slammed the door and she heard it lock. And there she was, standing outside in the alley behind the store, right next to the trash cans.

Maybe it all began there, right there in that alley. But Sherrylee had a feeling it began at the beginning and that there never had been much leeway. So anyway after that, at first just for entertainment, her and some of her friends would visit the dime store and finger everything. They would maul the stuff on sale and pick up every single little card of earrings and costume jewelry. And, after a while, they just naturally palmed a card or two, tucked some stockings in their pockets. But eventually even that became boring. When you were that far down on the social scale, there simply weren't many people you could steal from—not in a small town—just people like yourself who didn't have anything anyway, or members of your own family. Before long, it required more effort and imagination than it was worth.

So finally, in desperation, she had married Jewell Ray. After it was done, she realized that she had always been going to do it anyway. As if the two of them had figured on it, been joined, ever since they used to play in the cool dirt under the chinaberry tree, but somehow had neglected to mention it either to each other or anyone else. The thing about Jewell Ray was that at least he was willing to leave. The rest of the men thought they had had the good fortune to be born in paradise and they planned to stay. Their horizons ended at the edge of town and the summit of their ambition was to sit in the shade, trade jokes, drink beer and spit. Not Jewell Ray. He was excluded from the drinking and spitting crew by virtue of his questionable ancestry. He had appeared in town one day, a skinny, big-eyed and bone-white boy about four years old and been taken in by his "aunt." Nobody knew where he came from and he didn't seem to, either. His "aunt" ran a rooming house which catered to overnight boarders and was known around town as Daisy Mae's Hotel. Daisy Mae herself was large and tolerant. She began and ended her day standing in the doorway holding a can of beer. She hardly seemed to notice Jewell Ray but fed and clothed him and otherwise demanded nothing other than that he swat flies now and then. When he announced that he was getting married, she looked mildly surprised that he was old enough, wished him luck and gave him ten dollars. So he went—though only across the state line—signed some papers, gave up half his fortune and that was that.

At first, Sherrylee had taken him home with her. That was a mistake. The minute they walked in the kitchen, holding hands and looking kinda sheepish, her father had a wall-eyed fit—which was surprising, considering the state of his own morals. It did no good whatever to show him the marriage license—his reaction was to throw it on the floor and stomp on it. Then he dragged Sherrylee up to her bedroom, locked her inside and threw Jewell Ray out of the house. It was all very mystifying, the more so because he knew very well that she and Jewell Ray were not unacquainted, you might say, in the marriage way. Instead of being pleased that things were legal for a change, he stomped and swore and cussed that they sure as hell weren't going to do anything like that under his roof. (Or over his head, for that matter, since Sherrylee's bedroom was directly above the one her parents slept in.)

Well.

Jewell Ray, he sulked. His maleness had been insulted, his manhood challenged. He went and stole a shotgun off Jed Rankin. After that, Sherrylee realized that they better get out of there in a hurry. So the following Saturday night, while her dad was drunk and in jail, they snuck across the state line one last time and kept on going.

And all the time, Jewell Ray with that damnfool gun. Its presence made things difficult, to say the least. Folks would pull over, offer them a ride and then take off the minute they got an eyeful of that shotgun. Sherrylee lost track of how many times they had been left by the side of the road, showered not by buckshot but by gravel. But he refused to give it up. Every time she even mentioned it, he clutched that gun to his chest and snarled, exactly like a dog with a bone. She despaired of ever making him part with the thing. It worried her plenty, though. So one night when they had to jump from a freight car in a hurry and he couldn't lay hands on it in the dark, had to leave it behind, she was immensely relieved. He had cried afterwards. Then he sulked and declared the loss to be her fault. She had tried to reason with him but knew before she began that reason was no earthly use with Jewell Ray.

What did he want with a gun, anyway?
Well, he didn't plan to spend his life messing around with

this here punk stuff. He figured to do something big . . . make a haul and then lay around and take it easy for a while.

What did he think he was going to do with a gun, though?

Well, didn't nobody fool with a man who had a gun.

"Those railroad cops would have fooled with you, all right! Back yonder in that yard? They'd have fooled with you for good if you'd had that gun. Whoo! We barely made it out of there as it was. What in the world would you have done with that damnfool gun?"

"I'd a shot 'em!"

So Sherrylee sighed, gave up, folded her hands in her lap. Folded her hands in her lap the way her grandmothers had done and their mothers before them. Folded her hands on her jeans as hands had been folded on gingham, over aprons, between shellings and around baskets. Settled her hands, sighed, squinted into the distance, her forehead recalling all the crease lines of worry over men and the harsh light angling off the fields.

CHAPTER 22

. . . .

She yawned. "I guess I'm gettin' sleepy, Mr. Ferris. I feel like I done been run over."

His response was to order more coffee.

She looked at him and sighed. Then she told about the Christian couple and how she and Jewell Ray had run for their lives and hidden beneath the grandstand. And about getting cleaned up and selecting the right street for their operation. "There sure ain't many trees in this town, Mr. Ferris."

"I realize that. But tell me now, just exactly what did y'all do? I mean, what exactly was this system you been talkin' about?"

"Oh. Well, it was like this. I had me these magazines, see—just stuff I'd collected, some of it was from the post office and some of it I stole—and I would go to the front door of a house and pretend like I was selling subscriptions, usually for some eleemosynary institution." She looked at him to see if he understood the word, but it didn't seem to bother him so she went on. "Meanwhile, Jewell Ray would go in the back—sneak in the door or climb through a window or whatever he had to do—and take what he could find while I had the lady of the house busy at the front. He had to be fast and I had to keep her there as long as I could. I had me a notebook where I wrote down the names and addresses. . . ."

"Okay, so what about this town? What happened here?"

"Well, I done the best I could, picked me the least bare street I could find and went on up to this house that looked promisin'. Jewell Ray, he snuck off down the alley in back." She paused and sipped her coffee.

"I pushed my finger into that doorbell and I rang and rang and rang. I rang till I thought my finger was gonna fall off but nobody ever came. And it was so *hot*. Pretty soon them magazines started stickin' to me or else slitherin' and sneakin' out of my arms. And after a while, I began to get nervous. There wasn't a soul in sight and I felt kind of *obvious*, you know. Then, too, I didn't have the slightest idea where Jewell Ray was, whether he'd gone in the back, got locked in a closet or was layin' somewhere with his head split open. So I decided to leave that neighborhood. I gathered up my magazines best I could and went on down the street. At the end of the block I ran smack into Jewell Ray. I turned the corner and there he was—come jumpin' out of a bush and like to scared me to death. He was all red in the face and jittery.

" 'What's the matter with you?' I said.

" 'Nuthin',' he said, his teeth chatterin' like dry peas in a pail. He kept lookin' over his shoulder. 'Nuthin'. Let's just git on outta here.'

" 'Jewell Ray . . . ,' I said.

" 'Come *on!* '"

"So we go creepin' through town, all the way across, and end up standin' on the outskirts alongside the road with the sun blazin' down on us full blast, Jewell Ray shaking like a leaf and me wondering what on earth has got into him . . . when all of a sudden out of *nowhere*, just like a angel almost, this big, white convertible pulls over. Right off I noticed that the license plates were from California. The driver was a guy wearing a Hawaiian shirt and sunglasses. He grinned back at us.

" 'Hey!' he yells. 'Where you goin'?'

"And before I had time to think, the words just jumped out of my mouth. 'California,' I said.

"Jewell Ray, he turned and stared.

" 'Great!' hollers the driver and he blows on the horn. 'Get in!' "

And so they had. And spent the next eight hours pasted to the back seat of that car, glued to the leather by a mixture of heat, sweat, high wind and the constant uproar of the driver himself, who never shut up for one minute but shouted, sang and told stories the entire time. Stuck to the seat with fear, too, on account of that man never drove under ninety miles an hour even when he slowed down. It was a nightmare: cops would come swarmin' up behind them, whining away like yellowjackets, lights flashing ever' which way and the man would yell out, "Hey! Watch this!" and nearly mash the gas pedal through the floor. Police cars would disappear like dishwater going down a drain or something being swallowed by the wrong end of a telescope. "How about that?" shouted the man. "Pretty good, huh! I had this baby souped up in Mexico and those guys, they know how to do it."

After that, they would continue to cruise at about 200 miles an hour. Sherrylee wondered if the wheels even touched the ground.

At first, it was divine, especially watching the police cars fade away still whining into the distance. Jewell Ray in particular cheered and howled with delight, beating on the seat with both hands, hollering, looking back, "Yessir! Yesssiiiirrreee! *Gawddamn*!" Then beating on her for a while, grinning and hooting, sweating like a horse. "Whooo —eee! Ain't this somethin'? Ain't this *somethin'*, Sherry-lee?" But after a while his noise subsided and she noticed that he looked a little green around the gills.

On and on, over that endless desert . . . they seemed to be flying through space as white and dry as paper with the sun beating down on their heads and the wind whipping by so fast it stung. Around them, the scenery unreeled like a Saturday western, the same backdrop over and over as if the film had gotten stuck somehow—the same hills and gullies, the endless stretches of burning sand with islands of sad little towns and mountains so blue and far away they might have been in heaven. And all the time that crazy Californian shouting and singing. Then every so often he would switch on the radio and there would come a burst of static so loud it sounded like lightning had struck. "The reception out here is lousy," he'd holler and go back to singing.

"This is crazy," she yelled to Jewell Ray, hoping he could hear her over the wind.

"You mean *he* is."

"Yeah. But he's fixin' to get us all killed."

Jewell Ray looked glum. "Yeah. I reckon. Either that or them cops will catch up. And me, I sure don't want to see no cops right now."

"Whadda you mean? What did you . . . ?"

"SSSSSSTT!" He spun around and glared at her.

"Jewell Ray! What on earth did you do? I wish to God you'd tell me!"

"Nuthin'. I told you, I ain't done nuthin'. *Christ*, I don't know. I just gave her a little old tap, that's all."

"You *what*? WHO?"

"Oh, nobody. Jes' a old lady back yonder."

"Where?"

"That town where we was last. I didn't hurt her none . . . but she wouldn't turn loose of the money."

"Jewell Ray! Wha'd you have to go and do that for?" The wind whipped her hair into her mouth, carried off her voice in a shriek.

He turned like a cornered animal. "I *told* you! *Jesus* . . . Sherrylee . . . if you don't let me be . . ." His eyes took on a wild look and foam was starting to build up in the corners of his mouth.

So she let him be. But that was the first she knew of it and she didn't dare ask any more. Naturally she omitted that part when she told Mr. Ferris.

Toward evening, when they stopped for gas, she told the driver that they would get out.

"Christ!" He stared at her. "*Here?*"

She looked around. There was nothing but a leaning little house, all dusty and dispirited, one gas pump and a beat-up pop machine. Behind the house was an outhouse made of corrugated tin and off beyond that a junkyard of old cars with weeds growing out of their windows. The wind was blowing and this single, sad little settlement seemed pressed between twin slabs of sky and earth, white, indifferent and unbroken, stretching on forever.

"You sure you want out here?" asked the Californian.

The wind whined around Sherrylee's legs like a thin cat. Off up the road a short way was a kind of shelter. It had a flat roof of long, spiny cactus lashed together and a cement table squatting underneath in the square of shade. Past that, the highway ran straight as a ruler for what looked like a thousand miles.

*

Sherrylee turned to the man who had come out to fill the gas tank and who was now slouched against the pump looking them over. "Where are we?" she asked.

He shrugged and spat in the dust. He was shriveled and yellow-looking, with dirty blond hair and black fingernails. "Ya wouldn't know if I told ya," he drawled. He jerked his thumb at the highway. "Next town is Lordsburg . . . 'bout a hunnerd miles." He leered at her, narrowing his eyes.

Sherrylee stared back at him, wondering how in the world anybody could live way out there. Well, it would have to do. Jewell Ray was getting too weird. And they sure didn't need to take any more chances with that lunatic driver. Or with the cops, either.

"I reckon this will be all right."

The Californian shook his head, mystified. "Suit yourself," he said. He whipped out a twenty and gave it to the man at the pump. "Keep the change, Mac." Then he was gone, a swirl of dust and spitting gravel and a final blast on the horn.

In the sudden quiet, as dramatic in its way as the departure of the white convertible had been, the man who lived there leaned one arm across the top of the gas pump and pulled on his ear with the other hand.

"What in hell you kids want out here for?"

Jewell Ray was still white and sweating hard. "That guy! He was crazy! Man . . . he was fixin' to kill us!"

"Yeah?" The man shifted his gaze, studied the boy doubtfully.

"Now Jewell Ray . . . ," Sherrylee began. He was making her nervous.

"Well, Christ! He *was*! Crazy son of a bitch."

The gas-pump owner fingered the twenty. "Yeah. Well, there ain't much of anyplace to stay around here." He looked back over at Sherrylee, then up and down, his eyes slow and insolent. "But I reckon beggars can't be choosers, right? Might be room inside the house for *you*."

She pretended not to notice. "Thank you, but I reckon my husband and I will stay outside."

He gave a short laugh. "Don't make me no never mind." He waved a hand toward the roadside shelter. "Y'all can bed down over yonder."

"You got any soda pop?" asked Jewell Ray, pointing at the machine.

"That thing?" The man let out another snort of laughter. "The guy don't even stop to service her no more. He ain't been by here in five years."

"Well, you got any water, then?"

The man grinned, showing mossy teeth. "Nope. Not for you, sonny." He turned toward his sagging house, then paused in the doorway, smirking. " 'Nother thing, though. Better watch out for them snakes. Them big rattlers, ya know? They get real bad around here. Real bad. Sometimes I lie awake nights listenin' to 'em . . . sliding around in the sand on their bellies . . . damn near keeps me awake. Yessir. After dark, this whole place kinda gets up and moves. Ripples, you know? With snakes. Enough to make a feller seasick." Laughing softly, he went inside and the screen door slammed behind him with a gentle thud.

"Sherrylee. You must be outta your mind."

They fed the pop machine all their change. When nothing happened, they cussed it and kicked on it for a while. It was dented all over anyway, like maybe other people had had the same reaction. Then, just as they were ready to give up, it suddenly burped out five bottles of strawberry soda. The stuff was sickeningly sweet and warm but at least it was wet and they sucked at it greedily. They each drank a bottle straight down and then lugged the rest over to the shelter and huddled in the scraps of shade trying to make the soda last as long as they could. The cement table was sticky and smelled of old grease and barbecue. After the sun went down, they climbed up on top of the table and lay down. That way, they figured, the snakes wouldn't be able to get at them. They stretched out and watched the day burn off slowly into night. The darkness began in the shadows, which grew longer and longer, until finally they melted and ran together. Above, the sky was as polished as a pale stone. Eventually its luster dimmed into a velvet of midnight blue and the stars took over, thick as daisies in a field. Sherrylee sighed with contentment and declared that she never in all her life had seen a sky so beautiful. Jewell Ray looked up and grunted. Said he wished he had a dollar for every one of them stars.

Sometime later, a little night breeze came up and it got almost chilly. So they curled up together like two snails, the dry wind sliding over their skins like paper.

CHAPTER 23

. . . .

*T*he next morning they could hardly move. They woke up late and found themselves stuck to the cement and speckled with flies.

"I feel exactly like a Frito," declared Sherrylee. "Fried and salty and all hard edges."

Jewell Ray sat up slowly and considered. "Me, now," he decided, "I feel more like a old bed spring. Rusty and bent, you know?"

They crept out from under the striped shade of the shelter and limped to the edge of the road. It was very quiet. No sign of the man anywhere and very few cars on the highway. So they just stood there airing their thumbs, looking east and hoping. Before long, the heat began to shimmer on the blacktop like water. The same white-hot glare of the day before began to beat on them from all sides, not only down from the sun but up from the gravel and asphalt and from all around, the endless miles of caliche which reflected the power of the sun and threw it back with added strength. Soon three large, black birds began to circle high over their heads.

"Looky yonder, Sherrylee," said Jewell Ray, pointing. "Only thing gonna give us a ride is them gawddamn buzzards."

She squinted up at the birds and shook her head. She allowed that, being rendered down as fast as they were, there wouldn't be enough left to give even the buzzards a good meal.

Which was why they were amazed when a big semi loomed up out of the wavering heat and hissed to a halt. For a minute, they stood there in a state of shock, then scrambled to catch up. The driver leaned across the seat and opened the door.

"Howdy!" he said cheerfully. "Where y'all headed?"

They hadn't thought about it. They looked at each other while the huge diesel rumbled and smoked above them. Sherrylee didn't dare say anything on account of the way things had turned out the day before. Finally Jewell Ray said he reckoned they was just headed west.

The young truck driver grinned. He was a muscular guy wearing a tight-fitting T-shirt, jeans and cowboy boots. He had thick blond hair, light eyes and skin the color of a constant sunburn. "Looks like we got us a deal, then," he said. "Climb on in."

So they did, and spent another eight hours on the road. But this trip was as different from the one the day before as night is from day. This guy was more reasonable about the speed limits. And he would honk the big horn and wave to the other truck drivers or flash his lights as they passed. He seemed on good terms with the police, too— all in all, a real friendly bunch of people. He rode along with one arm resting on the open window and the other hand firm and strong on the steering wheel. For some reason, he made Sherrylee think of a high school halfback, although she couldn't say why since she didn't know anybody like him and had never spoken to a football player in her entire life. But there was something sturdy and quiet about him, something safe, whether it came from his open face or the curly blond hairs on his arms or the hard muscles in his thighs, she didn't know. It was just there and it made her feel good. He played the radio all the time, tuned to a country western station, and often he would whistle along. From time to time, he would turn and smile at them but for miles on end he never said a single word.

Sherrylee sat between him and Jewell Ray and at first she tried to make a little conversation. She asked the driver where he was from and he said Wichita Falls. She had her mouth open and all set to say, "Oh, we've been there!" when Jewell Ray landed a sharp jab in her ribs. So she just said, "Oh!" in a kind of gasp and let it go at that. Then she asked where he was going and he said the Valley. Sherrylee didn't want to appear ignorant but she had no earthly idea which valley he meant. She longed to tell him that she was from one of the biggest ones herself, but she was afraid Jewell Ray would give her another poke in the ribs. So instead, she inquired about what he was hauling. He replied, "Oh, just some boxes of stuff." So she gave up and left him alone to whistle and listen to his radio. But she admired him secretly from the corners of her eyes. Hours later, when they pulled into a truck stop for lunch and she offered to buy his meal, he turned his head and gave her a slow, quizzical smile. "Heck no," he said, swinging down from the truck. "You kids hang on to your money." And that was all anybody said until evening.

Through another long, white afternoon, the hours as seamless as a bolt of silk, they hummed across the desert. Jewell Ray fell asleep and his head slipped sideways onto her shoulder where it nodded and bumped gently with the motion of the truck. The highway stretched on straight and black, watery with heat, and on all sides unreeled the same endless scene of distant mountains, pale rock, listless brush and ragged cactus. Sherrylee thought to herself, "If the rest of life is as monotonous as this, I don't think I want to go on." Then she dropped off, too.

What woke her was the sun firing straight into her eyes. It had slid down almost to the horizon and they were heading directly at it. Presently, they pulled into a town—a real town—and the semi sighed to a stop. The young driver yawned and stretched. He smiled over at them and nodded. "Well, this here's Yuma. End of the line. I got to unload early in the mornin' then head on back home."

They climbed out and jumped to the pavement. "Thank you," said Sherrylee, looking back up at him. Then she gave Jewell Ray a painful dig in the ribs. Hot and puzzled, he scowled at her before he remembered his manners. "Oh, yeah," he mumbled. "Thanks for the ride."

"Sure thing." The truck driver grinned down at them, waved his hand and pulled out. They watched while he growled through the low gears and finally turned out of sight around a corner. Sherrylee looked a long time at the empty space where he had been. She thought about him driving all the way back across that desert, whistling to himself and listening to his honky-tonk music, then maybe next week turning right around and driving all the way out here again. She tried to imagine what kind of a life he had, whether he had a girlfriend (he hadn't been wearing any wedding ring) or what.

"Come on, Sherrylee," complained Jewell Ray. "What you moonin' at?"

*

They had some supper at a little cafe and hunted up a hotel where they could spend the night. When they walked into the hotel, the man behind the desk took one look at them and wagged his head. "Nope," he declared. "You two ain't married. I kin always tell. And besides that, you're under age." He was a heavy man with big sweat stains around the armpits and jowls the color of chicken fat.

"The hell we ain't," sputtered Jewell Ray. "And we come all the way from El Paso."

The man folded his arms across his paunch and belched.

Sherrylee spoke up. "I got a paper to prove we're married."

The man curled his lip. "Sure. And I bet you got a Juárez pedigree, too. Or is it Tijuana?" Still, he reached back, selected a key and threw it across the counter. He threw it so hard that Jewell Ray had to dive to keep it from going on the floor. "That'll be ten dollars," he said.

It sounded like about twice what it ought to be since the hotel was hardly what you'd call fancy. Glowering, Jewell Ray picked a ten out of his pants pocket.

"An' you gotta be outta here before eight in the mornin'," added the man.

"Horseshit," commented Jewell Ray as they started up the stairs. "I ain't never heard of no ho-tel that raised chickens before, have you?" He said it good and loud so the man would be sure to hear.

Sherrylee stared at him.

"Yessir," he went on. "Chickens. They got to be raising 'em in this dump. Stuff's knee deep. You can smell it. Ain't no ho-tel in the world checks folks *in* at eight o'clock in the mornin'. Only thing I know gets up that early is chickens— shitty chickens. They got to get off the nest in a hurry."

Enraged, the man roared out to the foot of the stairs. "Truckers!" he yelled. "Truckdrivers. Bed down early, pull out in the evenin'. Sleep all day and drive all night. Got to in this climate, specially if you're goin' east."

"Truckers, fuckers."

The man shook his fist. "Lissen here, boy. Don't you give me no sass. You do, I'll kick your ass right back out yonder on the curb."

Sherrylee grabbed hold of Jewell Ray's arm. "Come *on*, now. Let him alone. Don't go makin' more trouble than we already got."

"Well, ten dollars. Hell."

"Never mind. It beats sleeping on a barbecue table surrounded by snakes." She searched for the number stamped on the key ring. Then she turned the key in the lock and the door swung open. They stood for a moment in the doorway staring at the sagging iron bedstead and the ghastly stain in the middle of the carpet.

"Christ Almighty," breathed Jewell Ray. "It looks like there's been a killin'."

It wasn't until that night that he showed her how much money he actually had. Stopped her cold. The bed was covered with it; there must have been hundreds of dollars.

"Holy Jesus!" she breathed. "Jewell Ray? Where in the world did you get so much?"

Offhandedly, "I done told you already, Sherrylee. I got it from that old lady back yonder in that little town in Texas."

"But . . . my Lord! How come she had all that? It looks to me like you done robbed a bank."

"Nope." He told her about the kitchen table being covered with money and still more in an old tackle box.

She sniffed and then burst out laughing. "It smells like catfish!"

Slightly insulted, he stroked it. "Works, though. Looks good. Don't matter how it smells. Who's gonna smell it?"

Still tickled, she attempted to soothe him. "Well, the smell don't matter . . . it's just I noticed that you'd begun to smell mighty like mud the last few days." And, helpless, she fell out laughing once more.

He began to get white around the mouth.

"Never mind," she gasped. "How much you figure there is? Jewell Ray, I'm so *proud* of you!"

"I don't know," he said, still suspicious. "I ain't had the time to count it what with rides in white Cadillacs and all."

"Well, for heaven's sake . . . let's do it."

So they counted it and then sat staring at each other in disbelief.

"Lord have mercy," she said.

"Shove the mercy," he replied. "HOT DAWG!"

Sherrylee thought for a while. Then, drawing herself up, she spoke in her oldest and firmest voice. "Jewell Ray, you got to give me that money."

It was like the shotgun problem all over again. He tensed up immediately, eyes shut to slivers and glittering.

"Howcome?"

"Because I can . . ."

"Howcome I got to give it to you? I'm the one done stole it."

"Not without my help."

"Shit. You didn't do nothin'."

"Jewell Ray, listen. You can't go around with all that money in your pockets."

"Why not?"

"Well, whadda you think? Somebody stop us on the road, you know? What if them cops come along? How you think it's gonna look if you got all that cash? You give it to me now."

"What for? What are you gonna do with it?"

"I'm gonna hide it. . . ."

"*Hide it?* Now where in hell . . . ?"

She explained how she planned to sew it up out of sight in the lining of her purse. "See? That way ain't nobody gonna know and it'll be real safe, too. It's not like I'm taking it *away*, Jewell Ray."

He gnawed on his thumbnail and thought it over. He plainly didn't like it but he couldn't think of anything better. "Shoot," he said finally. "Give me fifty dollars then."

So she did and sewed the rest away, neatly folded behind the lining of her purse, all tidy and secure.

CHAPTER 24

. . . .

*T*he next morning they caught the bus for San Diego, California. Sherrylee sighed with anticipation. "I always did want to see the ocean." But it seemed like they were going to have to cross another section of the Sahara first. Or worse. For ages the landscape consisted of baked clay, blistering sand and lye flats. Finally they began a laborious climb up a twisty road into some hills lumpy with gray boulders and covered with thin, scratchy brush. They climbed higher and higher, the bus smoking and complaining all the way. The day grew steadily hotter.

"Hey, Sherrylee. When you reckon we're gonna see the ocean?"

After a while, the hills leveled out but the scenery was still arid, spread out under the arch of a cloudless sky. Then they dropped down into a valley and stopped for date milkshakes under palm trees which made a dry, whispery sound in the wind. The milkshakes were extremely sweet and made Sherrylee feel a little sick. They started up again and covered what looked like the same country they had just left.

*

"Sherrylee? You reckon we're goin' in the wrong direction?"

Then more mountains, bigger ones this time, and Jewell Ray fussing about his ears popping. And down into another valley, this one green with crops. Miles and miles of green. Jewell Ray thought maybe it was alfalfa but Sherrylee said it didn't look blue enough to be alfalfa, might be bush beans. There were some little towns, farms everywhere, and pretty soon the highway got wider and went to four lanes instead of two. More towns, trailer parks—acres of trailer parks!—all glinting in the sunlight, everybody with a car or a pickup parked under a tin or plastic awning . . . then they passed housing tracts laid out like sheet cakes with pastel frosting and little mint lawns. Suddenly, with no warning, San Diego itself was rushing past, all blue and white—a wide, clean freeway, a big, white city and an endless blue sky. The silver bus whished to a stop and they climbed down into a stench of exhaust fumes and a sea of sailors.

"My word!" marveled Sherrylee, and stopped dead in her tracks, so that Jewell Ray, coming along behind, collided and all but climbed up her back. "My *word!*" Everywhere there were sailors. They flooded the station, white hats bobbing like corks on a sea of navy blue and white duck. Sailors of every size, shape and description. Some of them were young and cocky. They wore their hats tipped so far forward that the brims barely hung onto their eyebrows. Underneath, their eyes roamed the station, bold and smarty. They tipped out their behinds in the tight, wide-bottomed pants and stood cruising with their eyes. The older men were thin and tired and looked around only if they had to, like they'd seen it all before. The colored sailors were shiny and their eyes moved quick and dark, like fish in the shallows. The white ones were pale, lack-luster, as if they didn't get enough sun even though it was coming down like thunder outside. Regardless, they all seemed to possess duffel bags which they either kicked ahead, or slung over one shoulder or sat on, depending on the situation. Mixed in with the sailors—floating among them like bits of driftwood—were heavy Mexican women laden with shopping bags of bright-colored twine or thick brown paper. The women stared fixedly ahead, moving only when the line did, and keeping a tight grip on their parcels. Suddenly, a door was sucked open and the whole flood shifted, eddied and then swirled away. Immediately others began to gather in their wake, collect, pool and lap once more against the wall.

"My Lord!" breathed Sherrylee. "The ocean must not be very far away!"

They began to push their way through the crowd. Music bawled from a jukebox and a loud, hollow voice read off a long list of times and destinations. Sherrylee was amazed at how young some of the sailors were. One kid grinned at her, showing a broken and dazzling front tooth. He couldn't have been any older than she was but he had a tattoo on his arm and the purplish shadow of a black eye. He winked the good eye and Sherrylee turned away. After something of a struggle, since they seemed to be moving against the tide, she and Jewell Ray emerged on the far side of the station and stood blinded by sunlight and breath-ing in the tangy, salt-flavored air. Presently they noticed that the huge, square building directly across the street was labeled in large silver letters: COUNTY JAIL. So they did not linger in that area.

*

Wandering up the street, agog at the rush and flash of
the city, overwhelmed by the noise and activity, they soon
found themselves in an area of older apartment buildings
going uphill like steps, two-story structures in a Spanish
style of pastel stucco, each with a little cast-iron railing
and some stairs leading up to the front door. It was quieter
up there so Sherrylee and Jewell Ray sat down on one set
of stairs to rest and have a look around. Across the street,
a woman popped out of her door like a cuckoo in a clock,
glared at them, shook a throw rug viciously and disappeared again inside, giving her door an emphatic slam.
Something about that slam struck Sherrylee as familiar. It
reminded her of a similar incident but for the life of her she
couldn't think what. Presently she forgot about it and gave
herself up to just gazing around. From where they sat, the
city seemed made of hills, all covered with light-colored
houses set in amongst trees and flowers. Below and in front
of them were broad streets fringed with palms, their huge
leaves flapping in the breeze like fans. Beyond, the water of
the harbor danced and sparkled, intensely blue. The wind
which came up off the water smelled of salt and fish and tar.

Sherrylee stretched out and let the sun soak into her
bones. Now *this* was her idea of living, so she lay back, lazy
and content. Jewell Ray, on the other hand, was restive. His
eyes ranged up and down the street searching and studying. While Sherrylee lounged back on her elbows and tilted
her face to the sun, he crouched, head down and squinting
all around.

"I reckon we better get to work now, Sherrylee."

Jarred out of any semblance of peace, she sat up abruptly.
"*Work?* We only just got here! What on earth do you mean,
Jewell Ray? I declare . . . crossing that desert . . . sun musta

fried your brains. Work—? When we got us all that money?"

"*Hsssssttt!*" he jerked around. "I wisht to *hell* you wouldn't talk so dadblamed loud! You want the whole damned world to know? You want to get us arrested?"

She ignored him. "Why, we could live for *ages* on that money."

He hunched over and went to nibbling on his fingernails, his eyes darting all around, furtive and jumpy. Sherrylee tried to put it away from her but sometimes he did remind her of a weasel—or a rat.

"It ain't enough, Sherrylee." His gaze shifted her way, turned crafty, slid away. "We got to have us a car if we're goin' to Mexico."

Her mouth dropped open. "*Mexico?*"

He sat back and folded his arms across his chest. She immediately recognized the pose and groaned inwardly. She was in for it now. How many times had she seen that same expression, that same posture back home? Must be hundreds. Usually it preceded a squirt of tobacco juice and it spoke for a whole way of life, a world view from the front porch—or maybe tailgate philosophy if you were younger and gathered in the haze of summer dust to air your views at some country crossroads. All that was needed were several boys or men who realized that they and they alone understood the mechanics of this world. As a rule, despite their wisdom, they elected not to participate, but chose instead to spit and speculate. Jewell Ray was at a disadvantage—he didn't have a tailgate or any tobacco juice handy but he did pretty well, considering. He sat back, remote, burdened by a greater wisdom and the lifetime responsibility for females.

"Thing is," he said loftily, "you got to have a car to get around down in Mexico. It's a foreign country, you know." He glanced over to make sure she was paying attention.

"You can't just go hitchhiking around like we done. Them folks don't like it. Might even take a shot at you. Sure enough steal all you got. Then, too, it's a pretty big country. And hot. Real hot. I come close enough to dyin' of thirst for one lifetime. Besides, you want to see it in style, don't you? Not just bounce around on some old claptrap bus packed with crates of chickens and pigs runnin' up and down the aisle." He paused. Time for the tobacco juice to hit the dust.

"Jewell Ray. This is the first I heard of any Mexico."

"Well, I been thinkin' on it all along. Or since Texas, anyhow. I even picked up a word or two of Spanish. Just imagine, Sherrylee. Our money will go three times as far and ain't nobody find us down there. We can spend all our time jes' settin' around listenin' to git-tars and drinkin' beer."

"We coulda done that back home."

"It ain't the same."

There was a period of silence.

"But a *car*, Jewell Ray? Don't a car cost a lot of money, more than we got? You figure on stealin' one?"

He appeared shocked by the very idea and waved his hand airily as if to dismiss it. "Christ no! Who said anything about stealing one?" He glanced around nervously and then pointed down to where they had walked from. "Hell, it's too dangerous. Didn't you see all them cops? Police thick as fleas. Besides," he added with authority, "they got some kind of roadblock at the border. Make everybody stop and they check on where you're from and your car and everything. Hell no, we can't go stealing no car. We got to buy us one."

Sherrylee sat debating with herself. She didn't know whether to believe him or not, but she did know that any further argument would prove useless. She would probably never find out *how* he had come by such information, or even if he knew for sure. Thing was, he *knew*. It was one of those male secrets—like engines and race horses. No mere woman would be able to understand. . . . Aggravated, she tried to make sense of it while he sat wooden-faced and sullen. If only he hadn't mentioned Mexico . . .

"Well, Mr. Know-It-All, just where and how are we gonna get money to buy us a car?"

His eyes strayed up and down the street. He waved his hand again. "Easy. Right here."

She considered the street in a different light. It did appear prosperous . . . clean . . . that was always a good sign. People who kept up appearances were forced to be charitable, or at least civil; otherwise, they ruined the whole picture. And this looked like one of those neighborhoods where outward appearance was important—flowers in the window boxes, nice cars along the curb, steps all swept. Still, she felt uneasy. This was no little town. It was a big city and one street led into a maze of others. What if something went wrong? What if they got lost? Or separated? Then, too, there weren't any other folks out walking around. In fact, it looked like nobody ever walked in California, everybody drove. Maybe he had a point. And yet . . .

"Oh, I don't know, Jewell Ray. Seems like the whole town would see us . . . anything we did, you know? I'd feel like a fly in a saucer of milk. And besides, I done left all my magazines and stuff back yonder in that Cadillac."

He snorted. "Shoot. All you gotta do is divert somebody. Ask directions. You're new in town, ain't cha? Gab a while at the front door. Then thank the lady real polite-like and be on your way. No harm in that, is there? Me, I'll be in the back and long gone while y'all are still trying to decide which way is north." He flicked the hair back off his forehead with a quick toss of his head. "What'sa matter, Sherrylee? You done gone and lost your nerve?"

*

Angry, she looked away, refusing to be goaded or shamed by him into doing something that she didn't want to. Yet she knew she had already lost. By allowing herself to be placed on the defensive, she had given way. But the whole idea seemed wrong to her; she was afraid of it. Desperately she made one last try.

"Jewell Ray. Lissen now. We don't *need* no more money. We got more than enough to last for a good long while. And a *car* . . . ," she shook her head. "Why don't we just wait a little bit . . . ?"

This time he did spit. Not tobacco juice, but nonetheless very much in earnest, hissing through his teeth in scorn and fury. He jumped up, wedging his body between her and the sun so that he stood looking down, throwing a shadow over her. His forehead creased into an angry V and the dark, heavy brows came together like the wings of a crow. Swaying lightly on the balls of his feet, he spoke in a voice that was low and almost threatening.

"You lissen at me now, Sherrylee. We can't just be hanging around. Folks will start to notice. You seen that woman yonder . . . ," he jerked his head in the direction of the woman with the throw rug. "You know how it is."

Sherrylee was tired. And she knew he was right about that part anyway. People dearly love to spy and complain and they are automatically suspicious of strangers. Strangers affect most people like an invasion of unwelcome insects and their first reaction is to slam the door and call somebody else to come with a spray gun. In this case, the somebody with the spray gun would most likely be the police. Police love more than anything to pick on people who look lost and homeless. They instinctively assume you've done something wrong even if you haven't. They will *invent* a crime, if necessary. And in this situation . . . well, she still worried some about what Jewell Ray might have done to that old lady back in Texas. Police have ways of keeping in touch with each other so they didn't want no truck with any of them. But maybe if her and Jewell Ray just looked a little better nobody would notice. Maybe get some new clothes . . . she could get her hair done. . . . Turning, looking up, she suggested this idea to Jewell Ray. Balling his hands into fists, he stood glaring down at her, bullying her with his shadow. Suddenly, cruelly, he stepped swiftly to one side, leaving her staring straight into the sun. Blinded, she sat helpless in the darkness while he crouched next to her, spitting softly into her ear. He was so nervous that she could hear him humming like a high-tension wire.

"No!" he whispered. "No, gawddamnit. Clothes, shit. That kinda crap can wait. I'm tellin' you, Sherrylee, we got to get us a *car*. Then we can go on down to Mexico, buy us all the clothes we want to." His voice smoothed out, took on a wheedling note which she knew well. "You'll see," he declared. "We'll get shed of this stuff"—he picked at his old shirt—"an' you can get your hair done ever day. Real purty. Whoo—eee! We'll buy us some real *fancy* clothes. Look real sharp, you know? Besides, after we seen all we want to down yonder in Mexico, I'd kinda like to take a little trip back to Texas."

"*Texas?*"

"Yeah."

"Jewell Ray, you gotta be outta your mind!"

Airily, "Nope, I jes' got me some unfinished business to tend to. Meantime, soon's we get across the border, I'm gonna get me a tattoo. Right here." He flexed his thin arm, bunching up a knot of muscle, then frowned, considering. "You think it would look good there?"

Still only half-sighted, she gave in. "Oh, all right. Where

you figure to start?" But something cold was taking hold in her belly. "Jewell Ray? Are you sure? Maybe we ought to . . ."

"There," he declared, furious. "Right there." He pointed across the street to a pink stucco building with a shiny blue Chevy parked out front. Sherrylee nearly laughed out loud.

"That ain't the car you're likely to get, Jewell Ray."

"Huh?"

"Oh, never mind. How do you know that place even has a back door?"

He smiled with the superior knowledge of males. "Fire escapes down the backs of all these buildings. I checked while we was walking up. All of 'em have one, even the first-floor apartments, cause there's a canyon in the back. It'll be easy, you'll see. Slick as a greased pig. I'll jes' climb in the window, have a little look around, then I can hide down yonder in the canyon."

He was like an animal, always searching, sniffing things out. She sighed. "Where are we gonna meet, though? I can't be traipsin' around in no canyon."

He thought for a minute, then inspiration lit up his face. "In back of the bus station."

"What? But . . . ?"

He grinned. "Not the jail side. We'll meet on the other side, behind the barn they have for them buses." And he was gone.

Sherrylee rummaged in her purse until she dredged up a scrap of paper and the stub of a pencil. She licked the tip of the pencil and, laying the paper out flat on her knee, wrote. She stood up, smoothed back her hair, and began walking slowly up to the next block, pausing often to examine the house numbers and glance at the paper held conspiciously in her hand. When she reached the end of the block, she crossed the street and went through the same routine coming down the opposite side. Every so often, she would stop and make a real production, studying the house numbers and gazing around in a puzzled manner. Jewell Ray would no doubt have laughed at her, said so much fuss was silly. But she still had her doubts about the venture and did her best to be convincing. Besides, she wanted to give him plenty of time. When at last she stood in front of the pink building, she made another little survey of the area, consulted the paper, then went up and rang the bell. While she waited, Sherrylee remembered that the woman who had been shaking her rug lived only two doors down. She would be just the kind to be staring out her window. Sherrylee could feel the curtains twitch. So she concentrated on the door in front of her and went over the words in her head. Beyond that door, she could hear a TV or radio playing. Then there was a shuffling noise and a woman opened the door. She was wearing rubber beach sandals, a cotton wrapper and big, plastic rollers in her hair, which was peroxide blond and going black at the roots. A little on the fat side, she was a good four or five inches shorter than Sherrylee and she peered out, suspicious, holding one hand away from her like maybe her fingernails were still wet.

"Yeah?" she said. "Whadda you want? And don't try selling me anything either, cause I already got a dozen . . . whatever it is."

"No ma'am," said Sherrylee respectfully, and hauled out her little piece of paper. "I was hoping maybe you could . . ."

"Or Bibles," declared the woman defiantly. "Deliver me from Bibles."

"Yes ma'am," Sherrylee agreed. "I ain't sellin' no Bibles. I ain't selling nothin'. It's just that I'm tryin' to locate my sister. She's gonna have a baby any minute now and my ma sent me out here to find her and maybe help. . . ."

"Yeah, well." The woman was tapping her foot. "This is a big town, kid. Full of girls having babies. All these sailors . . . !" She let out a throaty chuckle and rolled her eyes. "You out here all by yourself?"

"Yes ma'am. Leastways till I find my sister."

The woman narrowed her eyes, looked harder into Sherrylee's face. "She know you're coming? Is she expecting you?"

"Well . . . no. Not exactly. See, my ma gave me this here ad-dress . . . ," she fluttered the paper.

The woman snatched it from her hand. "Let's see. Hmm. Well, this is Del Mar Street all right but I never heard of 1821. This is 1820 and upstairs is 1822. That place across the street goes from 1819 to 1823. There ain't no 1821." She shoved the paper back at Sherrylee as if that took care of all the possibilities.

Sherrylee let her shoulders droop. Her face fell and she stared down sadly at the little piece of paper.

The woman folded her arms. "Maybe it's Del Mar Avenue. Sounds like it might be down in Chula Vista. Did you try Chula Vista?"

"No ma'am. I only just got here this afternoon and . . ."

"Your mom give you a phone number? Somebody you could call?"

"No ma'am." Sherrylee had never met anybody so eager to help before, and she was thinking that it was time to be moving on before things got entirely too complicated, when something happened which drove all ideas clean out of her mind and seemed to plant her feet forever on that concrete doorstep.

To her astonishment, the whole upper portion of the doorway filled suddenly with bare flesh—white, bold skin with a reddish cast looming up behind that woman like the hide of a harvest moon. Sherrylee gaped, felt the breeze in her open mouth. There stood the biggest, most bare-naked man she ever hoped to see, naked from the waist up, a massive torso which narrowed to an inflamed bull neck and a head as bald and smooth as an egg. A deep and angry voice rumbled forth.

"What's going on here?"

Sherrylee's stomach did a flip-flop and came down running but she willed her feet to stay where they were.

The woman simpered, tilted her head and looked up at the man. "Stade, this poor kid. She's out here all alone, looking for her sister. Must have the wrong address or something."

He arched his thick neck, squinted down at Sherrylee. His eyes were hard and round. "Oh yeah?"

Sherrylee backed up a step. She had suddenly understood that his head was shaved. "I . . . I'm real sorry to have bothered you. I guess I better be goin' now. I appreciate . . ."

"Hold on now! Just a gawddamn minute!" The man's huge hand snaked out, circled around Sherrylee's arm and yanked her inside. "*You!* Get your butt in here!"

The woman gave a little scream. "Stade!" she squealed. "Stade, what are you doing?"

He paid no attention to her but shoved past and pushed Sherrylee ahead of him down a little hall and into the living room. "Come in here, Connie," he bawled. "Get a load of this."

Across the room, sprawled out on the couch like something the cat drug in, was Jewell Ray.

The man regarded him with satisfaction. "Whadda you think of this, Connie? Huh?"

"Oh!" cried the woman. "What . . . ?"

Stade levered Sherrylee into the room and dumped her

alongside Jewell Ray, who lay there white as tissue paper with both arms up protecting his face. "Shitheads, that's what," he roared. "I went into the kitchen to get me a beer and guess who I found scratching around in there? This little turd—going through all the cupboards, digging in the drawers. He made a lunge for the window but I was too fast for him. I stopped him. Yeah. I stopped him, all right. Then I just picked him up and brought him in here." He paused and looked at Jewell Ray thoughtfully. "Dumb little son of a bitch. Looks kinda sick, don't he? Could be I shook him up a little. . . ."

The woman put her hands to her mouth. "Oh, Stade!"

"Aw, it won't hurt him none. He's too skinny. He's like a rubber band. I'd like to squeeze his gizzard but it really ain't worth the trouble. He couldn't even pass the first leg of the physical out at the base, and these days they're passing anybody who can even piss straight. Maybe this will teach him not to go sneaking in other people's back doors. When I heard you talking to somebody, I thought maybe they might be connected. Shitheads." He looked at the two in disgust.

Connie shot Sherrylee a look like a pit viper taking aim. "Well! I'll be damned! And here I was, all ready to let her come in and use the phone!"

Stade nodded. "You can't be too careful. Can't trust nobody these days."

Connie sighed with annoyance. "I guess I better call the cops." She gave Sherrylee another withering glance. "As if I wanted anything to do with cops."

Stade stroked his bald head with one hand. "Oh, I dunno. I'd kinda like to take this little shithead out to the base with me tonight. Make a man out of him. He could help me out on my watch. Or I could feed him to the guard dogs. Them German Shepherds like a little fresh meat now and then. Yeah. I think a day or two in the Corps would do him a world of good, don't you?"

Connie looked alarmed. "No, Stade! No, I'll phone the cops. We'll just have to."

The man stood stroking his bald head and musing.

"Stade? Go and put a shirt on, please." She went to the telephone.

The police came, two of them. All sunglasses and note-books. Handcuffs. The creak of leather and the clink of steel. They put away their notebooks and said, "Okay, let's go." The patrol car was hot inside and had no door handles in the back. They pulled around the shiny, blue Chevy and were on their way. But not toward Mexico.

CHAPTER 25

. . . .

Sherrylee leaned back in her chair. "I'll tell you one thing, Mr. Ferris, it was some kind of experience being in a place like that, that there Juvenile Hall, I mean."

"I'll bet."

"They was all kinds of girls . . . ," she shook her head. "Kinds I didn't even know existed. And I had to go before a judge twice."

"A judge? What did he have to say?"

"He said I belonged back home with my family . . . but he don't know my family, Mr. Ferris. Anyway, he ordered my P.O. to buy me a plane ticket and send me on back home."

"Your what?"

She looked at him. "My P.O. My probation officer."

"Oh. So she put you on a airplane and you went back home?"

She glanced away. "Well, I was *supposed* to go home but when the plane landed in Dallas there wasn't nobody to meet me. And they made me get off the airplane."

Joel Ferris shifted his toothpick. "Maybe you better elaborate on that just a little bit."

. . .

The pilot had announced through his microphone that they would be landing at the Dallas–Fort Worth International

Airport in fifteen minutes. Miss Peavy, the P.O. who had been sent along to accompany Sherrylee, dug out her compact and made a few repairs. Refreshed, she turned to Sherrylee. "Now, Sherrylee," she said in her bright, breathless way (she wasn't much older than the girl). "Now, Sherrylee, I'm going to get off here in Dallas. My boyfriend promised to meet me." She giggled. "We're going to have a *blast*! He's with a big aerospace company and he has a new Jag. I haven't seen him in three months! Anyway, I have to get off and another P.O., somebody from Dallas, will come to take my place. She'll go the rest of the way into Memphis with you, so you wait here on the plane until she comes. You wait right here, okay? They'll give you some supper on the flight so don't worry about that. Then you ought to be in Memphis about nine. I think that's right. . . ." She gazed off in a kind of pretty bewilderment, the same way, Sherrylee figured, that she had successfully faced and overcome all the difficult situations in her life . . . although it was hard to imagine Miss Peavy having much trouble or unpleasantness. She seemed to come from a suburb of perpetual sunshine. Her blond head to one side, Miss Peavy continued. "Then there's a bus . . . either tonight or in the morning . . . I really can't remember. . . . Anyway, I'm sure the new lady, your new P.O., will work it out." She beamed with a sudden burst of confidence.

The plane banked like it was going to plow with the right wing, came down, bumped and coasted to a stop before an immense building of glass and steel winking in the rose-gold evening light. The pilot crackled on the air again and said how much he had personally enjoyed flying with everybody, and the stewardesses sprang to attention, stationing themselves on either side of the exit with smiles pinned on. The other passengers collected their purses, briefcases, suit coats and scarves. They got up, jammed themselves in the aisle all at once and slowly shuffled out. Miss Peavy, now all a-flutter, gasped a brief good-bye and hurried down the aisle.

"*Wait!*" Sherrylee called out.

The young woman paused, long hair swinging as she turned.

"My purse. You've still got my purse." The people at the detention home had kept Sherrylee's purse in custody the whole time she was, locked away in a kind of hamper. She hadn't had a chance to touch it until now.

Miss Peavy was clearly perplexed. A shadow of worry stole across her face. "Oh! Well . . . I don't know. Nobody said anything . . ." she glanced down at the old white handbag with its imitation leather all cracked. It certainly did nothing for her outfit. "Oh well . . . here." She rushed back and thrust it into Sherrylee's hands. "You aren't going to run away, are you? Oh, I just *know* you won't. 'Bye now! Take care!" And she was gone, all breathless and radiant.

Sherrylee sat back and breathed a sigh of diesel-rich air. But before long, she was the only passenger left. The pilot came out, pulling on his jacket. He gave Sherrylee a big smile, cracked some jokes with the stewardesses and went on out. The two stewardesses rustled up and down, stowing and straightening and putting things to rights. They looked over at Sherrylee several times. Presently everything on the plane was turned off—the air conditioner, all but a dim little row of lights, the hum of the ventilator—and the only noise came from the other airplanes taking off and landing. Sherrylee looked out the window but there wasn't much to see, just some fuel trucks and big metal trailers full of baggage being hauled around. It began to get very warm inside the plane.

*

"Excuse me, Miss." It was one of the stewardesses, a small, dark girl, very pert in her flight outfit. "Will you be deplaning soon? This is the end of our flight." She paused, waiting for Sherrylee to say something. When Sherrylee didn't, she went on, kind of prissy. "This is the Dallas–Fort Worth International Airport. All passengers either terminate their flights here or change planes. Flight 405 is over."

Sherrylee had no idea what she was getting at. "I'm supposed to wait for somebody here. A lady."

The stewardess looked peeved. "Here? On the plane? Don't you mean that someone is going to meet you at the gate? I can direct you. . . ."

Sherrylee shook her head. "No ma'am. She said for me to wait right here."

Plainly annoyed, the stewardess bustled away and Sherrylee could hear the two of them whispering somewhere behind her. Pretty soon, she was back again. "I'm sorry, Miss," she said very primly, "but you will have to get off this airplane. We have to secure our stations and make certain that all flight passengers have departed."

"But . . . ," Sherrylee began.

"I'm sorry," repeated the stewardess firmly. The other stewardess came to stand beside her as if to lend moral support.

Sherrylee clutched her old purse and trudged up a long, carpeted hall, through automatic glass doors, past a whoosh of chilled air and into the gleaming acres of the airport terminal. She stopped and looked all around but there didn't seem to be anybody to meet her. In fact, nobody took the slightest interest. Feeling conspicuous, she located a restroom and went in. Once inside, she stopped short and gazed in amazement. It sure was a fancy place to pee in.

There was a luxurious powder room with a row of polished mirrors set in a gold frame above a marble counter. A thick, pale blue carpet covered the floor and there were several little armchairs set around and covered in gold velvet. Hollows like seashells were set into the marble for washbasins and all the fixtures were in gold. The ceiling was midnight blue with little points of light that blinked on and off like stars. Sherrylee had a good look around, washed her hands and then sat down in one of the gold chairs to consider her situation.

All of a sudden she felt very tired and wished that everything didn't always have to go haywire like this. She figured she better go to the airline ticket counter and ask them what to do. There must be a ticket . . . but somebody sure had messed up. Miss Peavy was gone, that was for sure, and nobody else had looked like a P.O. Sherrylee yawned. She began to feel hungry and she thought about the supper Miss Peavy had promised. "Boy, a hamburger sure would taste good along about now," she thought. "A hamburger and a cherry Coke. Or maybe a chocolate milkshake. Yeah, a milkshake." Well, it wasn't any use to think about it since . . . all at once she sat bolt upright and her heart took off like a panicky grouse. *She still had all that money in her purse!* How on earth could she have forgotten? She grabbed her purse and emptied all the contents into her lap—some scraps of grubby paper, an old comb, lipstick, chewing gum half-melted into the wrapper, her old pink billfold, a nail file—it all tumbled out in a messy heap. She snatched up the nail file and went to work on the stitches in the lining. Somehow they looked much bigger and sloppier than she remembered and she wondered that the counselors at Juvenile Hall hadn't noticed. The threads came away easily and with a great gulp of anticipation she plunged her hand into the gap and felt around for the bills. Ah! There! But somehow it didn't feel right. She frowned. It didn't feel right at all. Frantically she scrabbled around, got hold of the wad and hauled it out . . . stared in disbelief. What she saw tied in with the way everything else had gone. It wasn't money. It wasn't money at all. It was toilet paper. Plain old toilet paper, the kind that comes out of metal boxes in a public restroom. Little squares all jammed together. For a long moment she stared down at a whole lapful of little crumpled white squares. Then she lifted them up over her head, let go, and watched them float to the carpet like snow. Not a single bill among them, not even a dollar. Recklessly, she scoured the rest of her purse, ripped out the whole lining, but there was nothing there. So, too bone-weary to move, too sick to cry, she sat staring at the wreckage. After a while, she tried to think back and figure out when he could have done it. It must have been in Yuma, that old hotel room. He must have stolen her purse while she was asleep, snuck off with it to the bathroom and slit it open like he was gutting a rabbit. Then he tucked all that money on himself somehow, filled the lining back up with toilet paper (yes, she did seem to remember that the bathroom had been equipped with one of those little metal boxes) and made some effort at sewing. Funny she never noticed . . . but he could be crafty at times. . . . She sat back feeling blank. Seemed like he could of left her *some* of it!

Suddenly her thoughts were interrupted. Somebody was coming! A woman and her daughter, both dressed fit to kill, came in to use the restroom. When they spied Sherrylee, they stopped dead in their tracks. She was uncomfortably aware of how she must look—all that toilet paper lying around and her purse gutted, its insides hanging out. The mother cast a leery eye over the scene and made for the toilets. "Come along, Leslie," she said sharply. "Your grand-mother's plane will be here any minute." They disappeared into the other room and there were assorted sounds of running water. When they re-emerged, the woman gave a quick pat to her hair and dabbed on a dash of lipstick while the girl, who was overweight and probably about thirteen, slouched against the counter and gaped at Sherrylee. They left as abruptly as they had come, the mother sailing ahead and the daughter gawking back over her shoulder.

As soon as they were gone, Sherrylee got busy and cleaned up her mess. She crammed the comb and stuff back in her purse, jammed the lining on top and threw the toilet paper in the wastebasket. Then, as an afterthought, she took out her billfold and peered into it. Sure enough. She still had five dollars, money she had saved back a long time ago. At least she could get a hamburger. But the minute she thought of it, she discovered that she was no longer hungry. Well, she better get out of there, anyway. That mother would probably report her—and Sherrylee didn't want any more truck with the police. Maybe the best thing would be to go on home after all. But how in the world was she going to get there if she didn't have a ticket? Or any idea how to go about getting one? Sherrylee looked at herself in one of the mirrors. A faded, gangly girl looked back. The girl seemed sad and worried, homeless and maybe a little desperate, like her best friend had just stuck a knife in her back clear up to the hilt. Then very slowly, faintly at first, the girl began to smile. The smile spread to a grin. "Shoot," she told Sherrylee. "Other than being a little slow on the uptake, you're all right. It just took you a while—first of all to realize that there *ain't* no cotton-pickin P.O. and no use to wait for one—and second, why you are free as a bird! Ain't a livin' soul knows where you're at and you got five dollars to burn!" At that, the girl fell out laughing and pointed a finger at Sherrylee. "Girl!" she said. "You got it made!"

Sherrylee stepped back into the dazzle of the airport lobby. She spotted the ticket counters and made a wide detour around them. Then, lifting her chin, she marched across the blinding expanse of marble flooring to the glass doors which slid right open—just as if she was somebody. Outside, it was warm and smelled like a city. All around, the talc-blue Texas dusk was falling, catching here and there on points of light as they came on. Sherrylee stood on the sidewalk, uncertain what to do next. Long, shiny cars drove up and swept away again. Such *fine*-looking people, such an elegant coming and going. As it grew dark, a little breeze sprang up, and even though it was far from cold, Sherrylee shivered and pulled on Jewell Ray's old Levi jacket.

"God damn that fool Jewell Ray."

CHAPTER 26

. . . .

*J*oel Ferris regarded her, confounded. A rare and enormous grin unexpectedly split his face. He let out a hoot and slapped his knee.

"Well, I'll be a son of a *gun*! If that ain't the goddamnedest story I ever heard and believe me, I've heard a few." He leaned his elbows on the table and gazed at her with almost rapt respect. "If that don't beat all. So then what did you do?"

"Well, I did have some . . . some hateful thoughts toward Jewell Ray along about then. I coulda wrung his neck as a matter of fact. But it was a waste of time being mad at him. I didn't even know where he was and here I was standing outside an airport in Texas. So I just stood there for a while watching those big, fancy cars come and go. I tried to look like I was expectin' someone but of course I wasn't. Pretty soon this man pulls up right in front of where I was. He was driving a long black car as shiny as a beetle. He sat there looking at me, then he leaned across the seat and opened the door. 'Come on, little lady,' he said. 'Let me give you a ride downtown.'" Sherrylee glanced up at Ferris shyly, then away again. "He was real handsome, Mr. Ferris. Older, you know? But real handsome. Very distinguished."

Ferris had a little coughing fit and had to cover up his

mouth. He reached for a glass of water. "Please go on," he said in a choked voice.

Sherrylee studied him coolly. Then she tossed back her hair. "Well, it wasn't what you think. And anyway I was scared. Scared to go and scared to stay. 'Come on,' he says. 'Get in. I'm going that way myself. Be more than happy to give you a lift.' Well, that seemed real nice, real friendly, so I did. I got in."

Ferris shook his head.

Ignoring him, Sherrylee continued. "My word! What a car that was! Gray velvet and silver all over inside. It even had a little built-in bar. Wait till I tell Jewell Ray about that!"

Ferris had to have some more water but she seemed not to notice. Instead she went on dreamily about the car.

"It never made a sound, just glided off like a swan . . . a black swan." She gazed around the little Mexican cafe, her eyes full of wealth and luxury and Dallas. "That man, he was a beautiful driver. Slipped that big car in and out of traffic slick as . . . well, slick as anything. We rode along for quite a spell and it began to look like the traffic was thinning out instead of getting heavier like you'd expect. Then, too, them high buildings that must have been downtown were drifting away to the south and getting smaller. I was thinking on how maybe I ought to mention that, when all of a sudden he reaches over and puts his hand on my knee. Lordy! Like to scared me to *death*! I brung my knees together *fast* and scrunched way over in my corner, one fist ready to sock him one. Him, he looks at me and breaks out laughing. Then he gives my knee another little squeeze and lets go. Laughs and says never mind, I'm not even as old as his daughter and it's his mistake, or something like that. After that we drove and drove, way out on the edge of town. Finally he stopped the car and we got out at this little cafe or diner right next the highway and with fields all around it. It was dark by then, but I could smell the dust and water and the chemicals they use to spray with. Well, we went inside and had dinner and he introduced me to the man and his wife, the people who ran the place. He asked me if l would like to stay and work for them. Well, they seemed nice enough. And I sure didn't have no other irons in the fire, so I said okay. I think maybe they was relatives of his."

Ferris drummed his fingers on the table. "And just what was it exactly that they had you to do?"

She looked at him coolly again. "The whole world ain't bad, Mr. Ferris."

"The part I've seen of it is."

"Well, anyway, they gave me a little room all to myself in their own house and I worked in the cafe all day. I got my meals, tips and pay, too. Tips ain't much out there, though. Most of the customers were just Mexicans—field hands, you know. Over there around Dallas it's all cotton fields. The Mexicans would come in, eat and drink beer. I wasn't supposed to serve the beer—on account of my age, I'm only seventeen—but most of the time there wasn't nobody else to do it. So the lady, she showed me how to put up my hair," she paused to demonstrate. "Like this, see? That way, I looked older. It worked, too. Even the highway po-lice came in and they never noticed that I was under-age. So I served and washed up and even got to do some of the cooking. It wasn't bad. And since there was no place for me to go and no way to spend my money, I saved it. Then, too, the lady, she could sew real good and she made me some blouses and a skirt. That was real sweet, don't you think so?" She sat back and drank the last of her coffee. "It was real nice being there. I kinda hated to leave."

*

"Why did you?" Joel Ferris was laying out his cards one by one, face down.

She took a deep breath. "Well, like I said, I had saved my money. I wasn't really planning on goin' nowhere but then one morning I overheard a couple of truck drivers talking. They had come in for some coffee and they was settin' at the counter reading the paper and talking. One of 'em mentioned an article about a kid being sent back from California, how he was supposed to have kilt a old lady and stole all her money. Well, I just happened to be right there where I could hear—I was wiping off the counter and filling the sugar containers. Something about that article kinda rang a bell. Then when they said the name of the town, I like to died. I don't recall the names of all them little towns we been through but I sure did remember this one. So I knowed right off they musta been talkin' about Jewell Ray. Soon as they left, I got aholt of that paper. I seen what it said and then I knew for sure. I guess I musta gone white or something, cause the lady, she come over and asked me what on earth was wrong. Then she told me to go and lie down. I took the newspaper with me and I cut out the article. I read it and read it. Then one day I got my money together, flagged down the bus and got on it."

Ferris sat shaking his head. "But how come? I don't get it. Why did you leave a good job and come all the way over here? I mean . . . him swiping all the money and all . . . that was a mighty lowdown trick he done pulled on you."

Sherrylee nodded and traced a little pattern in the circle left by her water glass on the table. "I know. I know it was." She ran her finger around and around the ring of water. "But I guess he didn't mean no harm by it. Jewell Ray, he acts kinda crazy sometimes. But he don't mean no harm."

Joel Ferris sat silent, shuffling and cutting his cards. Finally, he pushed back his chair. "Well, come on then. I better be getting you home." He threw some dollars on the table and they went on out. He stopped the car in front of the rooming house and leaned across the seat to open the door on her side. In the light from the streetlamp, his face was outlined with black shadows. She could plainly see his sharp nose and the toothpick dancing underneath but his eyes were invisible, as if they were gathering up the darkness.

"You get a good night's sleep, you hear?" he said "We still got us a lot to talk about. I'll be by for you in the mornin'."

She got out and stood watching until the one taillight that was working disappeared around the corner and the sound of the engine died away. Then there was only her and the streetlight.

. . . .

Part III

CHAPTER 27

. . . .

*I*n that town, the county courthouse ruled stiffly from
the square like a stern grandfather over a spate of untidy
offspring. It was now nearly eighty years of age and the
town had grown up around it, a crowd of lesser buildings from which it withdrew as much as possible, retiring
into solitude and the lofty dignity afforded by its function
and stature. Once it had been raw and ugly—raised up in
the middle of a sun-baked prairie by reverent builders who
vowed there would be justice west of the Pecos and laid the
temple for it brick on brick. The pride of those early builders, it was to this day a source of civic self-esteem. People
were more inclined to believe that the world was an orderly
place when they contemplated the rust-red solidity of that
courthouse. And in May and June, the locust trees scattered white petals across the lawn and the air was heavy
and honey-sweet.

Inside the building, a haze of silence lay over years of
history like a veil of dust motes. On the top floor, in the
courtroom (often empty for long periods of time), the dust
and silence mingled freely, sifting slowly in the heat with
nothing to disturb them but the thickening of cobwebs and
the gradual fading of flags. The air in the basement was

cooler. It smelled of documents and mortar. The past hundred years were recorded there, filed away—history as it is interpreted by clerks: heavy books filled with titles, land disputes, births, marriages and deaths. The lives of that country, set down at first in flowing hands but later typed on forms, so that the ancestors seemed grand while their descendants, in comparison, were small and dry—the history of that country spelled out in spare words, settled in numbers somehow. Augusta Houghton's history was there, too. Her death but not the crime. Not yet.

.　　.　　.

On the day before jury selection was to begin, Joel Ferris paid a visit to Caleb Cartwright, M.D. He climbed the stairs leading to the office on the second floor over the drugstore, banged on the door and waited, kicking at the rubber runners on the floor, studying the gold letters and brass knobs. Then banged again, shaking the door until the old man, roused from his afternoon nap on the couch, came stumbling and cussing out. Expecting a dismembered cowboy or a snakebit wetback, the doctor blinked myopically at Ferris and said, "I don't know what you're sellin', fella, but I don't need any. Now git!"

Ferris held up a hand, explained who he was and said he needed some expert advice but would never be able to elaborate on what it was if he was made to stand out there in the hall all day.

Old Cartwright growled and grumbled but he let him in. Once inside, Ferris didn't waste any time but laid his cards right on the table, figuratively speaking anyway, since there was never any spare room on the surface of the doctor's desk. The old man sat down and listened reluctantly, sucking on a back tooth. The expression on his features was not encouraging. But Joel Ferris paid no attention and went on with what he had come to say.

They talked for over two hours. During that time the lines of skepticism deepened around the physician's mouth and Ferris went through a dozen toothpicks. Then, like a change in the weather, the old man's face altered. He tilted his head to one side. "Well, maybe," he said. "Just maybe. I wouldn't stake much on it myself, but you might have something. . ." He got up and began to rummage around his library. After discarding several volumes (What is this thing? I should have gotten rid of that years ago) and exclaiming in delight over a long-lost book of poems (My God! Rupert Brooke—now there was a fine man!), he returned and thumped down three texts in front of the lawyer. "There you are, boy. Take a look at those. Could be they'll help you out some." As the two men shook hands at the door, he gave the attorney a long, level look. "What you are suggesting has some value," he remarked thoughtfully. "Mind you, it's only a possibility. Still . . . there is surely that possibility. Can't afford to leave any stone unturned. I'm not a forensic man myself . . . but such things have been known to happen. Yes sir, they've been known to happen." And, ruminating dreamily, he closed the door in Joel Ferris's face.

That night both lawyers, the attorney for the prosecution and the attorney for the defense, stayed up late. Lights burned into the wee hours from the well-furnished study of the one and the dusty, cluttered trailer of the other. Austin Bailey studied the list of prospective jurors and made little notes in the margin. Then he read some law. Joel Ferris considered the list and made little dents next to certain names with the end of his toothpick. Whether that meant he was for or against a certain person, nobody would have been able to tell. Maybe Ferris himself didn't know . . . maybe he was just thinking. After a while, he put the list aside and read some medicine. When the two men met the next morning in the courtroom, they had two things in common: lack of sleep and an idea about mercy. Joel Ferris intended to seek it out, nourish it, to cause mercy to flourish in every heart. Austin Bailey's motives were different: he planned to seek it out . . . and destroy it. Stamp it out like a weed. Both men knew there was no room for it, that it had no use, but each of them would play on it in a different key and cause it to strike chords in the hearts around them. In unspoken acknowledgment, the attorneys nodded to each other across the room and the trial of The State of Texas vs. Jewell Ray Cantwell got under way.

Naturally the courtroom was jammed. Every wooden seat was filled and there were people standing all the way down the stairs and even outside on the grass. The courthouse square was surrounded by parked cars. Somebody said it looked like the Fourth of July and, as if to illustrate that view, several families appeared to be setting up for picnics on the lawn. Rowdy remarked to J. D. that they might just as well have summoned the entire county for jury duty since everybody whose name was not on the list already was there anyway. Inside, the clerk of the court sang out in a nasal tone, "All rise!" and Judge Ira Hainsworth swept in, black robes swirling. From the bench, he glowered down on the assembly, lowered the gavel with a mighty blow and declared the court in session. The little clerk hopped up, stirred in the wire basket and drew out a name. Johnnie Mae Spence was called to the stand. Both lawyers consulted their lists. Johnnie Mae looked out at them and the crowd and smiled uncertainly. She was a good juror for Austin because she was a friend of Gussie's and a ranch wife. She was also a good juror for Ferris because her only grandson had been killed just a year ago. If he had lived, he would have been the same age as the defendant. Johnnie Mae answered the lawyers' questions in a firm but gentle voice. Several times, her glance strayed to the defendant. Once, just as she looked, the boy did, too, and they studied each other for a split second. Ferris observed this exchange with a leap of joy in his heart and darted a quick glance at the D.A.'s table. But Austin had his head down and hadn't seen it. Ferris smiled to himself and before she knew it, Johnnie Mae was selected.

Jason Cartwright wasn't so easy. He was edgy on the stand and wanted to make sure that everybody understood that although he was devoted to the cause of mercy (had even taken an oath to that effect), he also possessed a strong sense of justice. Jason made it clear that he considered mercy to be the province of medicine and justice to be the province of law. He was suave, opinionated and very self-assured. He and the district attorney enjoyed such an affable exchange that they might just as well have been out on the golf course. To the questions which Ferris put, he responded with a cool and minimal courtesy conveyed from the heights of professional and social distance. Ferris, weighing the keenness of the young man's mind against his obvious snobbishness, remembered that Gussie herself had always gone to his father, and so let him on.

The next man up was Clay Weyerts. At the back of the courtroom sat his twin brother, Cliff, both of them slicked up in clean shirts and shined boots, their sandy hair identically parted and their light blue eyes identically calm. Each one folded his arms across his chest and waited. Ferris figured, as did most of the people there, that Clay would just as leave see that boy hang. So he twisted and turned his words and wrangled every objection he could think of, but Clay stared back at him with eyes the color of a Texas sky and gave all the right answers. To Clay, justice was a physical thing, the way objects confront each other and come together—or won't—like a fence post and a rock or a heifer and a rope. He was a little puzzled by Joel Ferris so he fell back on his experience when he replied. At the back of the room, Cliff's face never changed.

Then came another rancher, Asa (T. D.) Hines. Asa Hines had run cattle in that country for fifty years, as had his daddy before him. He was a big man, fair and going to gray, slow to speak and slower to anger. When he did get mad, however, he was relentless. Like most of them, he kept a pistol in his pickup and several guns at home, all of them loaded and ready. He had no use for strangers and he hated Mexicans almost as much as he hated Niggers. In response to the D.A.'s question . . . hell yes, he believed in capital punishment.

Joel Ferris was beginning to sweat, and not from the heat, either. Things weren't exactly going his way. Then it seemed that Austin Bailey gave him a present. For a few minutes, Ferris couldn't figure it out. Susannah Bledsoe simpered all the way to the witness stand and then drenched the poor prisoner with looks of abiding love. It was clear to everybody that even if he got off, by some miracle was set free, he would never escape the Christian charity she had in store for him. She looked like the answer to every defense attorney's dream. But Joel Ferris cut his cards and he concluded that even if Susannah wouldn't harm a gnat she sure enough would send a boy to the electric chair if it was put to her right. So he excused her, and she stepped down hurt, fluttered her fan and gave him a look which combined the pout of a spoiled child with the barely suppressed fury of a woman scorned.

Susannah's departure was followed by the arrival of Charlotte Buchanan, who sailed into position, a galleon of self-righteousness in a sea of sin. Bailey, all smiles, allowed her to fill her sails and she responded in full, unassailable glory. They made a splendid team. Ferris himself suspected that their performance might have had something to do with the fact that Austin and the senator had played poker every Friday evening for the last fifteen years. Still, shuffling his deck, Ferris held out a card for Charlotte Buchanan. She was a woman with a mind of her own, that much was certain.

Ferris had one of his hunches about Janelle French, the waitress from the Texas Cafe. She sat very straight in the witness chair, breasts straining against the white nylon of her blouse. Self-conscious in front of all those people, she held her head high and two spots of color glowed in her cheeks. Janelle had served coffee at one time or another to every single person in that courtroom and she knew them, you might say, from the other side of the coffee pot. In other words, she knew them better than they knew themselves, with the unpretentious honesty that comes of detachment and sometimes lack of interest. She observed and understood things that they themselves would never in this world have admitted to. On the stand, she was extremely poised. Lifting her chin, she answered the questions carefully. It was easy to see that she was flattered by Mr. Bailey's attention, but Ferris allowed himself another little smile and laid aside an ace.

*

He never was sure about Chuy Gallego. But then he figured that Austin never was either. Chuy was the only Mexican-American called for jury duty and he tried hard. Both attorneys realized that it was a gamble—whether Chuy's desire to win favor with the Anglos would win out over his natural sympathy for the dark boy so much like his younger brother, Martín. Oh hell, said Ferris to himself, and wished he could call it quits right there.

But they were a long way from the finish line. There were five more jurors to go plus extras in case of an emergency. There was the ranch foreman who had come up the hard way—literally—learning to ride by busting broncs out of Mexico and to rope by twisting through the catclaw after wild-eyed steers the color of raw kidneys and milk. Now he had it easy, loafing around mostly as host and bartender for a millionaire cattleman who liked to throw big parties by invitation only. The parties were so large and extravagant that printing costs alone ran into the thousands. And as for the liquor bill . . . People came from all over the country. The pasture above the house became a landing strip and the one below the lawn was packed with cars. The dust of arrival could be seen for miles and the smell of barbecue floated clear into town. Austin Bailey had been to one or two of these parties. Joel Ferris, of course, had not. But the question was, where would the foreman's sympathies lie? With the raw, unschooled boy so much like he himself had been? Or with life in the high grass where the paychecks and the whiskey kept flowing?

A pale, limp and spotless man approached the stand. He gave off a strong odor of benzine and admitted to owning the dry cleaning establishment in town. The smell of his occupation was so strong that Ferris suspected he was already embalmed in the stuff. "Give that fella a little lipstick and rouge, he could model a casket," muttered Ferris to himself. The dry cleaner, his eyes blank and depthless, was relieved of jury duty.

The son of a rancher from down in the badlands near the border was called up next. Both he and his father had tried to borrow money from Gussie at different times and for different reasons: the old man in order to survive the Great Depression and later during the 1950s when it didn't rain for nearly ten years, and the son in order to buy a fancy cutting horse and show off on the rodeo circuit. In both cases the answer had been no. The old man had finally gotten the cash he needed from a little old Mexican woman who was famous for her enchiladas that she cooked on a wood stove. As for his son (the one sitting in the witness box and being examined by the lawyers) he had meanwhile gotten drunk and smashed his pickup. By the time he got back to Gussie (who had originally sounded encouraging, "Why yes . . . I *might* . . .") he was all over bandages and splints and she changed her mind.

The clerk called a large woman in a wash dress. People saw her around town but few knew her name. She was the mother of three towheaded undistinguished and indistinguishable children. Nobody knew whether they were boys or girls, since they all dressed and looked alike. The child in the yellow shirt might be called Charlene one day and Charlie the next. The children seemed interchangeable and drove the schoolteachers to despair. As for their mother, the lawyers took their chances—Ferris betting on the maternal instinct (although it didn't look too promising) and Austin Bailey on the same response turned inside out (although he admitted that she seemed as placid as a pond).

Then, just about the time when everybody was longing to shade up for a little siesta, when the heat in the room was causing heads to nod, here came LaQuita Lightfoot. Three times divorced but still trim, her honey-blond hair pulled back so tight it made her eyes slant, wearing jeans which looked molded to her figure and diamonds big enough to choke a horse, LaQuita arrived like the main attraction. Immediately people woke up. It was rumored that LaQuita had been a heavy drinker in her day but somewhere along life's pathways someone had taken her by the hand and led her to an AA meeting. As a result of her conversion, she developed a smile like a blinking light—on/off—on/off—no matter what the circumstances, and sometimes her response seemed odd and out of place. She claimed to be part Indian, had an authentic whiskey laugh and enjoyed the benefits of a huge Oklahoma oil lease—whether on or off the reservation, she never would say. Despite all the loving and hugging and confession that went on at AA meetings, LaQuita took an embattled stance against the world. She kept a closet full of guns, two guard dogs trained to go for the throat, and fenced her property with six feet of chain link. From the witness stand, she eyed that boy sitting next to Joel Ferris like something she would gladly take a fly swatter to. With that barely restrained malice which makes some Texas women both svelte and powerful, she made sure she got on that jury. Nothing Joel Ferris could do would keep her off; he had used up all his challenges by then. His only consolation was a tale to the effect that when one of LaQuita's quarter horses had dumped her in a cactus, causing her to spend a restless week or so in the hospital, Gussie had sent by way of a floral consolation a prickly-pear cactus trussed up in red ribbons. LaQuita had been so furious that she hobbled home two days earlier than the doctors had predicted.

The final juror chosen was a sunburned young cowboy who was in the middle of a haying operation and stood to lose about ninety dollars a day by serving. That was just his luck. He was used to it by that time and didn't complain. All during the questioning, he kept glancing nervously out to where his wife was seated. She smiled back at him, obviously proud and even more obviously eight months and twenty-nine days pregnant.

By Friday evening, the jury was complete. Some said it was a hanging jury, that all the weight rested on the side of the prosecution and that Joel Ferris didn't seem to care, said he ought to be fired and a decent lawyer hired to take his place. Others declared that the jury was so wishy-washy it would hang itself. As for the prisoner, he sat unmoving, eyes cast down, a sure sign of guilt. Ever afterwards, people were to ask Joel Ferris why he didn't ask for a change of venue. Unhappily, he would shake his head. "Wouldn't have made no difference," he would say. "Ranch woman like that? From a old family? Shoot . . . would have been the same thing anywhere inside the state of Texas, anywhere in the whole damn state. Jury's supposed to be made up of a person's peers." Then he would shake his head again, shift his toothpick and look directly into the other person's eyes. "That boy never had no peers. No sir. Not in Texas."

CHAPTER 28

· ·

On Monday morning, the white-walled courtroom with its high windows, patterned tin ceiling and lazy paddle fans, was even more crowded than it had been the week before. Cab Stillwater commented to his old friend, Jiggs Skinner, that the stairs looked more like a Fort Worth loading chute than a passage to the chambers of justice. Jiggs nodded slowly, said he sure hoped somebody remembered to leave the windows open. Nearly all the ranchmen were there, bunched around Jiggs and Cab, their hair still ringed with sweat where hats had recently been, their boots shined to the high gloss of a good horse in July. Businessmen filled in the rows below the ranchers. They had all closed up shop and come, too. But next to the ranchers they were pallid and somehow smaller, a weaker breed with eyes that rarely took in horizons greater than a balance sheet. The Lone Star Bidders were present in a flock, and off to one side of the courtroom a phalanx from the American Legion had convened in full uniform. On the opposite side of the room, under one of the big windows and directly behind the railing which separated the observers from the participants in the drama, Bubba Houghton had selected his seat. He had chosen to wear a lightweight suit of tan linen, a green and gold tie and an off-white shirt. Just down the same row but toward the middle, behind the table for the defense, sat the defendant's wife. She was wearing a cotton dress and sandals and she stared woodenly ahead, paying no attention to all the whispering and nudging going on behind her back. If she knew that she herself was the source of most of it, she gave no sign.

In front of the girl and partway in toward the bench, Joel Ferris sat at the little wooden table especially reserved for him and the boy accused of the murder of Augusta Houghton. Ferris leaned back in his chair, stretched his legs and watched the crowd with interest. Between his lips danced the ever-present toothpick. Across the room, at an identical wooden table, sat the attorney for the prosecution, Austin Bailey. Cool, confident and poised, the D.A. appeared absorbed in some papers in front of him and wholly indifferent to the noise and bustle behind. In back of Austin, an extra row of folding chairs had been set for the press. Beyond and to the left was the door through which the defendant would have to make his entrance. Sheriff Killion paced the territory between the two lawyers, keeping a watchful eye on that door. The jury, newly-sworn and freshly scrubbed, sat in the box, self-conscious and perspiring with duty. Suddenly the clerk, a beetle of a man who always wore black, raised his head and listened. Several people in the crowd noticed and stopped talking, hushed each other. The clerk scuttled rapidly out, his large shoes making an unpleasant scrabbling noise on the bare floor.

Without any fanfare, without any warning whatever, and while the clerk was still absent, the side door opened and the defendant walked in. A hush fell over the crowd and everybody craned to look. The boy, in tan slacks and a white short-sleeved shirt, looked around in surprise at the crowd and then quickly ducked his head. A straggly lock of dark hair fell across his eyes. He moved hesitantly into the spreading quiet, eyes down, concentrating on his wrists, which were clamped in front of him by handcuffs. Next to him strode Deputy Rowdy Heywood, walking tall, the silver star of office winking and glittering on a brand-new red vest. Next to Rowdy, the boy looked frail and insignificant, incidental almost to the proceedings. When they reached the table, Ferris got up, scraped back a chair and the boy slid into it, still head down.

"He sure looks guilty to me," was the opinion of one onlooker.

"Yeah. And that little ole girl, his wife? She never moved a muscle."

"Hard. Kids like that. Hard and mean."

"Where are they from, anyhow?"

"Mississippi, I believe. But I heard that her folks were originally from Texas."

"Well, I'll be. Whereabouts?"

"Place called Uncertain."

"Come off it. Where in hell is that?"

"It's the truth. It's over there in Harrison County, right outside Longview."

"Well, I'd move away, too, if I was from a place called that."

"That's what I heard anyway."

"You think he done it?"

"Sure. Don't you?"

The clerk scurried back in, his beetle body swollen with importance. "All rise!" he sang out in his nasal twang.

Judge Ira Hainsworth made his entrance with dignity, his face set in granite resolve. Swinging his large head from side to side, he scowled at the assembled throng, sized up the jury with obvious misgivings and brought the weight of his gaze to rest upon the peaked and bony shoulders of the defendant. Then, lowering the gavel and himself, he settled to the business at hand. With a sigh of anticipation, the crowd settled, too. They had been craving a good trial for a long time.

There was some preliminary business. Then Austin Bailey rose and shot a cuff. "Your Honor," he intoned in a rich and mellow voice, "Ladies and Gentlemen of the Jury, Members of this Court, My Worthy Opponent . . . ," he touched each of them with his tongue and left them gilded, basking in the glow of his words. "We are gathered here to see Justice done." And the way he had of saying it even the prisoner felt gratified and proud to have a part in it. Jewell Ray lifted his head and gazed at this new man with wonder. Behind him, however, the girl looked more doubtful. Ferris, meanwhile, gazed off across the room like somebody fixing to take a vacation and trying to decide if the fish were biting yet. The prosecutor went on. And before long the boy realized that this man wasn't on his side at all. Mr. Bailey made it plain—he spelled it out in capital Roman letters—that in his own expert and professional opinion the death penalty was far too mild a retribution for such a *hay-knee-ous* crime—and the boy didn't rightly know what that word meant. Then as the prosecutor went on to talk about acts of unforgivable violence and wanton destruction, the moral chaos of a young man's mind—and shot a meaningful look at the prisoner—the boy figured that *hay-knee-ous* must mean something along those lines and so turned his face down and away, went inside himself so that this fancy man with the golden tongue couldn't get at him. Austin was eloquent in his belief that the only possible solution to such cruel and inhuman . . . "*Inhuman*, Ladies and Gentlemen!" . . . behavior was to put the animal perpetrator of same out of its misery. He was sure that the members of the jury would agree, being the intelligent and cultured people that they were, and having as their main, nay, their *only* goal, the pinnacle of Justice. Not to mention Law. And Order. Mr. Bailey felt confident that when they heard the evidence they would agree with him. He thanked them humbly and retired to his seat. But long after he had sat down, the syllables of his speech lingered, singing in the air.

Joel Ferris, when it was his turn, got up and addressed everybody in flat, expressionless tones. He rambled some but all he really had to say was that "this boy here, the defendant" had never killed anybody and they were going to prove it. This statement was received in dubious silence. It was all he could say, some folks figured. And all he needed to say, remarked others, and still collect his fee. After a while, he sat down again with the air of a man who has been trying to auction off a spavined horse and failed to raise a single bid.

Judge Hainsworth brooded over both opening statements with equal boredom. When Ferris had finished, he roused himself and ordered the prosecuting attorney to produce his first witness.

CHAPTER 29

. . . .

Bailey called Sheriff J. D. Killion. Rawboned and sandy-haired, J. D. sat tensed in the witness stand, painfully conscious of every eye upon him. The courtroom was very quiet, so that those nearby heard a rasp as J. D. ran one hand over his chin. But as he had done so many times before, Austin took charge. He led J. D. over the details just as he had done a hundred times previously but this time for the record: how the sheriff and his deputy, summoned by Dr. Cartwright, had gone immediately; how they had discovered the victim, Augusta Houghton, slumped across her kitchen table. Austin helped J. D. embellish the scene—the remaining loose bills lying around, the cash box rifled and the back screen door hanging open. J. D. described for the court in what position Gussie had been found and about the red mark on her head and neck. He explained that they had searched the area thoroughly but there had been no sign of anyone, only the screen door banging loose like that in the wind. His testimony gave the proceedings a cheerless overcast, leaving an atmosphere that was empty, hot and somehow ominous. The prosecutor thanked him and relinquished the floor to Joel Ferris.

Ferris sauntered to the witness stand and stood musing, his eyes fixed on some point in the middle distance.

The light from the tall windows which had favored Austin Bailey with a glow of dignity and righteousness fell upon the defense attorney with a harsh, pitiless gleam exposing every line in his face and every wrinkle in his Sears Roebuck suit coat. In that devious, near-noon blaze, he looked diminished. And the dust on his shoes was as much from where he was headed as from where he had been. He could have been peddling snake oil or eternal life—no matter. Everybody would have shut the door in his face. Joel Ferris squinted up at that light which left him overexposed against a landscape which showed up solid and successful—he shut one eye and squinted at that light as if he knew it well. Then he frowned, shoved one hand in his coat pocket and turned roughly toward the witness.

"Now Sheriff Killion, you've been an officer of the law around here for about how long?"

"Ten years," replied J. D., wondering whether it was too long or not long enough. You never could tell with lawyers.

"Ah," said Ferris. "And in the course of your career I imagine you have dealt with any number of assaults, crimes against the person?"

"Yes sir. I have."

"And you are familiar with any number of weapons and the kind of marks they leave?"

"Yes sir. I believe I am."

"Well, Sheriff, have you ever seen anything like this before?"

"I beg your pardon?"

Ferris was impatient. "I mean, naturally, the mark that was on Mrs. Houghton, on her head and neck, the one you just described to the court."

J. D. scowled. Out of the corner of his eyes he saw his wife, Shonda. Shonda looked worried. "Well . . . no, as a matter of fact. Not exactly, I mean. I guess any number of things could leave a mark like that."

"Such as?"

There was another scratchy little rasp as J. D. rubbed his chin. "Well, heck. Almost anything. A stick . . ."

"A *stick?*" There was a pause. "Sheriff, did you *see* any kind of a weapon laying around?"

"No sir. I can't say as I did."

"Did you make a search for some kind of weapon?"

"Oh, yes sir. We looked all around."

"But you didn't find anything?"

"No."

"Well then, what, in your professional opinion, could have caused such an injury?"

"Well, like I say. Coulda been almost anything." J. D.'s forehead was beginning to shine.

Ferris changed direction. "Now, Sheriff Killion, if you would just describe for the court the room in which you found Mrs. Houghton."

"Well, like I said, it was in the kitchen. She—Gussie, I mean—was laying across the table with her head down and one arm kinda flung out. . . ."

"The *room*, please, Mr. Killion, not the victim. For example, the table. Tell us about the table."

J. D. shot Ferris an angry look. "It was just a plain old table . . . a kitchen table. Pinewood. Had four legs and a top." There was a titter of amusement from the crowd.

Unperturbed, Ferris went on. "And can you tell us what was on that table?"

"There was some loose bills, an overturned Coke bottle and the cash box—actually it was an old tackle box—laying on its side."

"Was that all?"

"Yes sir."

Ferris pondered. "Would the Coke bottle have been used as a weapon, then? Does that seem possible to you?"

J. D. thought hard. The silence in the courtroom deepened. The sheriff sat in the witness box wrestling with the memory of that day when there was so much to look at and none of it made sense. He pulled the memory of that room and that table back for the millionth time and looked at it—the old woman sprawled out, indecent, her mouth hanging open in surprise, money clutched in one hand and that hand like a claw, holding on so tight that they had to pry the fingers loose, the cash box overturned and the Coke bottle sideways in a sticky brown pool. J. D. shook his head. "No."

Ferris glanced up. "Why not?"

"Because there was still some Coke left in the bottle. It was laying on its side, most of it spilled out, but there was still some left inside the bottle. If anybody picked it up, well it seems to me like it would have emptied out. And it was still laying in that puddle, too. Like it hadn't been moved after being turned over and spilled. It might have gotten turned over like that in a struggle," he looked at Ferris almost as if seeking approval, "but I don't think it was picked up, used like you are suggesting."

Ferris thought it over. After a while he said, "So you don't have any idea what might have made that mark?"

J. D. shook his head. "No sir. Like I say, it coulda been almost anything."

"Still, it looked to you like that was the cause of death? That mark, I mean. Like it was the reason?"

The sheriff seemed surprised that there should be any doubt. "Oh, yes sir. It sure does . . . did. It was a nasty-looking thing, let me tell you."

"But what from?" Ferris let the words form a question

mark in the air and stood looking at it, puzzled. After a minute he said, "Thank you," and sat down.

The next witness Austin Bailey called was the senior Dr. Cartwright. The old man raised his right hand, grunted assent to the Bible and shambled to the witness stand. From the jury box, his son Jason did his best not to look patronizing. Gracefully and melodiously, Austin took the old man through his paces, urging in one place and smiling encouragement in another. After a time, the old man started to get a little lockjawed. He began to answer in a curt and perfunctory manner which drove the clerk and the court reporter crazy. The reporter, a large woman in a jersey dress, complained in a carrying voice that she could not be expected to take down hums, haws and grunts. Dr. Cartwright nodded to her pleasantly and vaguely, as if he were searching his memory for the nature of her last office visit. Austin, ever tactful, intervened, asking if he would mind replying in more detail, in words, that is. The doctor looked baffled. "Course not," he said. "Do my best." But the questioning was strictly routine and there was nothing revealed that everybody didn't already know. Austin bowed out graciously. "Your witness, Mr. Ferris."

The defense attorney approached the witness moodily. "Now, Doctor—forgive me if I disremember—but I don't recall you saying anything about any kind of an object—a weapon—which might have caused this . . . ," he paused, consulted his memory, ". . . this *contusion* as you call it. Did you notice anything laying around which might have been used for that?"

The old man shoved out his jaw. "Nossir. I did not."

"Hmm. What do you reckon it was then? What do you think could have caused such a mark?"

"I don't have any idea."

"Then it didn't look like anything you'd ever seen before? In that line, I mean? A pistol butt, for instance? Or a old pipe, a fireplace poker? Something like that?"

The members of the jury were plainly shocked. The prosecuting attorney looked pained and Bubba Houghton looked downright ill.

Dr. Cartwright peered down at the lawyer. "No, I can't say that it did," he growled.

Judge Ira Hainsworth was regarding the defense attorney with growing suspicion. Ferris, oblivious, went on. "So we don't really know anything at all about that . . . *contusion* . . . do we? I mean how it got there? Or who put it there? Or what with? Seems like she could have fallen and hit her head . . ."

The physician beetled fiercely. "And gotten back up again?"

Mildly, Joel Ferris raised his hand. "All right." He rocked back on his heels and studied the ceiling. The big paddle fans turned softly, stirring the air but not cooling it any. "Now, Dr. Cartwright," Ferris resumed, "let's go back for a minute. You were the first person to arrive, were you not? Other than Mrs. Houghton's son, I mean? Nobody else was there?"

"That's right."

"So as far as you know, nothing had been moved or touched?"

Dr. Cartwright smiled. "Well now, Mr. Ferris. You are asking for supernatural vision on my part. How in the world would I know about that?"

There was appreciative laughter from the crowd.

Joel Ferris sighed. "What I mean, sir, is did either you

or Mr. Houghton move anything? Did you rearrange things any in the course of your examination?"

"Nossir. Soon as I laid eyes on Gussie I knew something was wrong. I checked for her pulse, that was all. Didn't have to turn her wrist, didn't even close her eyes."

A collective shudder ran through the courtroom.

"Thank you," said Joel Ferris. "Now would you please describe to the court everything that was on that kitchen table?"

"The table? Everything on the table?"

"Yes sir. Everything."

"Well now. Hmm. Well, besides Gussie herself, there was . . . ," he frowned. "Let's see. There was some loose bills and the box she kept her money in . . . that old tackle box of Carter's . . . it was upside down, empty. A Coke bottle next to her elbow . . . that was overturned, too." He paused, deep creases lining his forehead. Ferris turned and walked away, stood staring out the window. "Oh yes," continued the doctor after a moment. "Oh yes. Down at one end of the table there was a bunch of bowls set out. Mixing bowls. Like she was fixing to bake or something. And spoons lying around. Wooden spoons."

Ferris sighed again and spoke to the air. "Mixing bowls? And wooden spoons? Long-handled wooden spoons?"

The doctor nodded. Then, catching the gleam in the court reporter's eye, cleared his throat. "Yes. Yes, that's right."

"And that was all there was?"

"Best I can remember."

Ferris turned and walked back over until he was facing the witness. "Now, Doctor. Would you describe for us what that wound looked like?"

"It was more of a weal than a wound—a red mark, maybe six inches long—raised up, you know."

"Not a cut or a gash or anything like that?"

"Oh no. The skin wasn't even broken."

"How about the bones underneath?"

Doctor Cartwright looked at him. "They were fine, just fine."

"None of them broken?"

"No."

"But you have no idea what could have caused a mark like that?"

"Nossir."

Ferris leaned one arm casually on the witness stand. When he spoke, it was almost confidential, and so soft that people had to strain to hear. "Now Dr. Cartwright, I am going to ask you a very important question." He paused, waited until every iota of attention was focused on him and the witness, until the silence became intense, unbearable. Then he said, "Would you state, under oath, that that blow was the cause of Augusta Houghton's death? The *sole* cause? Could you swear that to be true beyond any reasonable doubt?"

Austin came up screaming. "Objection! That calls for an opinion from the witness."

"The witness is a professional man, Your Honor, and the question calls for a professional opinion," replied Ferris tartly.

"Overruled," rumbled Judge Hainsworth. "Witness will answer."

Dr. Cartwright gazed steadily at Ferris. "No sir," he said firmly. "No sir, I would not be able to say that."

There was a collective gasp from the spectators. A murmur ran through the crowd like a wind through grass. In the jury box, Jason Cartwright bent his head and covered his eyes with one hand. The defendant looked up, pale, his mouth hanging open and the judge looked down, stern,

his countenance dark. Of all the people in the room, Joel
Ferris was the only one who did not appear to be shaken
or surprised by the doctor's reply. Ferris scratched his ear
thoughtfully and went on.

"May we go over that again?" he inquired gently. "In
your professional opinion was that blow to the head and
neck of Augusta Houghton the cause, or the *sole* cause, of
her death? Would you swear to that beyond a shadow of
a doubt?"

"I certainly would not. I just got through telling you I
wouldn't." Dr. Cartwright glared at the attorney, plainly
annoyed.

"Well, why not?"

"Why not? Well, because it ain't the truth, that's why.
Or I couldn't swear to it. I simply can't be sure. That blow,
whatever it was, did not *in itself* cause sufficient damage
to *necessarily* result in death. I don't say it didn't cause her
death but I can't say it did. Please take note of these quali-
fications. At the time, I admit, I thought so. Since then I
have had reason to wonder."

"Why? What do you mean?"

"We don't get many murders here, Mr. Ferris. When we
do, I'm afraid that we may act too hastily, draw conclu-
sions that simply aren't there. We are inclined to accept
the obvious and look no farther."

"Are you saying, then, that the blow did not cause her
death?"

"Nossir, I am not saying any such thing. What I am saying is that there is a medical reason for doubting that such
a blow was *entirely* responsible, or that it even had anything to do with it. I simply *don't know*. I have seen many
people recover from much more serious injuries. It could
have been fatal—or it could have been just a bump on the
head. No way of telling now."

*

Everyone in the room was stunned. Some reacted with disbelief, others with dismay and still others with outrage. From his table, Austin Bailey's color changed from white to brilliant pink, going on and off like neon. Judge Hainsworth's face had a drained, gray look. The jury looked utterly confused and Jason Cartwright had by now covered his face with both hands.

Ferris continued his questioning, a flicker of interest brightening his usual dry, matter-of-fact manner. "Well then, what *was* the cause of her death?"

The doctor seemed suddenly weary. His look toward Ferris was vague and slightly puzzled. "My, my. It's hard to say sometimes. Gussie was no longer a young woman."

"Is it true that you had been treating her for a heart condition?"

"That's what I told her. Actually I was more afraid of a stroke. Gussie was very angry. . . ."

"Angry?"

"Yes. She carried anger around with her, old anger. I mean no disrespect, but Gussie was not one to forgive. And there she was hoarding all that money. . . ." He sighed. "Attitudes like that are not good for a person. And of course there was her blood pressure. It was high."

"Had you seen her recently, before she died, I mean?"

"Yes. She had been in to see me only the week before. I advised her to take it easy, get more rest. And I increased her medication. But Gussie couldn't tolerate the idea of slowing down. Said I was trying to make an invalid out of her . . . declared she would outlive me . . . and she might have."

"Are you saying she died of a stroke, then?"

Cartwright looked at Ferris in disgust. "Nossir. That is

not what I am saying at all. My opinion—if you would pay attention—is that there was a combination of factors. There nearly always is, come to it. At the time I examined the wound, we—Sheriff Killion, his deputy and myself—all assumed that somebody had killed her. But when you've practiced medicine as long as I have, you learn never to accept simple solutions." He paused, studied Ferris, seemed to reach a decision. "In any case," he continued, "I must allow that I entertain a 'reasonable doubt,' as you put it, Mr. Ferris, that the blow and the blow alone was responsible for her death."

A growing murmur rose from the crowd. Judge Hainsworth scowled it down. Ferris continued. "You said, 'a combination of factors'?" He looked at the court reporter, who nodded. "A combination of factors. . . . So a shock could have been responsible? A fright of some kind?"

The doctor gave a little smile. "A shock, maybe. But a fright? No, not with Gussie. If you mean that somebody came in the back door and scared her to death, it isn't likely." He chuckled. "Nossir, not likely."

"What would have been her response?" he spoke hurriedly, seeing Austin rise to his feet. "I mean the blood pressure and all?"

"Blood pressure, hell. It would have made her mad."

"Thank you, Doctor," said Ferris nimbly. "No further questions at this time."

The judge glanced inquiringly at Austin, but the prosecutor shook his head. He seemed depressed about something.

CHAPTER 30

. . . .

*J*udge Hainsworth pulled out an enormous gold pocket watch, consulted it gravely and declared a noon recess. People left the courtroom in a daze but it wasn't long before words started flying. Soon a steady hum could be heard all over town, and lunch—or dinner as most people called it—was loud with speculation. At two o'clock, when everybody had returned, Austin Bailey called his next witness.

"Mr. Hugh Merriwether Houghton!"

The witness proceeded to the stand in a gently sorrowing manner.

"Now, Bubba," said Austin warmly, "if I may call you by that name? It is the one most of us know you by."

Bubba inclined his head. "Certainly."

"Thank you. Now, Bubba," Austin continued, "would you please describe to the court what happened that day."

Bubba took a deep breath. Then, choosing his words with care, he revealed to the town, the judge and the jury how he had come home and found his mother. How he always came home for lunch to keep her company and to see how she was. And how, on that particular day, he had felt a premonition, a prickle of anxiety when she did not respond to his cheerful greeting from the door. He explained that he became concerned—she hadn't been feeling too well lately—but here he noticed Austin frowning so he hurried on and said how, his unease mounting, he had gone directly to the kitchen and found her there. His voice breaking slightly, Bubba finished by saying how he had immediately rushed to the phone and called Dr. Cartwright.

During his testimony, the jury sat transfixed. The whole courtroom exhaled sympathy. Poor man, it was surely all he could have done—and he was the picture of a dutiful son. Bailey spoke for them all when, in tones of gratitude tempered with deep regret, he thanked the witness and retired.

Joel Ferris, meanwhile, was busy mining one of his back molars with a toothpick. He studied Bubba through narrowed eyes and then strolled casually to the witness stand. Bubba, for his part, tried to be decent, but really, the man was seedy. His necktie was atrocious and he jerked it askew as if on purpose. His suit was cheap and unpressed, his shoes dusty and run-over . . .

"Now, Mr. Houghton," said Ferris in a grating voice, "how much money do you reckon your mama kept in that old tin box?"

There was a collective intake of breath. Bubba frowned. Then, drawing himself up, he gazed at a point above Ferris's head. "I really couldn't say."

Ferris seemed taken aback. "You can't say?" he repeated, incredulous. "You mean you don't know?"

"No," replied Bubba testily. "I have no idea."

"But surely . . . ," the little attorney stared at him. "But surely you were aware of the *contents* of her *cash box?*" The question quivered in the air like an accusation.

Bubba's hands were damp. He made an effort to pull himself together. This was the last thing he had wanted or expected, this nasty, sneaky prying into private lives. "Of course I was aware of the contents," he answered irritably. "She spread her money all over the kitchen table. I simply have no idea as to the amount."

"I see," responded Ferris in a tone flat with disbelief. Gloomily he studied the tips of his unshined shoes. Bubba took out his handkerchief and dabbed at his forehead. "I'm sorry, Mr. Houghton. I frankly don't understand. I thought I heard you to say that your mother spread her money all over the kitchen table . . . now why did she do that?"

"I believe her intention was to count it."

"Ah. And how often did she do that? Once a month or so?"

Bubba felt his face begin to flush. "She did it every day."

Both the defendant and his wife looked up.

"*Every day?*" Ferris's voice rose to a high filing sound. "She counted her money *every day?*"

"Yes," said Bubba tightly.

"My Lord!" said Ferris, filled with wonder. "My Lord!" shaking his head in amazement and sharing it with the jury. After a moment, he resumed. "Well now, Mr. Houghton, if that is the case, then you must have observed this . . . this *event* any number of times."

Bubba gritted his teeth. "Yes."

"Yet you insist that you have no idea how much money was there?"

"That is correct."

"You mean to tell me—to tell this court—that your mama counted out her money every day of the world, Sundays included, laid it out bill by bill, arranged it like a game of solitaire—and you don't know how much was there? I mean, you lived in the same house, surely . . ."

"Objection!" cried Austin. "The witness is not on trial!"

Judge Hainsworth beetled down. "Mr. Ferris? Perhaps you should make your point?"

Ferris nodded, indifferent. "Well, would you be willing to give this court an estimate, Mr. Houghton? The evidence against my client rests largely on the presence of this money. Could you at least give us *some* idea?"

Bubba sighed. "I really don't know."

"Well, Mr. Houghton . . . surely now. Would you say it was a *lot* of money? A hundred dollars or . . . ?"

"I would guess that it amounted to several thousand dollars."

The spectators murmured with gratification. The defendant's wife shot her husband a strange and almost hostile look.

"Several thousand dollars! My goodness!" Ferris rolled his eyes and appealed to the jury. "And did anyone else know about this . . . this habit your mother had of keeping so much money at the house and counting it every day?"

"Oh my yes."

Ferris looked up sharply. "And who was that?"

"Well, I guess almost everybody."

"*Everybody?* What do you mean—everybody?"

"That is exactly what I do mean—everybody in town."

Ferris stared at Bubba. He took out a toothpick and began to suck on it delicately. Finally, astounded, he repeated, "You mean to tell me, this court, that everybody in town knew that your mother kept all that money at home and counted it every day?"

"I believe that is what I said, Mr. Ferris."

"Well now," drawled Ferris. "That is interesting . . . very interesting. Not the kind of thing a stranger would be likely to know, is it?"

"I beg your pardon?"

"I say, a stranger, a newcomer to the community or somebody just passing through, he wouldn't be likely to know about that, would he?"

"I really couldn't say."

Ferris wandered off, stared out the window for a few minutes. When he returned, he planted one foot on the step to the witness stand and leaned forward confidentially. Bubba withdrew slightly in distaste.

"Now, Mr. Houghton," began Ferris, "just how much of that was your money?"

Bubba reddened. "None of your . . . none of it!" he snapped. And wished, too late, that he had said it differently.

The Lone Star Bidders leaned forward to a woman.

"*None* of it?" gasped Ferris. "Not one nickel?"

"No." Bubba fought to keep his voice level. "It was entirely my mother's money."

"But you had access to it."

"No, I did not."

"But it was right there. Mr. Houghton, you strain . . ."

"She kept it locked up in that nasty old tackle box, locked up and hidden away. I had no call to touch it."

"What would have happened if you had?"

Bubba looked at the attorney with loathing. But it was not Ferris he saw, it was his mother, smirking, taunting, eyes bird bright as he passed the table.

Bubba? Honey? Would you run down to the store and get me some Cokes?

I don't have any money.

What do you mean, you don't have any money?

Exasperated—*That's what I mean. I don't.*

Well, I swear, I don't know what you do with it. I thought the school paid you enough. They ought to. Trouble is, you spend it all on clothes. I saw your bill last month.

He said nothing.

She went on, wetting her thumb, counting out bills. *My word! I didn't realize there was so much here!* Then, for his benefit, *I guess I'll have to cash a check, then. Surely you can do that for me.*

He exploded. *For God's sake! You've got money right in front of you! The whole damn table is covered with it. Give me one of those filthy fifties and I'll go get you some Cokes.*

She glanced up, sly. *Ha! Now wouldn't you just love to get your hands on this money! This* filthy *money! Now wouldn't you just love to do that?*

And once he had screamed *YES!* Yelled it right in her face, his own gone purple and hers mottled with rage. *YES*—and grabbed a handful and waved it over her head, just out of reach. *YES!* And to his horror, she came up clawing. Shrieked and scrabbled across the table making wild grabs at his upraised hand. Appalled, he had dropped the money and fled. For the next several days, his students had exchanged knowing grins and giggles about the scratches on his face. But he could never tell that to the court, not for the world. He could never tell anyone. He would have to bear the shame of it himself—his own and his mother's. He was the one on trial, not this boy. And he, Bubba, already stood convicted, not only of his solitary sins but of some greater guilt which was hideous, inherited and had no name.

Austin Bailey was howling. "Objection! Objection, Your Honor! This material is irrelevant! Defense attorney is intimidating the witness!"

Judge Hainsworth scowled down. "Perhaps not entirely irrelevant. . . . Still, Mr. Ferris, do you wander from the issue?"

"Your Honor, I have only one further question."

"Proceed then, but remember your duty."

"Mr. Houghton," Ferris rasped, "to whom did your mother leave all her money?"

Bubba's voice was strangled with fury. "To me." There was a silence.

"Thank you. No further questions." Ferris concluded crisply and turned his back.

Visibly shaken, Bubba stepped down from the witness stand and walked back to his seat. As he did so, he looked directly at the prisoner for the first time. The boy, sensing it, raised his head and stared back. For a brief moment, a look of sympathy or even complicity passed between them.

CHAPTER 31

. . . .

*T*he following morning, the courtroom filled early. Even Old Lady Reeves was present, shuffling in on the arm of her daughter, Lady Lynn. As the woman who had ruled over that community longer than anybody, longer even than Gussie herself, and who relinquished the attention unwillingly, old Ada Reeves stopped in her tracks, peered around angrily and announced in a voice loud enough to be heard by all, "Going to hell in a handbasket!"

Heads were turned.

Presently everyone had appeared except Joel Ferris. Even the defendant had been brought in and sat alone at the defense table, head down, picking a hole in the wood with his thumbnail. The girl, his wife, sat behind him with the other spectators. A couple of times she seemed to want to lean forward and say something. She made a movement or two in that direction but didn't follow through. Maybe she was afraid to. And since the boy ignored her, she finally sat back and folded her hands in her lap. Meanwhile the temperature in the courtroom was on the way up. Overhead, the fans flapped feebly at the air.

*

Still no Ferris. Then all of a sudden he appeared, came in walking fast, his suit rumpled and his tie flying. His hair stuck up like grass that has been stepped on and is slowly coming back to life. The girl looked at him and her shoulders went up and down in a big sigh. Ferris skidded to a stop at the table, leaned down and spoke fiercely into the prisoner's ear. The boy, sullen, shook his head. Ferris straightened and gazed down at his charge in disgust. Then he turned and looked at the girl. Raising one hand, he made a throat-cutting motion by running his thumb across his windpipe. The prisoner's wife faded to an even paler color. Ferris scraped up a chair and sat scribbling on a piece of paper. Austin Bailey, the jury and the spectators observed all this with great interest. Shortly thereafter the clerk whined out his sing-song: "All rise!" and the judge swept in. He frowned down at the table for the defense. "Glad to see you could make it, Mr. Ferris. If you are ready, sir, we will begin. The prosecution advises me that it rests its case so you may call your first witness."

Ferris looked momentarily stunned, like he hadn't been expecting this maneuver. He glanced across at Bailey, who was gazing idly into the air, the smirk of a fat cat lurking around his lips. Ferris's dun-colored eyes rested thoughtfully on the district attorney, then he got to his feet and to everyone's amazement and delight, called the banker to the stand.

Elegant and cool, Lincoln Winters seated himself with precision in the witness stand. His suit was the color of pale smoke and a silver cuff link flashed whenever he moved a well-groomed hand. Joel Ferris approached him wearily in a dark brown suit which looked like it had been slept in. To some observers, the scene called to mind a picture right out of the Great Depression—a man who was down and out looking in a plate glass window at a figure on display.

"Now, Mr. Winters," Ferris rasped, "you are the president of the First National Bank of this community, is that correct?"

The banker inclined his head in assent but before he could speak, if indeed he intended to, the little clerk barked in a sharp voice all in one breath and every word on the same note, "Witness-will-be-so-kind-as-to-please-speak-up-court-reporter-is-unable-to-record-gestures-therefore-all-replies-must-be-of-a-verbal-nature." He took a deep breath.

Startled, Lincoln Winters stared at the little man. There was a fleeting sense of malice in the air—not for justice being considered by the judge and jury, but a petty, baser form of retribution, a flicker of old resentments over loans requested and denied, of small revenge being exacted at last. The clerk sat back, a grimace of satisfaction lighting his face in what might have passed for a smile on a bigger man.

Slightly embarrassed, Lincoln Winters cleared his throat and replied, "That is correct." There was just a hint of ice around the edges of his words.

"How long have you held that position?"

"For the past twelve years."

"And were you employed by the bank before that, before you became president?"

"Certainly. I have been with the Bank for over twenty-five years." It was plain to everybody that Lincoln Winters spelled bank with a capital *B*. To him it was more than a building, it was an institution.

"So I imagine you handled any number of accounts personally—the larger accounts, I mean—giving of your own time and experience, acting as financial advisor and investment counselor, all that kind of thing."

"You describe some of the duties of a bank president, Mr. Ferris."

"Was Augusta Houghton one of those preferred customers?"

"Mrs. Houghton—Gussie—banked with us for over fifty years."

Judge Hainsworth leaned forward uneasily.

"I must ask you to answer the question, Mr. Winters," said Ferris.

"I am not certain that I understand the question, Mr. Ferris."

"Let me put it this way: Did you have a long-standing and intimate knowledge of the financial affairs of Augusta Houghton?"

Lincoln Winters replied with pained delicacy. "I suppose you might put it that way. Yes."

"So you advised her on transactions, investments, stocks —that sort of thing?"

Lincoln permitted himself a chilly smile. "I am afraid it would be more accurate, Mr. Ferris, to say that Gussie advised *me*."

A little ripple of laughter swept around the room.

"She was a good businesswoman, then? Astute?"

"Astute is too mild a word. She was a remarkable woman."

"She managed her money wisely?"

"I should say extremely well."

"Would you be good enough to elaborate on that?"

Winters smoothed his graying hair with one hand. A silver cuff link caught the light. "For one thing, she was an absolute wizard on the cattle market. I never met anybody better. Gussie knew exactly when to buy and when to sell and when to sit tight. She had exceptional ability—almost uncanny." He shook his head, marveling. "And she displayed the same . . . talent . . . when it came to buying property, diversifying her holdings."

"And she was smart when it came to stocks and bonds and so on?"

"Well, the cattle market was her specialty. But oil was discovered on a little patch of land she had picked up at a foreclosure auction. With some of that money she bought the rights to a toll bridge down on the river from DuPont. . . . You might say she had the Midas Touch."

"Would you say she was well off at the time of her death?"

Lincoln suppressed a smile. "Well off? Surely you understate the matter, Mr. Ferris. Gussie died a very wealthy woman."

Bubba shifted uncomfortably in his chair. From the back of the room, Houston Carr observed him thoughtfully.

Ferris droned on. "Could you give us an estimate of her wealth, Mr. Winters?"

The banker stiffened disapprovingly. "Well, I don't know if that would be proper. . . ." He glanced inquiringly at Judge Hainsworth, who nodded. Lincoln continued, "Well, then, I should say that Gussie was several times a millionaire."

A murmur of interest rose from the crowd. People looked at their neighbors and wagged their heads, some in disbelief and others pretending to have known about it all along. Charlotte Buchanan, in the jury box, bent forward from the waist and gave the matter her undivided attention.

Ferris's next question snapped rudely out. "Then why,

Mr. Winters, did she keep so much cash in an old tin box at home?"

Winters gazed down at the defense attorney with enormous distaste. "I really have no idea," he replied coldly.

"Oh come now, Mr. Winters. You have just testified that this woman was your friend and customer for many years, that you had personal knowledge of her financial affairs and that by your own estimation she was a millionaire several times over. Now why would such a woman keep her cash in an old tin box at home?"

Once more the banker appealed to the judge for aid. Judge Hainsworth raised inquiring eyebrows at Austin Bailey but the prosecutor shook his head. "Please answer the question, Mr. Winters," said Judge Hainsworth.

The banker spread his hands in a gesture of dismay. "How should I know? Perhaps in her heart Gussie distrusted banks. She was forever complaining that I was parsimonious when it came to interest earned. She said that my instincts were . . . were, well, those of a dog with a bone. And just about as profitable."

This time a hearty laugh erupted from those assembled.

Slightly miffed, Lincoln resumed. "However, I must make it clear that Gussie was very . . . *attached* to her money. Very fond of it. She liked to have it nearby. She once remarked to me that money was the only thing which had never let her down, the only thing she could rely on. She said that everything else in her life had turned out to be a disappointment."

There was a painful silence. Ferris considered this last statement. Bubba, by this time, had slid so low in his seat that only the back of his scarlet neck was visible. Charlotte Buchanan released a terrific sigh—she had not breathed for some time.

Joel Ferris rocked back on his heels. "Just one or two more questions, Mr. Winters."

The banker waited.

Ferris gazed up at the ceiling, apparently lost in contemplation. The paddle fans beat the air weakly with a soft, monotonous flap. It became so quiet that the people who had been itching to cough or sneeze or move around a little bit had to put it off still longer. Joel Ferris brought his eyes back to the banker's and said in a clear, twanging voice, "Did Miz Houghton ever mark her bills in some way? Did she put a sign or a symbol of some kind on them so that they were distinct or different from others?"

Lincoln Winters bestowed a tiny smile of respect. "Yes," he replied evenly. "She was in the habit of always drawing a small Lone Star in the upper right-hand corner of each bill. In ink."

"On every single bill?"

"Yes."

"Like a brand, you mean?"

"I suppose you could say that."

The prisoner jerked up staring and gave a choked yell. His wife said, "Oh my *Lord*!" The murmur in the courtroom became a roar.

"Thank you, Mr. Winters," sang out Ferris. "That will be all."

The prosecution showed no desire to cross-examine.

Lincoln Winters stepped down into a tumult.

"*Goddamn!*" declared somebody. "A Lone Star on every dollar! Don't that beat all?"

"Shoot!" grinned another. "Could be we ought to get 'em printed that way."

Several members of the Daughters of the Confederacy

gave the matter some serious thought and vowed to bring it up at the next meeting.

"Order in the court!" demanded the judge. He pounded his gavel.

Joel Ferris ran his fingers through his hair. "Your Honor, at this time I request permission to recall Sheriff Killion to the stand."

Hainsworth looked over at Austin Bailey. The D.A., bored or irritated, gave a shrug and nodded.

"Sheriff Killion? Remember you are still under oath."

Reluctantly J. D. took the stand.

"Now, Sheriff, if you will just bear with me for a moment." Ferris spoke with unusual smoothness. "You have heard the testimony given just now by Mr. Winters?"

"Well sure. Of course I did."

"Would you please explain to the court what bearing this testimony has on the present case?"

J. D. turned stubborn. "I don't believe I . . ."

"You heard Mr. Winters describe the marked money?"

"Oh yeah. Yes sir."

"Well, in what way is this marked money relevant to the case?"

"Oh. Well, they found it on him."

"Who is 'they'?"

"The police out in California."

"They found this marked money?"

"You bet. See, we had sent out an APB . . ."

"An APB?"

"All Points Bulletin."

"I see. Now you said, 'they found it on him.' We have established who 'they' were. Who was 'him'?"

J. D. looked at Ferris in amazement. "Why, the kid over yonder." He pointed at Jewell Ray.

"So the authorities in California found money marked in the manner in which Mr. Winters has just described on the person of Jewell Ray Cantwell."

"Well, not on his person, exactly. It was in his stuff, though."

"And that's how he came to be sent back here and charged?"

(Austin Bailey and Judge Hainsworth were gazing at the defense attorney in total disbelief.)

"Yes sir. They had picked him up for breaking into a place in San Diego, put him in that there ju-ve-nile home. Then they come across that money and called us on the phone. We told 'em he was wanted for murder. . . ."

Ferris quickly interrupted. "Thank you. But what verification do we have that these events took place? The arrest and the discovery of the money?"

"They sent us a . . . ," he implored the judge. "A disposition?"

"You mean deposition?" suggested Ferris drily.

"Yeah. That's it."

"And where is this document now?"

"Well, uh . . ."

Judge Hainsworth intervened. "Mr. Ferris? If I may speed matters along a little? The deposition from the San Diego County Sheriff's Office was entered into the records at the preliminary hearing. It is available for all who wish to see it."

"Thank you, Your Honor." He looked directly at J. D. "So it was on the basis of this deposition that this boy here, Jewell Ray Cantwell, was brought here and charged. It is because he had this marked money in his possession that he is on trial today."

J. D. appeared confused and defensive. "Well, heck yes. I mean . . ."

"How much money was actually found?"

"About five or six hundred dollars."

"Thank you, Sheriff." A fleeting grin tucked up the corner of Ferris's mouth as he saw a flushed district attorney rising to his feet. Then, briskly and all business, he requested permission to approach the Bench. Austin Bailey joined him and the three of them conferred. The judge took out his watch and studied it. He surveyed the restless audience and nodded. "Court stands adjourned until two o'clock this afternoon."

CHAPTER 32

. . . .

When court reconvened, it was observed that the defendant was all dressed up. He came in wearing a pearl-button western shirt with blue piping across the shoulders and flared around the cuffs. His slacks were navy, he had on a western belt and some attempt had been made to polish his shoes. The slacks were just a little bit too long but otherwise he looked nice, more like a boy you'd see in the Baptist church than a jittery jailbird. Soon after the boy arrived, Ferris hurried in carrying a long, thin package wrapped in brown paper. He laid the parcel on the table and Jewell Ray shot it a look of distrust. Ignoring him, Ferris sat down. Immediately thereafter, Austin Bailey made his entrance and everybody noticed that he hesitated just the merest fraction of a second when he saw Jewell Ray. Houston Carr, sunk in his chair at the back of the courtroom, sat up and grinned. "Hell!" he said softly to himself. "*Now* we're gonna get *down* to it!"

Looking somewhat the worse for lunch, the jury trailed in and took their seats in a sleepy and dyspeptic manner. Nothing happened for several minutes. Joel Ferris laid out some scraps of paper on the table, stood up and leaned over them, studying. Charlotte Buchanan put on her glasses.

Looked to her like he'd dragged out his cleaning bills. If that's what they were, then they must be old ones, she decided—and took her glasses off again. Ferris continued to hunch over them, working his toothpick. The room was becoming increasingly oppressive, heavy with heat, like a thunderstorm might be building. Ladies fluttered whatever they could that would stir a breath of air. Gents mopped their foreheads. Suddenly the door to the judge's chambers slammed. People barely had time to execute a kind of reverse curtsy before Judge Hainsworth hammered down the gavel. In a visual repercussion of the sound, he lowered his gaze on Joel Ferris. "Are you ready, Mr. Ferris? Very well, then. Call your next witness."

Joel Ferris stood straight, shoved one hand in his sagging coat pocket, shifted the toothpick to the other side of his mouth and said quietly, "I call the defendant, Jewell Ray Cantwell."

A collective "OH!" went around the room. Charlotte Buchanan put her glasses back on again.

The boy stood up, biting his lip. Ferris was waiting by the witness stand. "Come on, son," he said gently. The boy moved forward, mumbled to the clerk, gave the Bible a pat and slipped into the box with quick, catlike grace. The attorney for the defense studied him for a moment. Then he took a deep breath.

"Please tell the court your full name."

"Jewell Ray Cantwell."

"And what is your age, Mr. Cantwell?"

"I'm six . . . ," his voice faltered, "sixteen."

"Speak up, please."

"*Sixteen.*"

"Thank you." Ferris went into a brief study from which he emerged smiling. "Now, Mr. Cantwell, there are a few things which I would like for you to explain to the judge and jury here."

Jewell Ray worked his eyebrows and nodded uncertainly.

Ferris rose lightly on his toes. "Am I correct in saying, Mr. Cantwell, that you visited this town on . . . ," he consulted a slip of paper from his pocket, ". . . on May 12 of this year, and at that time you did willfully and unlawfully enter the dwelling of Mrs. Augusta Houghton, taking from her an undisclosed amount of money? Is that statement substantially correct?"

Jewell Ray shifted his feet, scowled. "Well, I never . . ."

"Just a minute now." Judge Hainsworth peered down, concerned. "The defendant cannot be required to testify against himself, Mr. Ferris. Just whose side are you on?"

Ferris shook his head impatiently. "Believe me, Your Honor, I have no wish to malign this defendant. I have asked him about an act of burglary. But the defendant is not on trial for burglary. He has never even been charged with burglary. He is on trial for murder. I seek to show that the guilt of the former has nothing whatever to do with his innocence of the latter and is, instead, germane to proof of that innocence."

Everyone sat back pondering this remarkable burst of rhetoric. Austin Bailey and the sheriff exchanged glances. The D.A. looked uncomfortable and busied himself with his papers.

"Hmm," Judge Hainsworth mulled it over. "Hmm, I see. Very well then, proceed, Mr. Ferris. But I urge you to keep your legal obligations foremost in your mind."

Unruffled, Ferris continued. "It is true then, Mr. Cantwell, that you entered the back door of Mrs. Houghton's residence and took her money?"

Jewell Ray continued to work his eyebrows. He scowled,

glanced up and then down again. "Well, I reckon. Yes sir. I done that. Leastways, I guess it was her. I went in the back door and there was a old lady settin' there. Money layin' all over the table. So I took some of it."

"What kind of a table was it?"

"Well, a kitchen table, I guess. That's where she was— in the kitchen."

"And there was money all over this kitchen table?"

"Yes sir."

"And was there anything else besides money on the table?"

The boy stared down at his hands. "Well . . . seemed like there was a bottle of pop. A Coke, I think it was."

"Anything else?"

The boy was very pale. He shook his head.

"Witness will please answer . . . ," began the clerk.

The boy jerked up, stared at the clerk wide-eyed. Mumbled something.

"What was that?" demanded Ferris, pouncing.

"Just some old bowls and stuff."

"Stuff? What do you mean—stuff?"

Jewell Ray slanted his face away so that he seemed to be talking to somebody behind the bench. His voice was barely audible. "Oh . . . you know. Spoons, I guess. Stuff like that, stuff for cookin'."

"Then what did you do?"

"What?"

"What did you do when you saw all that money?"

"I grabbed me a handful of it and ran."

"Where to?"

"Huh?"

"Where did you run?"

"I run out the door, hopped over the fence and took off down the alley."

"Did you see anybody else?"

The boy looked surprised. "No, I didn't see nobody."

Ferris walked around in a little circle, then stopped and stood staring hard at the center of it. He shook his head. "It's mystifying," he said. "It's downright mystifying."

That got everybody's attention. Clay Weyerts, the jury foreman, sucked on a side tooth. Cliff, his brother, sitting in the back of the room, looked from Joel Ferris to Clay and back again. Houston Carr grinned hugely, slapped his knee and leaned forward. Austin Bailey was watching from the corners of his eyes and Judge Hainsworth rubbed his chin.

"It is most mysterious," Ferris went on. "In fact, it is beyond me. Why, I knew Gussie." He turned and swept his arm to include the whole room. "Everybody here knew Gussie. And it is a mighty curious thing, a very *uncharacteristic* reaction, that Gussie would take a thing like that laying down."

The boy glanced at him with deep mistrust. Over at the prosecution table, Austin Bailey narrowed his eyes and tapped gently on his front teeth with a pencil.

"Amazing!" rhapsodized Ferris. "Simply amazing! Why, we have heard testimony from many people—sworn testimony! From the banker himself . . . from her own son even . . . about how Gussie loved her money. Now I, for one, find it hard to believe that she would set there—*idly*—while some young . . . ," he glanced doubtfully at the defendant, "while some young *kid* grabs onto it and runs."

A murmur began to rise in the room. The girl sat stiffly, elbows locked to her sides, hands knuckle-white in her lap. The judge, his brow furrowing, began a preliminary rumble. Ferris stepped neatly up and confronted the defendant directly.

"Would you have us believe, Mr. Cantwell, are you asking us to assume that she offered no *resistance*?"

The boy shook his head but seemed numb, confused, and before he could reply, Ferris held up a warning hand.

"Remember you are under oath, boy! You swore an oath to *God*!"

Now God had not figured largely in Jewell Ray's life but fear had. At Ferris's words, his eyes became very dark. Like leaf shadows on a night wind, they darted and flickered in the pale surface of his face. He glanced quickly at Ferris and away again. Ferris said nothing more but allowed the silence to accumulate, pile up like a thunderhead, until the room was ready to burst from the weight of it.

Jewell Ray twitched and mumbled something to his lap.

"What was that?" snapped the lawyer.

Stubbornly, "I *said*, she fussed some."

" 'She fussed some,' " repeated Ferris, his voice rich with sarcasm. "Now ain't that somethin'?" He turned to the jury. "Can you imagine?"

The defendant looked up, fury written all over him. He tossed back the lock of hair which dangled over his eyes and glared at the defense attorney with pure hatred.

Ferris turned his back and walked over to the little table. "She fussed some," he muttered, shaking his head. "Now ain't that amazin'?" He picked up the package wrapped in brown paper, went over and stood respectfully in front of the Bench. "Your Honor, I would like to enter this item as Exhibit A for the defense."

The judge peered over and down. "What the . . . what is it?"

Ferris shucked the wrapping and let the paper fall to the floor. He held the object up for all to see. "It is a long-handled wooden spoon. An ordinary wooden spoon like you would find in any kitchen."

A shocked silence prevailed. Suddenly an animal-like cry came from the witness stand, a groan of the wildest desolation and sorrow. Jewell Ray shuddered and covered his face with both hands. Austin Bailey, midway to the Bench, stopped as soon as he saw what the object was, turned on his heel and went back to his seat. Charlotte Buchanan took off her glasses and strained with her bare eyes.

"Mr. Ferris," said Judge Hainsworth drily. "Mr. Ferris, are you feeling all right?"

"Never felt better, Your Honor."

The wooden spoon was duly entered into evidence, the clerk barely deigning to touch the thing.

"My stars!" Mrs. Reeves was heard to exclaim. "Did you see that? What is this world coming to?"

For the first time in his career, Joel Ferris shot a cuff. He shot a cuff and smoothed his hair. "Ahem!" he said loudly. "*Ahem!*" People quieted and turned to look at him. A faint but unmistakable odor of witch hazel hung in the air. "Now," he spoke into the pool of quiet. "Now, Mr. Cantwell, would you kindly describe to this court what you mean by the words 'she fussed some?' Please be so good as to tell us exactly what this 'fuss' consisted of."

But the boy was rocking back and forth in the witness stand, rocking and moaning, covering his face with his hands.

"Mr. Cantwell?" repeated Ferris sharply. "Will you please respond to the question?"

The boy continued rocking back and forth. The moan grew louder until it became more of a howl.

"STOP IT!" cried the tall, pale girl, his wife. She jumped to her feet and grabbed hold of the railing in front of her. "Stop it! Lookit what you're doing to him!"

Immediately J. D. went over and laid a hand on her arm. She subsided into the chair, shoulders shaking. The boy raised his head and looked at the girl. His face was streaked with tears and red marks where his hands had been. Suddenly he leaped up and took hold of the edge of the witness stand so hard it looked like he might throw it. His knuckles stood out white against the wood, shiny as bone. Ferris took a step back but the boy leaned out and spat the words directly into the attorney's face, yelled them out, spit flying.

"ALL RIGHT YOU SONOFABITCH! ALL RIGHT! I DID HIT HER! Like you been wanting me to say all along. She come at me clawing, grabbed aholt of my arm and hung on. Then she glommed onto one of them there spoons . . . came down hard acrost my knuckles . . . wham! It hurt like hellfire! And laughing! Her laughing the whole damn time! I pulled back my hand cause it hurt, let go. But she wouldn't. Just kept hanging onto my arm that way and laughing. Screaming, more like. Then she drug herself up and grabbed aholt of my shirt—like this"—he gathered a fistful of his shirt—"commenced shoutin' and yellin'. Goin' on about that money—it being *hers* and how she loved it and how she sure as hell wasn't gonna let some . . . wasn't gonna let *me* take it." His voice wavered and nearly stopped. He went on in a hoarse whisper, his eyes wild and looking at nothing, remembering. "Then all of a sudden her eyes went funny—glassy-like—and kinda rolled back in her head. She started to sag. But her mouth was still laughing, the drool coming out of it on one side. Her head flopped over but her hand was still hung up in my shirt. Like a claw or somethin'. I couldn't get rid of it. I tried to pull loose . . . but it was like she was hanging on with all her strength. I couldn't get shed of her to save my life." He gulped. His face was all wide and staring, the color of paper. "That there spoon was still laying on the table where she dropped it. I picked it up . . . and I hit her with it." He stopped and took in a long, shuddering breath. "I only hit her once. And it didn't make no difference. Didn't even break the spoon. Her hand was hung up in my shirt and she wouldn't let go."

His words reverberated in the silent room:
Let go.
Let go.
Let go.

Ferris spoke very quietly. "What did you do then?"

The boy, now very damp and sweating, drooped and slid back down in the chair. His hands fell away from the railing and he seemed to be fighting for air, staring into that nightmarish memory and gasping for his own life. "I . . . I took hold of her shoulders . . . tried to push her away. They was all sharp . . . gristle and bone. I thowed the spoon away . . . took hold of her shoulders . . . and pushed. Finally she come loose."

"What did she do? Did she say anything?"

"Oh no. But I never killed her, Mr. Ferris." He looked at the attorney, dazed. "I swear it. I never. I gave her a little tap with that spoon . . . but there was somethin' mighty wrong with her already."

"She was starting to fall back even before you hit her?"

"Yes sir. But she wouldn't let go my shirt. Her head kinda rolled back and her mouth fell open and stayed that way." He shivered, swallowed and went on. "And her eyes got all funny . . . like somebody who was drownded. I only hit her to make her let go. No harder than you would a horse or a mule. But it didn't do no good. I kept backing up and pushing. Her hand finally fell out—just like a fishhook."

Ferris sighed. He seemed drained, about to fold up, sucked dry. "Okay," he said softly. "That's all then." He turned his back on the boy and walked away. "Your witness," he said to the prosecutor over his shoulder. But Austin Bailey wanted no part of it. He folded his arms and shook his head slowly. No questions.

CHAPTER 33

. . . .

By morning the weather had turned sultry. Off to the southwest, thunderheads began building and the air in the packed courtroom was as hot and heavy as a flatiron. Austin Bailey arrived very well-turned-out and gleaming with hair oil. Jovial and expansive, he joked with the reporters and gazed around the room with satisfaction. Joel Ferris, coming in a short time later, amazed everybody by showing up in a navy suit which was nicely pressed, a fresh white shirt and a sober tie. He walked quickly to the defense table, poured some water from the pitcher into a glass, and took a long drink. Then he hitched his hands in his back pockets and stared out over the crowd. Rowdy brought in the prisoner. The boy was dressed in the same clothes he had worn the day before but there was something stale and wasted about him, as if he had neither slept or eaten. He slid into his chair and sat hunched over with his eyes on his hands. Joel Ferris sat down next to him, laid a hand on his shoulder and began speaking earnestly into his ear. The boy made no response. The jury filed in solemnly. The clerk sang out and the judge sailed in. Both attorneys remained standing at respectful attention while the judge seated himself. Ira beetled down, brows heavy beneath a shelf of thick, gray hair. Did either one of them wish to recall any witnesses? No, neither one did. Very well. Then they would proceed with the final arguments.

Austin Bailey consulted the neat packet of notes in his hand and commenced to address the court. "Your Honor," he began, "Ladies and Gentlemen of the Jury, my Worthy Opponent . . . we are here to do our Duty." He paused to let it sink in. "Now, any one among us would rather be somewhere else . . . ," he scanned the jurors' faces and moved closer to the box where they were seated. "We have our families, our ranches, our businesses . . . a thousand things we need to tend to . . . but all these things must wait. They must wait, must hang in abeyance, indeed must rest and be patient while we perform a greater obligation. It is not a pleasant duty . . . by no means is it a pleasant or easy duty. Nevertheless," he said sternly, "it must be done." He paused and then resumed in the resonant tones for which he was known. "Now we all knew Augusta Houghton, some of us all our lives. I myself knew Gussie when she was just a girl." He smiled, reminiscing. "As a matter of fact, Gussie made it possible for me to advance to the fourth grade when otherwise I might have languished. My older sisters had no time to help a little boy with his spelling—but Gussie did. Oh yes," he went on, hitting his stride, "she was a good friend and neighbor to us all. And now," he turned and confronted the jury, "*now she has been struck down and taken from us years before her time.*"

His words hung burning in the air, white-hot and righteous, a scalding evangelical indictment. "Struck down," Austin whispered in an aftertaste of sulphur, "and taken from us, Ladies and Gentlemen, as if *she*, as if her *life*, as if *human life* were of no consequence whatever. And that," he continued more loudly, "is wherein our duty lies.

*

"Gussie was a fine woman. A remarkable woman. She was strong and she loved life. She will be missed by us all for years to come, years which she herself could have enjoyed had not this . . . this *despicable* act of random and incomprehensible violence occurred." He stepped back and took a tiny sip of water. "I beg your forgiveness, my friends, for opening these wounds of grief and anguish which have hardly had a chance to heal. But I find that today I must assume the office of a surgeon with a knife . . . ," and these words, steel-bright, glittered in the air, ". . . open old wounds and tear away the tissue that time has kindly made so that we may see the truth. It is my sworn duty to do so. My task is to aid you to see wherein your greater duty lies—your duty to Augusta Houghton and to all of us who go about our lives in the hope that *we* and our *children* will never be struck down as she has been."

Bailey turned and looked at the defendant. The boy sat, head down, unmoving except for the twitch of a muscle in his cheek. "We see here a lad," said the district attorney, "a boy only sixteen years old. This boy is charged with the murder of a woman who was near and dear to all of us. We have heard what this boy did—he admits it himself. He has not acted rightly. He stole and robbed and otherwise behaved in a criminal manner. An unlawful manner. But," and here Austin's voice rose to a crescendo, "but, Ladies and Gentlemen, *the excuse will be made that he is young*. Oh yes. There will be those who will try to excuse him because of his youth. Much pity will be played upon. Human kindness will be milked. But, I ask you, was *he* kind? Did *he* behave with compassion?" Austin shook his head. "Far from it. He showed no pity whatsoever. And I say to you, Ladies and Gentlemen, that *because of*

his youth, *such behavior is inexcusable. Indefensible.* Indefensible." He paused and allowed the full impact of the
word to fall. Then, in a stage whisper which carried to
the farthest corner, "Are we going to let him go *so that
he can do it again?* Are we?" His voice began an effective
rise. "Have we even the slightest proof that he will not?
Have we? Even the slightest inkling? No. In fact, that he
has already done such a deed *when he is only sixteen* is
proof to the contrary. It is a very bad sign."

With no warning, he whirled and stabbed a finger at
Jewell Ray. "This boy here struck and killed an elderly
woman! And he is only sixteen years old. I ask you . . .
what will he be like when he is thirty? Will he be a bank
president? A Scout Master? An honest worker? I think not.
I think not. Here he is, only coming of age, and already he
is a killer. And not merely a simple killer, a man who reacts
in the heat of passion, but a thief who sneaks in the door
and commits cold-blooded murder for a handful of money.
A young man who attacks an old woman quietly sitting at
her kitchen table and brutally beats her to death. Do we
want to let him go so that he can do it *again?*"

Burdened by the weight of sorrow, Bailey turned back
to the jury. "No, my friends, we do not. Our duty is clear
and we must perform it without flinching. We owe it to
Gussie, to ourselves and to our children, that they may
walk these streets in safety. We have only one choice. And
so I urge you to act as your conscience and your sense of
justice compel you to act—nay, *demand* you to act—and
find the defendant, Jewell Ray Cantwell, guilty as charged.
You can follow no other course and be true." With that,
he bowed slightly and withdrew. There was a smattering of
applause.

*

Judge Hainsworth roused himself and brought down the gavel. "We will take a brief recess—fifteen minutes—" he said. "Then, Mr. Ferris, we'll hear from you."

Even all spruced up like he was, Joel Ferris looked small and insignificant after the splendor of Austin Bailey. Still, it didn't seem to worry him any. He flung back his shoulders and stepped forward, his thin voice rasping through the heat in tune with a chorus of locusts which had started up outside.

"Your Honor, Ladies and Gentlemen of the Jury, Mr. Prosecutor—I, for one, wish to compliment Mr. Bailey. We would have to go some to find a better performance—I hope y'all appreciated it—and I must admit that we agree on several points. One of which is Duty." He bent a stern gaze upon the jury. "He's right about that at least. You *are* here to do your duty. We all are. But our duty is to the living—not the dead." He paused for a moment. "The other point which I and Mr. Bailey agree on is the presence of tragedy. There is much tragedy here, no doubt about that. But the thing is, when one tragedy has occurred it makes no sense to add another one. That would be like saying one bad deed deserves another. Then, too, a person has to live with any tragedy he has been a part of—it kind of sets around, uneasy-like on his conscience. Some folks think you can ease the first one by adding another one to it but it don't work that way, it don't help. No matter what fancy name you give to it, it still don't help. 'Two wrongs don't make a right.' "

He turned his back to the jury box and stood contemplating the opposite wall. The jury looked uncomfortable and confused.

"No," said Ferris to the wall, "revenge has never been the solution.

"Thing is, in a court of law like this one here, you can't afford to deal in emotions. Emotions, feelings . . . they have to be left out yonder in the hallway along with the hats and guns." He turned back to face the jury. "What we have to deal with in the courtroom is facts. Facts, Ladies and Gentlemen. *Facts and only facts.* If we quit looking at the facts and go to trading in emotions, why we might just as well go back to burning folks up whenever we feel like it. Set up stakes all over the countryside. That way we wouldn't have to bother with the evi-dence. Judges or juries either, for that matter. All we'd need is some kindling and a match." He smiled oddly. "That's certainly one way of doing justice. Or what passes for justice. But there is another way—the way of evi-dence. Evi-dence. Weighed and carefully considered. We all know about the Goddess of Justice—the lady with the scales? Well, it ain't emotions she's weighing, it's evi-dence she's trying to balance. And that is what I beg you to do, Ladies and Gentlemen. I beg you to weigh the evi-dence for it is there that the truth will be found."

He paused and scratched his ear. "Now, this evi-dence here before us . . . let's have a look at it. First of all there are the medical facts—testimony given by a man who has practiced medicine right here in this very town for fifty years. And what did he have to say? Well, he said two things: first he said that in his professional opinion the death of Mrs. Augusta Houghton was not the result of a blow to her head. Not entirely, he said. Or maybe not at all. According to him—and he ought to know—she could have died from any number of things. He has seen folks recover from far worse injuries. Those were his words.

"And secondly, Dr. Cartwright stated that he had been treating her for high blood pressure, that she had not been well of late. She was an elderly woman, he said, and I believe it is fair to imply that she might have gone at any time. I believe I do not misuse his words. So I ask you to consider these facts, please. This testimony." And he walked back over to his table, leaving them to do so.

After a few moments, he resumed. "Now, Ladies and Gentlemen, consider if you will the woman herself, Mrs. Houghton. I wonder . . . was she always the good friend and kindly neighbor that my opponent makes her out to be? Think back now, honestly, over her life. Mr. Winters tells us she was a wealthy woman, very wealthy. But did she *share* any of that wealth? I have looked and I was unable to find her name at the head of any charities, any eleemosynary institutions. Do you know of any?" He shook his head and moved a few paces looking down at the floor. "I wonder . . . just how many of you owed her money?" Ferris looked directly at Clay Weyerts, who shifted uncomfortably. "How many folks did she help out in times of drouth and trouble?" He turned to the boy whose daddy ranched down south and to whom Gussie had denied loans. "How many times did she throw out a rope when your ox was in the ditch?" The boy turned red. "I ask you to consider these things . . . not so as to malign a woman's character . . . oh, certainly not . . . but merely to place the situation in a proper perspective. So that we understand exactly who it is that we are talking about."

Ferris poured some water into his glass and swallowed noisily. "Now, once we get rid of the emotion and all them other trappings—false sentiment and so on—once we do that, we are left with the facts. And just what are these facts? I will state them once again: A woman, an elderly woman who loves money more than anything else in the world, sits at her kitchen table of a morning. And what is she doing? She is counting the cash she keeps at home in an old tin box. Consider that for a moment. She is very particular about that money—won't even let her own son lay a hand on it. Won't allow him to use it for the most ordinary errands, but collects it, packs it into that old box and *counts it every day of the world*. There she sits, counting, enjoying her most solitary and precious pleasure . . . when *out of nowhere* this here *boy* jumps in the door and tells her to give it to *him*! Picture it, Ladies and Gentlemen! A boy she's never seen before in her life"—he broke off and gestured at Jewell Ray, who was gloomily chewing a thumbnail and staring at the floor. "This boy sneaks in her back door and tells her he wants her money, makes a move to touch it even. Picture it to yourselves." Doing so himself, he gazed up at the ceiling, a smile widening on his face. "Do you reckon she *gives* it to him—her most cherished possession, lets him lay a finger on those bills? Hands it over just like that?" Grinning, Ferris shook his head. "Not hardly. We might suppose that she gets a mite angry . . . but then she *laughs*. Laughs at him—this two-bit boy out of nowhere—what does he think he's gonna do? We can imagine a momentary stand-off. Then he makes a grab for it and—*smack!*—she hits him!" Ferris clapped his hands and everybody in the room jumped. "So what does he do? He does what anybody would do—he grabs hold of her wrist to keep her from doing it again. A perfectly normal reaction. We can surmise that they struggle for a moment. And it's not too uneven a match—he ain't a very big boy. But then . . . then she snags onto his shirt with the other hand . . . raises up . . . and *won't let go*." Ferris dropped his voice to a carrying whisper. "*And then she starts to die*. Ladies and Gentlemen, *she starts to die*." Gradually he brought his voice back up to normal, increasing the volume with each word. "She raises up already dying . . . and when she starts to fall back he can't get loose from her. She is clamped onto his shirt front and he can't pry her off . . . so he loses his head and he hits her. Oh yes, he hits her. Can you imagine how scared that boy is along about then? I myself can smell that fear. . . . Yes, he hits her. He has admitted doing so himself. But what does he hit her with? A blackjack? A crowbar? A pistol butt? No. He hits her with the only thing available—a wooden cooking spoon."

Jewell Ray let out a groan and buried his face in his arms. Ferris, taking no notice, continued. "Now I ask you," he went on, his voice chafing the hot air like sandpaper, "I ask you. Do we need expert medical testimony to tell us that a wooden spoon like this here"—he picked up the spoon and waved it—"is not a lethal weapon? That it could not— not even in our wildest fancy—have caused the death of Augusta Houghton?" He wagged his head. "No, Ladies and Gentlemen, we cannot convict a boy of murder just because he got scared, lost his wits and took a swing with a wooden spoon . . . ," he paused and looked searchingly at the jury, ". . . at a woman *who was already dead*."

Joel Ferris walked up and down studying the jury intently. "Now you are thinking that he shouldn't have been there in the first place. Of course not; he had no business to be. And he has stolen and run off and generally behaved in a very improper manner. But the point is—*he did not kill anybody*. He was there . . . oh yes. And a woman died. But no man has ever been convicted of a murder just because somebody happened to die while he was in the room. And the curious thing is, we don't even know what she did die of. But I think we can make a guess: Gussie died of *rage*. This kid creeping in the back door, threatening to take her precious money, making a grab for it—! Think about it, friends. Gussie Hoot didn't die from the tap of a wooden spoon—Gussie died of rage."

He took another noisy drink of water. "That leaves us with only one more point: if you want to convict this boy of murder—to send him to the ee-lek-tric chair—then you are obliged to establish in your own hearts and minds— *beyond the shadow of a doubt*—that he done this thing." Ferris took the wooden spoon in both hands, held it up before the eyes of the jury—then snapped it in two like a wishbone. The sound, like the crack of a twig, was both alarming and revealing; it jarred certain beliefs and startled old secrets into the open.

Later, in the midst of intensifying heat, Austin Bailey delivered his summation. Strolling slowly to the jury box, he rested one hand on the railing. "It is a sad thing," he began in a conversational tone. "A tragic thing that such events occur in this world. Not off in some big city; not something we read about in the paper; but right here in our own town, shattering the lives of our citizens for years to come. Not a one of us will go from here untouched. All our lives we will remember this . . . unnecessary . . . death and these proceedings. That is why it is so important that we do the right thing." He paused and directed his gaze on each juror in turn. Chuy Gallego smiled, then realizing his mistake, quickly frowned, rubbing out the smile like a misspelled word. Next to Chuy, Jason Cartwright sat back, bored, one ankle crossed casually over the opposite knee. Beside Jason, Asa (T. D.) Hines stared over the prosecutor's head at the prisoner with the look of a cattle buyer weighing out a calf. When Johnnie Mae Spence looked at the defendant, she saw only a boy and her face was white and strained. Janelle French seemed somehow older, aged by the whole experience—or maybe it was only the light. Her face had a pliant, sleepy look and she studied Austin Bailey with the concentration of a person trying to stay awake. Charlotte Buchanan, upright and alert, was not so much listening to Austin as she was suffering from the pain in her back, a sure sign that it was going to rain. Clay Weyerts was suffering, too, but he was more occupied with the heat and wishing to hell it *would* rain. LaQuita Light-foot watched through narrowed and inscrutable eyes accented by green eye shadow and a thick crust of mascara. Other jurors slumped in their chairs and tried to pay attention. But their minds were hazed over by the heat and the ominous weight of the still air.

"So important," resumed Austin Bailey. "These others now, will go on about their business: the defendant to the fate he so rightly deserves, a fit punishment for so vile and unspeakable an act done to one of our own, to Gussie and to us, our little town; the honorable counsel for the defense to other cases in other towns, and soon he will have forgotten all about us and about this boy here, he will be busy elsewhere; and," he turned and looked at Sherrylee, who was pale and all elbows but nonetheless maintained a sort of defiant dignity, her chin lifted and her eyes steady, "and this young lady, back to her family where she belongs— All of them, gone. Tomorrow, next week, sometime soon. But we remain, Ladies and Gentlemen. We remain. We stay behind and the memory of this crime stays with us. The effects of it will be felt for years. Our children will grow up with it, with the knowledge that once, in this year and at this time, a murderer came—a thief in the night—and literally *stole* the life of one of our oldest and most respected citizens. What will they say to us, *of us*? Will we be able to answer their questions? What will we say? Will we be able to hold up our heads and say that we did the right thing? That we performed our sacred duty and kept the world safe for them? I hope so, Ladies and Gentlemen. I sincerely hope so."

He paused, rocked back slightly on his heels, gazed unseeing out one of the tall windows. "It is an awesome thing—life. When you come right down to it only the good Lord can give it or take it away; all the rest of us can do is to follow his laws to the very best of our ability. And we base our laws on his. They are all we have against a world of chaos, war and random violence. A universe of anarchy and terror. Law is the fragile shield we hold up to protect civilization against the tides of darkness and the shoals of death. To be without law—lawless—is to be without humanity or hope." He dropped his gaze and stood, head bent in repose, his hands quiet on the railing of the jury box. Then he lifted his head and spoke to the jury, to them and them alone. "Listen," he said. "Listen and do not be confused by cheap tricks and circus acts. Listen to your own hearts and to your wisdom. It is the law which you must heed. The Trumpet of Justice must be heard in the land! As mortals, we must consign mercy into the hands of God."

A cheer went up from the Legionnaires. There was a fervent "Amen!" from somewhere in the crowd. Bowing his head, Austin Bailey retired. Then Judge Hainsworth raised himself up and gazed down upon the jury with all the power conferred on him by centuries of God and history. In a deep, omniscient voice, he declaimed their instructions.

He was thorough, imposing and Judaic. He left no stone unturned and nothing to chance. When he was satisfied that they understood, he ceased and let the silence gather. Then he spoke from the mountain. "I charge you to do your duty," he thundered. "And may God help you!" Outside, a more distant thunder rumbled, lolling in the mountains to the south.

CHAPTER 34

. . . .

*T*he jury had no sooner filed out than public speculation began on how long it would take them to reach a verdict and just what that verdict might be. Opinion was divided and often loud. Some folks were certain that the jury would return within the hour with a verdict of guilty. An equal number insisted that it would be at least this time tomorrow and that the boy was sure to be cut loose. A sensible few held out for a hung jury: nobody, they said, could come to any kind of a decision in a case like this one. Bets were offered and taken up all around.

The actual participants in the drama affected a relaxed manner, trying to appear casual about the whole thing. J. D. leaned against the jury door looking bored and sleepy. Austin Bailey, hearty and confident, saw the intermission as an opportunity for campaigning and he made the rounds backslapping and handshaking.

At the table for the defense, the atmosphere wasn't so cheerful. Sherrylee had been permitted to join them and Joel Ferris had sent somebody out for coffee, but the three of them sat without saying much, each busy with private thoughts. After a while, Sherrylee put down her cup and sighed.

"What do *you* reckon's gonna happen, Mr. Ferris?"

He looked at her, shrugged. "You never know. You simply never know. Jury like this? They're like a bunch of spring heifers—just as likely to head up one draw as another."

She considered this estimate of the situation. "But can't you even make a guess? Whether it'll be good, I mean . . . or . . . not?"

Ferris fished out a toothpick and went to work on it. "Nope. Like I say, a jury is the most unpredictable animal in the world. They're just as apt to go straight up as straight down. Or nowhere at all. This one now"—he thought about LaQuita Lightfoot and Chuy Gallego, Jason Cartwright and the cowboy whose wife was ripening before their very eyes, Johnnie Mae Spence—"I plain don't know. They might lock horns and we'd be here all summer." He wasn't really interested in the conversation; he had done what he could. He was busy watching the district attorney lining up votes. Bailey had hooked both thumbs in his vest and was rocking back on his heels with a broad smile. Joel Ferris eyed him thoughtfully.

Jewell Ray deepened his frown and worked his eyebrows. "I just wisht you hadn't a brought up all that spoon business."

Ferris shifted his gaze to the boy and regarded him bitterly. He opened his mouth to reply, apparently changed his mind and shut it again.

Meanwhile, the spectators were faced with a dilemma. Perishing of thirst but at the same time unwilling to give up their seats and maybe even miss the verdict, they sat sweating in that courtroom which by then had built up heat and steam enough to challenge a pressure cooker. At last a compromise was reached and delegates were sent across the street to the drugstore for carry-out orders of Cokes, limeade and coffee. The ladies generally desired something cool while the men, as always, ordered coffee. Some of the orders got mixed up. However, the Lone Star Biddies agreed that it was worth it—drinking hot coffee on a sweltering afternoon—just to observe certain grizzled ranchers puckering up over paper cups of limeade. The ranchers, on the other hand, were elated about the error as soon as they discovered that Gus McIntyre had smuggled in a bottle of tequila. "Not bad," they agreed, and smacked their lips while the bottle made furtive rounds. "Not bad at all."

The Biddies were amazed. And before long, the tension gave way to a festive if not downright rowdy atmosphere among the men. J. D., hunched against the jury door, crossed his arms and scowled.

After a couple of hours, the court clerk suddenly burst in, slamming the door behind him. He thumped some papers on his table, faced the crowd and drew himself up like a locust preparing to fly. "*Oyez! Oyez!*" he sang out in a loud, reedy voice. "This court is now called into session." There was a stand-up scramble for seats as the judge made his way in. Gus McIntyre spilled some of his punch and swore. Somebody hawked. There was a crash of unknown origin. Judge Hainsworth gazed down upon this assembly from his bench much as Moses must have glowered from the mountain, stone tablets under one arm and little hope in his heart.

Poker-faced, the members of the jury filed in and took their places. Austin Bailey fixed them with a winning smile. Ferris squinched up his dun-colored eyes and peered at them like he wished he had x-ray vision. Deadpan, they settled themselves with considerable rustling and scraping and then stared glassily at the Bench.

Judge Hainsworth rumbled forth. "Members of the Jury, have you reached a verdict? If so, who will speak for you?"

Clay Weyerts unwound himself to a standing position. "I will . . . er . . . we have. I am the foreman and I will speak."

The judge swung his head back to face front. "Will the defendant please rise and attend upon the verdict of this jury?"

Terrified, Jewell Ray jerked around and faced Ferris, the fear of betrayal hovering in a white line around his mouth.

"It's all right, son," said the lawyer quietly. "Stand up."

But the boy would not move.

The judge beetled down. "Mr. Ferris? Will you bring the defendant before the Bench?"

Ferris took Jewell Ray by the arm and led him before the judge. Then the attorney stepped back a few paces and left the boy standing alone.

Judge Hainsworth swung his head back around to the jury. In a voice straight from Sinai, he commanded. "How do you find, Mr. Foreman?"

"We find . . . ," Clay began, and stopped to lower his voice a notch. He started over, reading from a slip of paper in his hand. "We, the members of this jury, find the defendant, Jewell Ray Cantwell, not guilty as charged."

That courtroom was as still as the world in the instant before Creation. Clay stood there for a second, then not knowing what else to do, sat back down. Jewell Ray, standing before the judge, started to fold at the knees. Ferris leaped forward and caught him under the arms. But the boy dropped to his knees and stayed there. He looked up at the judge, disbelief and hope at war in his face.

"Did . . . did he say *not guilty?*" he whispered.

The judge's face moved in just a suggestion of a smile. "That's what he said, son. That's what the man said." Then, brusquely, he turned back to business, searching out the sheriff. "Sheriff Killion? I charge you to hereby release this prisoner from custody." As J. D. approached with the key to the handcuffs, the judge spoke to the clerk. "Let the record show that Jewell Ray Cantwell stands acquitted of the murder of Augusta M. Houghton. This court now stands adjourned." He brought down his gavel with a mighty blow. Outside, a clap of thunder caused the windows to shake and the rain broke loose in a torrent. Sherrylee laid her head on her arms and cried.

CHAPTER 35

. . . .

*E*arly the following morning, Effie Sue Ethridge was out in her back yard fussing with her rose bed. The night's storm, hail mixed in with the rain, had played havoc with the flowers. Effie Sue was busy cutting away the wrecked blossoms. She was just bending over to examine her Isabella Sprunt when she noticed a big hole at the back of the bed, a place where no hole had any business to be. Effie Sue, doubting her vision, peered more closely. Sure enough. Right there up against the alley wall was a round pit like a dog hole. No . . . not exactly like a dog hole . . . Effie Sue eyed the place with a certain apprehension. Ever since that business with the twenty-dollar bill she had been very sensitive about her garden and about that flower bed in particular. In fact, this was the first morning she had ventured out in the back yard for some time . . . and now here was this hole. She leaned over to get a better look . . . then jumped back like she'd been stung. The object which had caused her dramatic reaction was a U.S. currency bill worth twenty dollars. Caught on a thorn, it hung gently fluttering in the morning breeze.

"Oh my, no," moaned Effie Sue. "*Oh my no!*"

She searched around in the garden until she found a long stick. Then she poked at the bill until it fell to the ground. With sure-handed vengeance, she jabbed a hole in the middle and drove the stick right through the heart of the thing. Then, very gingerly, she lifted the bill on the end of the stick and bore it at arm's length back to the house. Once inside, Effie Sue lit the burner on her gas range and stood toasting that bill over the flame until even the tip of the stick dropped off in a soft flake of gray ash. After that, she retired to her bedroom, where she rested for the remainder of the day with a cool cloth pressed to her eyes.

.   .   .

Later that same morning, several men convened in Austin Bailey's office in the courthouse. Houston Carr was there in high spirits, openly gleeful, his bulk filling one of Austin's big leather chairs. Judge Hainsworth stood to one side, maintaining an air of detachment and studying the D.A.'s shelves of books. The sheriff lounged against the window frame. Austin was at his desk.

"Har!" guffawed Houston, and slapped his knee. "That was the goddamnedest thing I ever heard! Why, I thought toward the end there that Ferris was going to plead *self-defense* for that damnfool boy! Damnedest case I ever heard in my life!"

The others laughed, Austin a shade less heartily.

"Quite a case, all right," remarked the judge. "Certainly one of the more unusual ones it has been my privilege to hear. No offense, Austin, but I must say that Joel Ferris acquitted himself very well. Very well indeed."

"Is that supposed to be a pun, Ira?" inquired Austin drily.

His Honor chuckled. "Just checking."

"Where in the hell is Ferris, anyway?" asked Houston.

J. D. hawked, hit the spittoon. "Shoot. That son of a gun's been gone for hours. I saw him having breakfast down at the Texas Cafe. He hitched up that old trailer of his and pulled out early."

"Where was he headed?"

J. D. shrugged. "Damned if I know. He ain't the most talkative cuss. Said something about a case over in Stockton County. Some gal shot up her boyfriend."

The others thought over this news in silence.

J. D. planted one foot on a chair, leaned forward resting his arms on his bent knee. "Thing I can't figure out . . . coming back to this case, I mean . . . thing I can't for the life of me make out is what that kid done with the money."

Judge Hainsworth gave him a sour look. "What money?"

J. D. looked up, surprised. "Why, Gussie's money, of course. When they picked that kid up in San Diego he had about five or six hundred dollars on him. Y'all heard what Bubba said . . . and Lincoln Winters, too. I reckon Gussie kept a lot more money than that in her old tin box, don't you?"

There was an awkward silence. J. D. looked around, puzzled. Then Houston grinned. "Well, maybe you ought to ask him about it next time you see him."

The sheriff reddened, scowled down at the tip of his boot. "Aw, hell. He's long gone. Him and that girl? They done hightailed it outta here this morning on the early bus."

.   .   .

Far to the south and east, a silver Continental Trailways bus labored through the hot hours of early afternoon. The long, narrow window high in front spelled out the letters L-A-R-E-D-O with only the bottom half showing, as if the goal had been overshot or would remain forever in limbo. The bus driver, probably the one responsible for this carelessness, was an open-faced, friendly young man who was thinking about Nuevo Laredo. While not in the same league as Juárez or Tijuana, Nuevo Laredo had its attractions. The young driver, who lived in Uvalde, had been to Nuevo Laredo any number of times but it held less interest for him now that he was married and working steady. As he drove, he remembered a little song he had learned from one of the girls down there and so, in order to pass the time, he sang it. Usually he was able to strike up some kind of conversation with his passengers but on this particular day he gave up and started singing to stay awake. There were only four passengers—a Mexican woman with a straw shopping bag, a Mexican truck farmer with a bushel basket full of cantaloupes and two skinny teenagers who were pale, like they hadn't seen the sun for a good while, the boy especially. The bus driver liked kids—hell, he liked anybody except drunks on that long haul—and he had tried his best to interest either the dark-haired boy or the tall, thin girl in some kind of talk. But they were as skittish as colts. Soon as he said, "Howdy!" they showed him the whites of their eyes and streaked for the back of the bus. They'd been holed up back there ever since. The bus driver glanced in his rearview mirror from time to time trying to make out just what it was they were doing back there. Whatever it was, they sure were secretive about it. Looked like some kind of game to him. A game using play money. Monopoly—sure, that must be it. He had played it plenty of times when he was a kid. These two looked a little old for it, but you never knew. Sure, that's what it was, all right. The manufacturers must have improved on it some since his day—the money looked almost real. Well, it was a good game for passing the time. The bus driver yawned.

All through the long, glare-white hours of that afternoon the two teenagers sat intent over their work. It took a whole lot more time and patience than they had figured— inking out the little stars in the upper right-hand corners of all those bills.

ABOUT THE AUTHOR

I was born on a cold January morning (1/12/36) to Scottish parents in the small town of Alpine, Texas. As I seemed reluctant to emerge into the world, the attending physician finally slapped down a silver dollar on the table in disgust. That did it, but I have often wondered since if I should have held out for more.

I grew up in Alpine, profoundly attached to the landscape, deeply aware of a sense of place. While my high school classmates drifted on clouds of crinoline, I wandered the mountains, enchanted by cloud shadows, attuned to the creak of saddle leather and the unsurpassed smell of a sweaty horse. At the age of eighteen, I was rudely awakened and sent to college—the University of Texas at El Paso. After four years there—some of them good, some spent in 1950s *angst* and *anomie*, plus some highly educational tours of Juárez, Mexico—I graduated and fled, convinced by a friend that "the only good thing that ever came out of Texas was Highway 80." (This was before the interstates paved the entire country.)

I spent about ten years in San Diego, California, working as a juvenile probation officer, a position which granted an unparalleled opportunity to observe human nature and which I took complete advantage of. Eventually, swamped by kids who had OD'd on Jimson Weed and ended up crawling the walls of the psycho ward, sensing the early stages of political rebellion and the drug culture, I resigned and took the quiet road to library school.

After two years at the University of Washington in Seattle and an MA degree, I returned to San Diego and worked for a time as a reference librarian. I held some very interesting jobs but I was not cut out to be a 3 × 5 person. Something seemed to be missing. Maybe I had had too much freedom as a child. I resigned, migrated north to the Oregon coast and opened a bookstore known as Innisfree Books with all the philosophy of the Yeats poem behind it and not one ounce of business sense. It was pretty much a clay and wattles operation but I did find some peace there, and others seemed to also, rejoicing in the careful selection of books and the congenial atmosphere. Eventually, the business became a modest success.

However, something was still missing. Weary of accounts and publishers' hype, I sold the business and moved to several acres on the Nehalem River, a bucolic paradise where I took up serious gardening as well as cooking on a wood stove. It was a beautiful time, living in the tall trees and listening to the river. But, as if a gnat had gotten in my ear, I began writing, first for pleasure and soon out of that inescapable obsession which consumes us all. To my surprise, I found myself scribbling about the Big Bend country, about wetbacks and canyons and very open, dry spaces. In order to get the details right, I was forced to rediscover Texas—that was about 1980—and I have been here ever since with the exception of a puzzling year spent in New England.

All of which adds up to the fact that I did not begin writing "seriously" until about the age of forty-five. At first this worried me but I have since decided that it was exactly the right age. At eighteen I had composed an absolutely dreadful play which was performed at Sul Ross State University complete with choir and philospher-king. Later, I edited *El Burro*, the monthly magazine at UTEP which, to the total annoyance of the engineers, I turned from snide-cum-porno fun into a literary rag which won some awards. I fiddled around with poetry, wrote some awful short stories, but never for a moment considered trying to make a living "with words," as they say. As I have always been taciturn, it did not seem a promising career.

Still, eventually the bug bit. *Gussie Hoot*, begun in a cedar loft in Oregon, returned to her origins in West Texas. I now write full-time and am currently at work on two additional novels as well as a collection of short stories set along the border.

MARGOT FRASER

Odessa, Texas

1990